Dear Miss Richardson,

We regret to inform you that your great uncle, William S. Delcambra, passed away on the twenty-fifth of last month. It is our responsibility to notify you that he has left you property that is located approximately a hundred miles from Albany, New York.

It was the wish of your great uncle that you have the first opportunity to take possession of his property, but that you be given only forty-five days from the date of this letter in which to do so.

It is imperative that you make claim to this property before the end of next month. Otherwise, the property will be disposed of as directed in your great uncle's will.

Please contact me at your earliest convenience.

Respectfully,
Franklin P. Cosgrove

René quickly realized that Franklin P. Cosgrove was one of the partners of the law firm who had sent the letter. She sat staring at the letter still unable to believe what it said.

The first thought that crossed her mind was what property? The letter only said that it was located approximately a hundred miles from Albany, New York. That could be almost anywhere, as it didn't even specify in which direction from Albany.

The second thought that came to mind was just who was William S. Delcambra? She had never heard of him before, at least not that she could remember. If he really was her great uncle, how was it that she could not remember hearing of him? Why had she not been notified of his death earlier?

* * * * * * *

Other titles by J.E. Terrall

Western Short Stories	Western Novels
The Old West	Conflict in Elkhorn Valley
The Frontier	Lazy A Ranch (A Modern
Untamed Land	Western)
Tales from the Territory	The Story of Joshua Higgins

Romance Novels	Mystery/Suspense/Thriller
Balboa Rendezvous	I Can See Clearly
Sing for Me	The Return Home
Return to Me	The Inheritance
Forever Yours	

Nick McCord Mysteries
  Vol – 1 Murder at Gill's Point
  Vol – 2 Death of a Flower
  Vol – 3 A Dead Man's Treasure
  Vol – 4 Blackjack, A Game to Die For
  Vol – 5 Death on the Lakes
  Vol – 6 Secrets Can Get You Killed

Peter Blackstone Mysteries	Frank Tidsdale Mysteries
Murder in the Foothills	Death by Design
Murder on the Crystal Blue	Death by Assassination
Murder of My Love	

THE INHERITANCE

by
J.E. Terrall

4

Printed in the United States of America
First Printing and Second Printing / 2010 – www.lulu.com
Third Printing / 2015 – www.createspace.com

Cover: Cover photo taken by author, J.E. Terrall

Book Layout/
Formatting: J.E. Terrall
              Custer, South Dakota

THE INHERITANCE

To my father,
who always believed in me.

CHAPTER ONE

Dark clouds hung over the city like a wet, dirty gray blanket draped over several pairs of clotheslines. It had been raining off and on for the past several days. The gloomy days and almost constant drizzle were taking its toll on the morale of the local residents. The usually friendly souls that lived along Cutter Street in Utica, New York, seemed less willing to greet each other and less willing to smile at one another.

René Richardson was no exception. The dreary weather was wearing on her, too. As she walked up the wet steps to the front door of her apartment building, she walked right past Mrs. Casteel without saying so much as "Hello".

Not only had the weather been depressing for René, but also her week at work had been very grueling, very long and very exhausting, with one problem after another cropping up. It seemed that nothing had gone right for weeks.

René had a good job that paid her reasonably well, but she was getting frustrated with nothing but problems day after day lately. Her job lacked the excitement and the stimulation that it had once held.

Her life had become as routine and dull, and as gloomy as the weather. And it was just as depressing. She had tried to wear clothes that normally would make her look and feel good. There was no doubt that she had a very nice figure and she always got compliments on her shoulder length hair and her sparkling brown eyes. But lately she didn't feel very pretty. Not even some new clothes seemed to help brighten her spirits.

She wished that there could be a little excitement in her life, and a little sunshine to brighten her days. René needed something that would stir her into some sort of action, something that would give her mind something new to think about, something fun. Life in general had been very tedious for her.

The weekend had finally arrived and she was looking forward to a week off. She had not planned to go anywhere. She just wanted to spend a quiet week at home away from the difficulties at work. René had no special plans and that suited her just fine. She was ready for a week of sleeping in late, watching a few movies, reading a good book and just relaxing in the peace and quiet of her small mid-town apartment.

After making a brief stop in the entryway of the building to get her mail, she climbed the stairs to her second floor apartment. Once inside, she dropped the mail on the end table next to the sofa. She kicked off her wet shoes, then hung her coat over the back of a chair to dry before hanging it in the closet. She flopped down on the sofa, tipped her head back and let out a long sigh.

Resting her tired feet on the footstool, she looked over at the mail. Reluctantly, she reached over and picked it up. She began flipping through it, taking a brief look at each envelope.

The first couple of envelopes had colorful stickers and bold print on them. They were from different companies offering her chances to win millions of dollars by just entering their sweepstakes. She quickly thumbed through them, silently wishing that she could win one of them so she wouldn't have to go back to work next week.

"I could go to far away places and meet a tall, dark and handsome stranger," she said out loud, but there was no one there to hear her.

Knowing that her chances of winning such a contest were next to impossible, she tossed them off to the side to dispose of later. The next letter was her utility bill. She opened the letter and let out a long sigh as she looked at the amount due, then laid it on the end table to take care of later. There was one remaining envelope in her lap. It was an envelope with her full name and address on it. She wondered what kind of a contest this one could be since the letter looked so official, so important. There were no colorful stickers or bold print on this envelope. A glance at the return address quickly caught her attention. The return address was that of a law firm located in Albany, New York. It read in bold print "Cosgrove, Wentworth and Smith, Attorneys at Law".

She sat and stared at the letter for a long time. René was almost certain that she had heard of this firm before, but she couldn't remember where or under what circumstances at the moment. She wondered why a law firm from Albany would be writing to her. It occurred to her that it was probably bad news and that someone was probably suing her for something she couldn't even remember doing. It certainly would have fit in with how things had been going lately.

Unable to come up with any logical reason why she would be receiving a letter from what appeared to be a prestigious law firm, she proceeded to open it. Unfolding the letter, she began reading it. When she reached the end of the letter, she dropped her hands in her lap, tipped her head back and looked up at the ceiling. She could not believe what she had just read. Her mind filled with questions so fast that she could not deal with them rationally. The only thought that raced through her mind that she could understand was the letter couldn't possibly be for her.

She looked back at the letter and began to read it again. Only this time she read it slowly and carefully in an effort to absorb each and every word that was neatly typed on the clean white paper.

Dear Miss Richardson:

We regret to inform you that your great uncle, William S. Delcambra, passed away on the twenty-fifth of last month. It is our responsibility to notify you that he has left you property that is located approximately a hundred miles from Albany, New York.

It was the wish of your great uncle that you have the first opportunity to take possession of his property, but that you be given only forty-five days from the date of this letter in which to do so.

It is imperative that you make claim to this property before the end of next month. Otherwise, the property will be disposed of as directed in your great uncle's will.

Please contact me at your earliest convenience.

Respectfully,
Franklin P. Cosgrove

René quickly realized that Franklin P. Cosgrove was one of the partners of the law firm who had sent the letter. She sat staring at the letter still unable to believe what it said.

The first thought that crossed her mind was what property? The letter only said that it was located approximately a hundred miles from Albany, New York. That could be almost anywhere, as it didn't even specify in which direction from Albany.

The second thought that came to mind was just who was William S. Delcambra? She had never heard of him before, at least not that she could remember. If he really was her great uncle, how was it that she could not remember hearing of him? Why had she not been notified of his death earlier?

Puzzled by the letter, she looked over the letter again. In the letterhead was a telephone number. She decided that it would be a good idea to call the number and find out what it was all about. She reached for the phone on the table next to the sofa, but instantly realized that it was probably too late to get hold of anyone in the office tonight. It was well after six o'clock in the evening. She decided that her call would have to wait until morning.

René set the letter down on the coffee table, stood up and went out into the kitchen to fix something to eat. As she was preparing her dinner, she kept turning over and over in her mind the contents of the letter. She wondered just what property was being left to her.

The letter had simply mentioned "property". It failed to mention what kind of property, where the property was specifically located, or anything else that would help her decide if she wanted it. But then why wouldn't she want it?

The location of the property continued to hang around in her mind and cause her to speculate. She tried to remember what was within a hundred miles or so of Albany, New York.

Her mind started coming up with all sorts of thoughts as to what the property might be. It could be almost anything. It could be a plot of land, possibly a town house, or a building in one of the towns near Albany. It could even be a whole farm or a large estate hidden away in the Five Finger Lakes Region of Upper New York, she thought. Or it could even be one of those fancy houses overlooking the Hudson River.

She smiled at the thought of the fancy house overlooking the Hudson River. With the way she had been feeling lately, that didn't seem very likely.

The smile on her face faded as she began to think of other less pleasant possibilities. She began to think that it might be nothing of any value at all. There were a few old rundown farms, several small cabins on little marshy lakes, and a lot of areas where there was nothing but marshlands full of snakes, mosquitoes, and other bugs within a hundred-mile radius of Albany. There were also a number of little towns with old houses and buildings that would not be worth very much.

The evening passed rather slowly for René. She had to mentally shake herself to get her mind off the letter and back to what she had been planning to do. The contents of the letter continued to haunt her mind and disturb her thoughts. She found it impossible to concentrate on the movie that she had been looking forward to seeing all week. When she sat down and opened a book that she had wanted to read, she found that her mind would wander back to the letter. She simply could not concentrate on anything.

When it was time to go to bed, she found herself lying wide-awake looking up at the ceiling. She once again began to think of the possibilities, but all that would come to her mind were the old farms, the rundown cabins on small lakes and large areas of marshes that she had seen.

"If I know my luck, I will have inherited a moldy old cabin in some marsh in the middle of nowhere with ten years of back taxes due on it," she said out loud, her voice showing her disappointment at the thought.

Remembering what it said in the letter, she began to smile.

"If I don't claim it by the end of next month, I won't have to pay the back taxes."

That thought seemed to help her mind settle down. At least she had a way out if the property was nothing she wanted. With that thought firmly planted in her mind, she was finally able to relax a little and finally got some much needed sleep.

* * * *

René woke early in the morning still not very rested. She had spent the better part of the night tossing and turning. The letter had kept her mind too busy for her to get any real rest. The one good thing about this morning was that the rain had stopped and sunlight was shining through her bedroom window.

René sat up on the edge of the bed and stretched. Her eyes were automatically drawn to the nightstand where she had left the letter. It was almost as if the letter had been a dream and she needed to see if it was there to make it real. The letter was still there, waiting for her to pick it up. It had not been a dream.

She picked up the letter and carried it into the kitchen. After setting it down on the table, she made herself a cup of coffee and sat down at the table. René found herself staring at the letter as she sipped the hot liquid from the cup. It was as if the letter had some mystical power over her that continued to draw her to it.

Her mind would not let her relax and forget it, not even for a moment. Yet, with all the thoughts of what she might inherit running through her head, her mind could not let go of the one question that continued to creep into her mind every once in awhile. Who was William S. Delcambra?

It suddenly occurred to her that the letter might have been addressed to the wrong René Richardson. She almost instantly rejected that idea, but she knew that there was only one way to find out. René found it difficult to get up from the table and walk across the room to the phone for fear that the letter was for a different René Richardson.

"God, you're such a coward," she said to herself as she shook her head. "This could be your way to something exciting."

She gained some courage from the thoughts of adventure and excitement finally coming into her otherwise dull and lonely life. The thought of meeting a handsome man who would sweep her off her feet put a smile on her face. She shook her head in disgust as she censured herself for dreaming of something that she was convinced would never happen to her.

"You've been reading too many romance novels," she said, scolding herself.

René took in a deep breath, then let out a long sigh. She picked up the letter and looked at it again. It was Saturday. She wondered if the law office would even be open. There was only one way to find out.

She stood up and carried the letter with her to the phone. Hesitating only for a moment as she looked at the letter, she picked up the receiver and began dialing the number on the letterhead. The phone rang several times. She was about to hang up when it was answered.

"Hello?"

"Ah, yes. Is this the law firm of Cosgrove, Wentworth and Smith?"

"Yes, but I'm afraid we are not open today."

"Oh," she said a little disappointed. "I was hoping to talk to someone about a letter I received yesterday from your firm."

"I don't know if I can be of any help to you, but if you will tell me what the letter is about, I might be able to be of some assistance."

"Yes, of course. My name is René Richardson. I received a letter telling me that my great uncle, William S. Delcambra, had passed away and left me some sort of property."

There was a long moment of silence before the man on the phone responded.

"Ah, I'm sorry, but, ah, I'm not familiar with the letter," he said, seeming a bit unsure of what to say. "However, I have heard Mr. Cosgrove speak of Mr. Delcambra before. I believe that Mr. Delcambra is, or was, one of Mr. Cosgrove's clients. I'm sure that Mr. Cosgrove would be able to tell you more about the letter."

"The letter is signed by Mr. Cosgrove. How do I get in touch with him?"

"I'm afraid that he is not in today, but I am sure that he would be most interested in talking with you in person. I'll tell you what. I'll give him a call and ask him to call you back as soon as possible. How would that be?"

"That would be very nice. Thank you."

After giving the man her phone number, she hung up. Her mind was racing. She could hardly believe that the letter didn't appear to be a fake or some kind of terrible scam to get what little money she had saved away from her. She was going to actually inherit something, but she didn't have any idea what it might be.

The realization that she still didn't know what it was that she was to inherit caused her to stop and think. She wished that she had asked the man if he might know what it was. Now she would have to wait for Mr. Cosgrove to call back.

Suddenly, René found herself thinking about the man she had just talked with on the phone. His voice sounded soft and gentle. He seemed to want to help, which pleased her. She even began to wonder what he might look like. She wondered if he was tall, dark, handsome and single. She also wondered if he was a lawyer, or just an office worker in the law firm.

René mentally shook herself. What was wrong with her? Was she so lonely for companionship that the pleasant voice of a man on the phone would cause her to fantasize about a man that she had never even met? And to make matters worse, she didn't even know the man's name.

She tried not to answer her own question, but deep down in the recesses of her mind she knew the truth. Yes, she was that lonely. It had been weeks since she had had so much as a date, and that was not much of a date. It was more of a business dinner with a male friend from work. She began to feel depressed.

René sat down and sipped her coffee as she waited for the phone to ring. All the time she waited, question after question continued to fill her mind, but none of them were getting answered. There was nothing she could do now, but wait for someone to call her back.

After waiting for what seemed like eternity, but it was just barely an hour, the thought had passed threw her mind that she might not get a call back until Monday. She decided that she should take a shower and get dressed rather than sit around waiting for a call that might not come today.

She went to her bathroom, undressed and stepped into the shower. The warm clean water washed over her body causing her skin to tingle. The light, pleasant fragrance of her soap soon filled the shower and stirred her senses. The feel of the soap on her skin relaxed her tired muscles and relieved some of the tension that her work and the letter had caused.

After the refreshing shower, she dried herself off with a large soft towel. The ringing of the phone suddenly interrupted her thoughts. She quickly wrapped the towel around herself and rushed to the phone.

"Hello?"

"Is this Miss René Richardson?"

The voice was not familiar to her. It was deep and gravelly with a thick eastern accent. Yet, it was pleasant.

"Yes," she replied.

"My name is Franklin Cosgrove. One of our office assistants told me that you have been trying to reach me."

"Yes. I received a letter from you informing me that my great uncle Delcambra, William Delcambra, has passed away."

"Yes, that is correct. Please accept my deepest sympathy at the loss of your great uncle."

"Thank you," René replied. "I'm sorry to say that I don't believe I knew him. Could you please tell me what I am to inherit?"

"Well, your uncle, I should say your great uncle, has left you some lake front property on a private lake in the Essex Lakes region of the Adirondack Mountains. Your great uncle, Mr. Delcambra, lived there."

"He lived in the Adirondack Mountains?"

"Oh, yes. It is a very beautiful estate."

"An estate?" she asked excitedly.

"Yes. Would you like to see it?"

"Yes, I certainly would. I would like to see it very much. Who do I have to talk to in order to get directions to his estate?"

"I can certainly arrange that for you, if you would like?"

"Yes. That would be great."

"Would it be all right if I have Mr. Hanover call you back in a few minutes? He will provide you with directions and any assistance you might need."

"Yes. I understand that I have the option of not taking it. Is that correct?"

"Yes. That is correct, but I think you will like it. Be sure to take your time looking over the estate before you decide," Mr. Cosgrove suggested.

"I will, and thank you very much, Mr. Cosgrove." she replied then hung up the phone.

René stood there looking at the phone. Mr. Cosgrove had told her that she was to inherit an "estate". He had not told her how big an estate it was.

The word "estate" turned over and over in her mind. She had seen a number of estates, but they were all different. Some were large and some were small. He had given her no help in what she was to inherit except that it was on a lake and that it was beautiful. The idea of owning property on a lake was an exciting prospect for her. It would give her some place to go on weekends and during her vacations, she thought. It would provide a place to get away from the riggers of her work.

She began to feel a chill and realized that she was standing in the living room wearing nothing but a towel. She began drying her hair as she went back to the bathroom to get her robe.

René no more than slipped into her robe when the phone began to ring again. She hoped that it would be the nice man she had talked to earlier. Sitting down on the sofa, she picked up the receiver.

"Hello?"

"Hello. Is this René Richardson?"

"Yes, it is," she replied, immediately recognizing the voice of the man.

"Mr. Cosgrove has asked me to direct you to the lake front property of your deceased great uncle. Would I be correct in assuming that you would like to visit the property as soon as possible?"

"Yes. Yes, I would," she answered, hoping that he might let her see it today. "If that is not too much trouble?"

"It's no trouble at all. How would this afternoon be?"

"That would be fine," she replied excitedly.

"Since we live in opposite directions from where the property is located, I think it would be a good idea if we meet somewhere close to it. It would save a lot of time and we could be there in about two hours. That way you could return home this evening before it gets too late. You do have a car?"

"Yes, of course," she replied, thinking that was a strange question.

"Good. Looking at the map, - - I think we should meet at, - ah, - say, Blue Mountain Lake. If we leave within the next hour, we could meet there about noon."

"That sounds good," she agreed.

"Good. I will see you at about noon at Blue Mountain Lake."

"Where?"

"Excuse me?"

"Where do we meet in Blue Mountain Lake?"

"Oh. There's a lodge that has a little cafe and store in it. We could meet there, have lunch, then go out to the property."

"That sounds good," René agreed.

"I'll see you there."

"Just one more thing," René said. "How will I recognize you?"

"I drive a black BMW, and I'll be wearing a red polo shirt and dark blue slacks," he replied as if her question was unnecessary.

"I'll be wearing a flowered blouse and gray slacks. I drive a green Dodge."

"I look forward to meeting you."

As René hung up the phone, she looked at the receiver. Although the man had sounded pleasant enough, there was something in his voice that troubled her. She couldn't put her finger on it, but it caused her to wonder if he really wanted to drive all the way to Blue Mountain Lake to meet with her. She got the impression that he was not nearly as excited about visiting the property as she was. But then, why would he be? He was not the one inheriting it.

René tried to push her thoughts of him aside as she went to her bedroom to dress, but they kept creeping back. As she dressed, she began to wonder if she was doing the right thing.

Although Mr. Hanover had mentioned that she could return tonight, Mr. Cosgrove had told her to take her time and look over the estate. René decided that she would pack an overnight bag just in case she might need it. If she liked what she saw at the estate, she might want to stay a little while to take a better look around. If not, she could always return home. Either way, she would be prepared.

By the time she was ready to leave and was about to put the key in the ignition of her car, she was once again having some serious doubts about her decision to meet the man. What if this was some kind of terrible joke or game someone was playing on her?

"I asked for a little excitement in my life, and now that I have it, I'm going to carry it through," she said to herself with a note of worry in her voice.

"If nothing else, I will have taken a long drive for nothing," she told herself as a way to justify her reason for going.

In spite of her doubts and concerns, René was determined that she was not going to let anything stop her. It was about time that she took charge of her life and put a little excitement back into it. If this were some kind of a prank, she would just turn around and come back home. She figured that the most she could lose would be a tank of gas and a few hours of her time, and she had plenty of that.

With a new burst of determination and excitement, she turned the key in the ignition and started her car. She pulled away from the curb and headed out toward the highway that would take her to Blue Mountain Lake.

CHAPTER TWO

René drove north out of Utica following the highway that would take her into the Adirondack Mountains. As the miles rolled by, she began to let her mind wonder back in time in an effort to remember if she had ever met a William S. Delcambra. She tried to remember if she had ever been in the Essex Lakes Region before. The only time she could think of when she might have been in that area was when she was a little girl, maybe five or six years old.

That thought took René back many years when her parents had taken her on a trip from Troy, New York, where they had lived at the time, to a big old house on a blue-green lake surrounded by trees. She couldn't remember the name of the lake, but it seemed to her that it had taken them a very long time to get there. The one thing she could remember was that the house had impressed her.

Although her memory had dimmed a little by the passing of the years, she could still remember the old house with its large covered porch that ran around three sides of it. The house was two, maybe even three, stories high with a steep roof and several gables. It had been painted in a deep dark red with white trim around the windows and under the eaves. The railing on the porch had been white, too.

The windows in the front of the house were large and looked out over a crystal clear lake that was surrounded by a thick forest. There had been a long dock that stretched out into the lake, and a boathouse about halfway out and off to one side of the dock.

She could also remember a large powerboat tied to the dock. Her memory of the boat reminded her of those big wooden powerboats that were in those old black and white movies. Her father had taken her for a ride in it around the lake. The feel of the wind in her hair and the splash of water on her face were as clear to her as if it had been only yesterday.

Remembering the house and lake brought back memories of the man who had greeted them when they first arrived at the lake. She could visualize him in her mind standing on the large porch as she came around the end of the house. She walked up to the front of the house with her mother holding her hand. The man stood with his hands clenched in fists resting on his hips and his feet spread apart. He was a tall man with a long gray beard, bushy eyebrows, and dark blue eyes that at first seemed cold as ice. He seemed to be very big and old to her, but he was probably only in his mid-to-late fifties. He reminded her of a sea Captain standing proudly on the deck of his sailing ship much like Captain Ahab in the old movie, Moby Dick.

She remembered peeking out from behind her mother's skirt as she hung onto her mother very tightly because his appearance had frightened her. René smiled to herself at the thought of how much he had frightened her at first, but how gentle and kind he had been to her during her visit.

It suddenly occurred to René that the man at the house might have been her great uncle, William S. Delcambra. As much as she tried, she could not remember ever hearing the name of the man. All she could remember was that everyone had called him "Captain", but she didn't know why. She wondered if that house was the "property" that she was to inherit.

Without warning, her thoughts were suddenly disturbed by the earsplitting sound of an air horn. She had not seen the large semi-truck cross the centerline of the road, but it was headed straight at her. In a state of sheer panic, René jerked the steering wheel hard to the right, just barely avoiding a head-on collision with the big truck.

Her car swerved first one way, then the other before it started to skid sideways. She fought the steering wheel in an effort to regain control of her car as it skidded off the edge of the pavement onto the shoulder, then onto the slippery wet grass along the side of the roadway. It seemed to René that her car skidded a very long way before it finally came to rest only inches from a large tree.

She sat unable to move, her eyes were open wide with shock as she looked out the rain splattered windshield at the big tree directly in front of her. Her heart was pounding so hard that she could feel it as she tried to catch her breath. In her effort to regain control of herself, she took a deep breath and tipped her head back against the headrest. She closed her eyes and took a couple more deep breaths. René tried to relax and get her nerves settled down so she could continue on her way, but it was not easy after such a close call. It had been close, much too close.

As she sat quietly trying to regain her composure, she began to think that the near accident might be some kind of an omen of what was to come. She quickly shook off that thought. René had never considered herself to be a superstitious person.

René opened her eyes, straightened up and looked around. The trucker that had crossed the centerline and had almost hit her had not even slowed down, let alone stop to see if she was all right. There was no doubt in René's mind that he had to have seen her go off the road. What was wrong with him? Was he drunk, or on drugs? Was he trying to kill her?

A strange feeling slowly began to creep into her mind. Something was not right, but she could not immediately put her finger on it. Then it struck her. It was deathly quiet. There was no traffic in sight, no cars, no trucks, no nothing. It was eerie. All of a sudden there was not a single vehicle on the road when just minutes ago she had seen several. She had to wonder if she might have missed a turn, but how could she? There had not been any place to turn off for several miles. Besides, she could see a road sign just a short distance up the road showing her that she was still on state highway 28.

Something else was different, too. For the first time she realized that the sky was filled with ominous dark gray clouds and a light mist was falling. She had been so preoccupied with her thoughts that she had not even noticed the change in the weather, a change that had made the pavement a little slippery.

A chill slid down her spine as if someone had dropped an ice cube down the back of her neck. She had a sudden urge to get away from this place. She reached for the key and restarted her car. Shifting into reverse, she stepped on the gas, but the wheels just spun on the wet grass. The car would not back up. René's chest began to tighten again as she began to realize that she might be stuck out here on this deserted road, miles from anywhere and without any help.

As fear began to grip her, she shifted into drive. The car lunged forward, coming to rest against the tree with a heavy thud. She shifted back into reverse again and felt the car move backwards a little, but the wheels quickly began slipping again.

Shifting between drive and reverse, she rocked the car back and forth until the wheels suddenly grabbed some gravel near the edge of the road. She was finally able to back the car out onto the highway again. Putting the car into drive, she stepped on the gas. The car lunged forward and fishtailed a little on the wet pavement, but she was able to regain control of it quickly.

She sped on down the road as she looked for some sign of life, any life, that would let her know that she was not alone, but there was no one. The road was deserted. She continued on down the road, but had not seen another car for several miles. She could not remember a time when she felt so alone, so isolated, and so scared.

It seemed like it took forever before she finally saw another car. When she did, she breathed a sigh of relief and let her car slow down a little. Simply seeing another car reassured her that she was not as alone in the world as she thought she might be. As her senses returned to normal, she couldn't believe how she had let her imagination run wild to the point of scaring herself half to death.

"I wanted some excitement in my life, but this was not what I had in mind," she said out loud, mostly to hear the sound of her own voice.

Just the sound of her own voice helped her feel better. It was one time when her habit of talking out loud to herself seemed like a very normal thing to do.

As she once again settled into driving, she was more mindful of her surroundings and kept a watchful eye on the road. The mist had turned into a slow, steady rain. Her wipers kept a steady rhythm as they moved back and forth across the windshield as the miles rolled by.

René began to think that what she was doing might not be the smartest thing she had ever done. She even thought about turning around and going back to the safety of her apartment. All she knew was that the man she was to meet was named Mr. Hanover. She didn't even know his first name. She also knew that he worked in Mr. Cosgrove's office, part of a law firm in Albany, New York.

She shook her head in disbelief. Never in her life had she done anything like this. She had responded to a letter from someone that she didn't know, about someone she didn't think she knew. And as if that wasn't bad enough, there she was driving about ninety miles to a remote town in the middle of nowhere to meet a man she had never seen before in her life. And to top it off, she was doing it alone. She wondered what she had done with her common sense. How had she gotten herself into this?

René began to realize that she was letting her frayed nerves and imagination get the better of her. She took a deep breath and tried to think it out logically.

The letter she had received was from a law firm in Albany. She would be meeting a man from that same law firm at a cafe. There would certainly be other people around if they were meeting at a cafe, she concluded.

The thought of other people being around helped her decide that it would be a safe place for her to meet with Mr. Hanover. She could decide from there if she wanted to proceed any further, or turn around and go back home.

* * * *

Blue Mountain Lake was not much more than just a wide spot in the road with a few small businesses and a few houses. René had no difficulty finding the cafe. She pulled up in front of the building and looked around. Parked near the end of the building was a big black BMW.

"Well, I see you're here," she said to herself with a sigh. "I might as well find out what you look like."

She took a moment to look in the rearview mirror to make sure that she still had lipstick on and that her hair was not a mess. She could not remember a time when she had been so nervous. This was a business meeting and nothing more, she assured herself as she reached for the door handle. She got out of the car and walked up onto the front porch of the cafe.

René hesitated briefly before entering the café. There was still a twinge of doubt in her mind. Taking a deep breath, she opened the door. Once inside, she took a moment to look around. She noticed that there were only a half dozen people in the old fashioned cafe. They all seemed to be looking at her. She reasoned that they were local residents and were simply checking out the strangers that were passing through their part of the world.

"Excuse me."

The sudden sound of a man's voice from behind her startled her, causing her breath to catch. She swung around and looked at the tall man standing about two feet from her. He was so close to her that she felt the need to take a couple of steps backward to put some space between them.

"I didn't mean to frighten you," he said rather uncaringly.

René took a deep breath in an effort to calm her already frayed nerves and get her heart beating normally again. The man had said that he had not meant to frighten her, but the slight glint in his eyes and the hint of a grin at the corners of his mouth made her think that he might not be as concerned about her as he would like her to believe. The thought crossed her mind that he might have actually enjoyed frightening her.

"Are you Miss René Richardson?"

"Yes," she replied, still a little shaken.

"Please, come sit down," he said as he pointed toward a booth near the corner.

René turned and walked toward the booth. She sensed that he was looking her over as he followed her across the room. The feeling did not set well with her. It made her feel like he was stalking her.

After she sat down, he slid into the booth across from her. For the first time, she really looked at him. She found him to be a very handsome man, probably in his late twenties or very early thirties. He had dark wavy hair and dark brown eyes. His features were strong, yet pleasant to the eye. This was simply his outside appearance. René wondered what he was really like on the inside.

"I suppose I should introduce myself. I'm Martin Hanover, Mr. Cosgrove's assistant."

"How do you do, Mr. Hanover."

"Please, call me Martin," he said with a smile.

René did not reply. She simply acknowledged his request with a slight nod of her head and a bit of a smile. It was best to use a certain degree of caution, at least until she got to know him better, she thought.

"I thought that we could have something to eat here before we go to the property, if that's okay with you?" he asked, even though it sounded more like the way it was going to be.

"Certainly," René agreed, as she was not ready to go off alone with him, not just yet, anyway.

René watched him as he turned and motioned for the waitress. There was something about this man that gave her the impression that he might not be what he seemed. It was nothing he said, but more of a feeling than anything that she could actually describe. It was not anything that frightened her, but rather something about him that intrigued her. Yet, it heightened her need to be cautious. He was certainly handsome by any woman's standards, and the clothes he was wearing were expensive, yet conservative. There was also something about him that made René think that there might be a lot more to him.

"Is there something wrong?" he asked after turning around and finding her looking at him with a very concerned look on her face.

"No. No, nothing at all," she replied, feeling a little embarrassed that he had caught her staring at him.

Just then the waitress arrived at the table and handed them each a menu.

"Can I get you something to drink?"

"Yes. Coffee, black, please," René requested.

"Make that two," Martin added.

As the waitress went to get the coffee, René found herself looking at Martin over the top of the menu. When she realized what she was doing, she tipped her eyes down and looked at the menu.

"I think I'll have just a cup of soup and a sandwich," he said as he closed the menu and looked across the table at René.

"That does sound rather good on such a gloomy day," she replied. "I'll have the same."

Martin smiled at her, then laid the menu down on the corner of the table. He folded his hands together and put his elbows on the table as he leaned slightly forward. Putting his chin on his hands he looked across the table at René. He did not speak for a minute or so, though it seemed much longer to René.

René didn't like the way he looked at her. It was almost as if he was looking through her. It was a bit unnerving for her. He startled her when he finally did speak, putting her a little off balance.

"I'm sure that Mr. Cosgrove would have come to show you the property himself, but he is very busy at the moment."

"I'm sure," she replied as she tried to gather her senses.

It seemed to René that Martin understood that he made her a bit nervous, even frightened her a little. It also seemed to her that he rather enjoyed doing it, but she couldn't understand why. She tried to push that thought aside telling herself that it was just her nervousness at meeting a complete stranger.

"I understand that you did not know Mr. Delcambra?"

"No. That's not what I said," she replied, once again in control of herself. "What I said was that I didn't recognize the name. If William Delcambra was my great uncle, I did not know him by that name, only by sight. I do remember meeting a man once when I was about five or six years old, but I don't remember his name. He lived in a large house on a lake in the woods. I would recognize him if I could see a picture of him."

"Oh, I see," he said as he removed his elbows from the table, then sat back and looked at her.

René watched his eyes. They seemed more interested in what she was thinking than in actually looking at her. There was something about the way he looked at her that made her feel uncomfortable. It was almost as if he was trying to see into her soul.

René began to wonder what Mr. Hanover's function in the law firm really was and decided to ask him.

"Are you a lawyer, Mr. Hanover?"

"Please, call me Martin, but to answer your question, no. I'm Mr. Cosgrove's assistant."

"And just what does an assistant do?"

"I show pretty women to estates that they are about to inherit," he said with a pleasant smile.

Although his smile was a pleasant smile, his eyes did not convey the same message. His eyes looked hard and piercing. He seemed pleased that his answer might have irritated her just a little.

"I see," she replied as she returned the smile.

Although Martin seemed pleasant enough, there was something about him that made René wonder what was going on in his mind. The fact that he had simply avoided answering her question by using a smart aleck remark made her even more suspicious of him. She felt that it would not be a good idea for her to trust him too easily, and that she should be leery of what he would tell her.

The waitress interrupted her thoughts when she brought them coffee. René watched the waitress as she set a cup in front of her, then turned her attention to Martin as the waitress set a cup in front of him.

René noticed the way he looked at the young waitress. It reminded her of the look of a predator and the pretty young waitress was his next victim.

The waitress was a pretty young girl, but there was more to it than that. It was clear to René that Martin considered himself to be handsome. She could hardly argue with that assessment, but it was also clear that he thought of himself as very charming.

René got the feeling that Martin used his good looks and charm to play on people, especially women. If she had to describe him to her best friend, she would have to say that he seemed very conceited, even a bit egotistical and very much wrapped up in himself.

"Are you all right?" Martin asked as he looked across the table at René.

"I'm fine. Why do you ask?"

"I'm worried about you."

"Why would you be worried about me?" she asked as she looked at his face for some indication as to his real interest in her.

"You seem so, so distant."

"I guess it was the trip up here. I was almost hit by a large truck. It ran me off the road and the driver never even stopped to see if I was all right or not. I guess it was more upsetting to me than I thought," she explained as she watched him for some reaction.

"Oh, I'm sorry to hear that," he said, but the tone of his voice and the look on his face lacked any signs of sincerity.

There was something about the way Martin said he was sorry that didn't set well with René. It was almost as if he were patronizing her. It did not seem to her that he was one bit concerned about her near accident. The thought occurred to her that he almost seemed disappointed that the truck had not hit her, but that thought seemed to be way out of line, even as skeptical as she was of him.

She took her coffee cup and lifted it up to her lips. As she did, she looked over the rim of the cup at him. The liquid in the cup was hot, but it did not relieve the cold chill that ran through her. There was something very wrong with the whole thing. She was glad to see the waitress coming across the room with their order. It would give her time to think.

She sat back and watched while the waitress set their lunch on the table. She especially watched Martin.

He sat back and turned his attention to the waitress. He smiled up at her. The waitress smiled back.

"Can I get you anything else?" the waitress asked, directing her question to Martin.

"Not at the moment, thank you," he said as he smiled up at her.

René watched him as he watched the waitress turn around and walk back across the room. She found it interesting that he never asked if she needed anything. As he turned back around, René looked down at her food.

"Nice girl," Martin commented casually.

René looked up at him and smiled briefly, but didn't say anything. She was sure he would think so. After all, the waitress had been nice to him, and she obviously didn't mind having a handsome man take a little interest in her.

If Martin was really here just to show her what she was to inherit and nothing more, why was she having these strange and disturbing feelings of distrust about him? What was it about him that she didn't like?

"Aren't you going to eat?"

The sound of his voice caused her to look up at him. She hadn't realized that she had been just sitting there staring at her cup of soup.

"Yes. Yes, of course," she replied. "I was just thinking about something."

"About what, may I ask?" he said with a pleasant smile.

"Oh, nothing important," she said, then smiled at him.

As she took a bite of her sandwich, she watched him. The change of expression on his face indicated that he didn't seem to like the answer she gave him. She got the impression that the fact that she wouldn't answer his question actually angered him just a bit.

During the rest of the meal, René didn't say anything. She continually glanced at Martin as she tried to figure out what it was about him that she didn't like. She wasn't even sure that her suspicions were well founded. After all, she had nothing to go on but her instincts, and they hadn't been very good lately.

They ate their meal in silence. When they were finished, Martin commented, "Well, that was pretty good for a simple lunch."

"Yes, it was," she replied thinking that the use of the word "simple" seemed unnecessary.

Remembering the type of car he drove and having noticed the expensive clothes he had on, it was probably a very simple meal to him. Martin was probably used to fine wines and expensive dinners in high-class restaurants, not soup and sandwiches in some small town café in the middle of nowhere.

"Are you ready to go see the property?"

"Yes. I think that would be a good idea."

"Don't get your hopes up too high. It may prove to be more than you can handle. You might not want to accept it."

"Have you seen this property before," she asked, curious about his comment.

"Well, ah, not exactly," he replied nervously, as if caught in a lie.

"Then why might I not want it?"

"I don't know. I just don't think you should expect too much."

"Oh," she replied, wondering why he would make such a comment if he had never been there. Was it just something to say so she would not get her hopes up, or was there something else behind his comment? The part about "more than you can handle" seemed to stick in her mind. It made her wonder if he was just a male chauvinist or if there was some hidden meaning behind his remark. She wondered if it might be some kind of warning.

Martin didn't say anything more. He turned away from her and walked to the cash register. After he paid the bill, he turned and gestured for René to lead the way out of the cafe. Once outside, René started to walk toward her car.

"You can leave your car here and ride with me," he said, the tone of his voice and the way he said it made it sound more like an order than a suggestion.

René was not used to taking orders, especially from someone she didn't trust. She stopped, turned and looked at him before replying.

"I don't think so. I think I will drive my own car. You never know, I might want to stay overnight."

"Why would you want to do that?" he asked, the look on his face and the tone of his voice indicating that he thought she was not using good judgment.

"I would like a chance to look over the property. I'm sure that Mr. Cosgrove would want me to look it over before I decide if I want to claim it or not. Don't you think?" she asked.

She stood looking at him and waiting for his answer. She had challenged him, and now it was his turn to make a move.

"Ah, yes, I'm sure he would," Martin said, his voice showing a hint of disgust in it.

René smiled to herself as she turned her back to him and walked toward her car. She had noticed that he did not seem very happy with her because she wanted to drive herself to the "property", as he kept calling it. She knew that if she rode with him, he would be in control. She would be forced to leave when he wanted to leave and not necessarily when she was ready to leave. If she had her own car, she could leave anytime she wanted to, with or without him.

Besides not wanting him to have any control over her, there was her lack of trust in him. She was convinced that he was keeping something from her, but she had no idea what it might be.

There was also the fact that she did not think she would feel comfortable with him. The idea of being alone with him in his car did not set well with her. The thought of being alone with him set her nerves on edge for some reason, almost like a warning of some impending danger.

Once she was behind the wheel of her car, she looked over at him in his BMW. The expression on his face indicated that he was upset with her. Martin glanced over at her, and then he pulled away from the cafe rather quickly.

René quickly pulled in behind him. The way he took off from the cafe, leaving deep tracks in the loose gravel simply supported her notion that he might be angry with her. The only question René had was, why? Why was he so angry with her? What possible difference could it make to him if she stayed the night or left early? And what difference could it make to him if she took her car or not?

CHAPTER THREE

René followed Martin's black BMW a few miles down the highway before Martin turned off onto a winding dirt road. She continued to follow him, but he was gradually pulling away from her. It seemed to her that he was intentionally trying to lose her, which didn't make any sense. After all, he was supposed to show her where the property she was to inherit was located, not lose her on some deserted country road in the woods.

When René refused to follow him at such a high rate of speed on the wet, slippery dirt road, he slowed down and allowed her to catch up. There was no doubt in René's mind that he was angry with her, but she could not understand why? His reaction to her not wanting to ride with him had been like that of someone who was used to getting his way and didn't like it when he didn't. Martin's reaction reminded her of a spoiled little child who would throw a temper tantrum when he didn't get what he wanted. His actions simply reinforced her suspicions that she should not trust him.

The rain was coming down in a slow, steady drizzle. René smiled to herself as she watched the back of Martin's fancy car slowly get covered with mud from the wet dirt road. It wasn't long before she could hardly see his taillights for all the mud on them. It struck her as a small bit of justice.

"It serves you right," she said silently to herself as she followed him at a distance.

Suddenly, she saw his brake lights come on and he slowed down to almost a stop. He turned into a narrow driveway in among some trees. René followed his car down the long narrow tree lined dirt driveway until she came out into a large clearing. Straight in front of her was a large two story house.

She stopped her car and sat staring out the rain-splattered windshield at the house. René's breath caught and she could hardly believe her eyes. She had been there before and now that she was seeing the house again, she remembered it. She had been there with her parents when she was a small child.

The view was magnificent, and the house was just the way she remembered it. Off to the left and in front of the house was the large beautiful lake. Off to the right was the narrow drive that led around behind the house to the large garage, which looked like it had been a carriage house at one time.

The house was a large old Victorian style home with long narrow windows. The covered porch had delicately carved woodwork along the railings and at the top of each of the beautifully turned posts that supported the porch roof. There was similar woodwork around the top of each of the six tall, sharply pointed gables.

René glanced off toward the back of the house just in time to see Martin stop in front of the garage and get out of his car. She could see him standing beside his car with his hands on the roof as he looked up the hill toward her. The way he stood gave her the impression that he was wondering why she had stopped. He also seemed impatient for her to come down to the house.

She casually slipped her car into drive and then took her time as she drove down the winding drive to the back of the house. She parked her car next to Martin's car and shut off the engine. She got out and looked up at the house. The memories of the time she had spent there rushed through her senses and filled her mind with the joys that she had experienced.

She remembered the two weeks that she had spent in this beautiful old house and on this lovely lake with her parents. She could remember the hours that she had spent in the kitchen helping her mother and the cook bake pies using the fruit from the cherry trees out behind the carriage house.

She could also remember the hours she spent in the early morning fishing on the lake from a small rowboat with her father. He told her stories when the fish were not biting. That was the summer that her father had taught her how to swim.

It had been a time in her life that she would probably never forget. It was also the time before her father left for war, never to return. Seeing the place again brought back a lot of memories for her, not all of them good ones.

The one memory that she had hidden deep in the recesses of her mind was that of William S. Delcambra. Seeing the old house brought back her memories of him. She suddenly remembered what she and the others had called him.

"Captain Del," she said softly as a smile came over her face.

"Excuse me?"

The sound of Martin's voice startled her. She had not heard him walk up behind her. She turned and looked at him.

"I'm sorry?" she asked wondering what it was that he had said to her.

"I heard you mention a name, at least I think it was a name. What was it?"

"It was nothing. I was just remembering something from a long time ago."

René didn't want to confide in him. It was almost as if recalling her great uncle, Captain Del, was too personal a memory to share with a stranger, especially a stranger that she didn't like.

"Would you like to go inside?" Martin asked, the tone of his voice indicating he meant it as a statement rather than a question.

"No," she replied flatly.

René didn't wait for him to respond. She started walking around to the front of the house. It was still drizzling a little, but René hardly noticed. She was too busy looking at the house and bringing to mind the memories the old place held for her.

The house looked just the same as she remembered. It had the deep red siding with white trim around the windows and the porch. The tree in the front yard seemed much bigger, but that was to be expected. The grassy yard was well trimmed and gently slopped down to a narrow sandy beach that ran along the edge of the lake.

René stood in front of the house and looked toward the lake. She smiled to herself as she remembered her mother spreading out a blanket and sunbathing on the beach while she waded in the warm water close to shore and built castles in the sand.

Tears came to her eyes as she thought of her mother. It had been only a few months after the news of the death of her father that her mother got sick and died. The doctor had said it was pneumonia that caused her death, but René knew that her mother had died from a broken heart. It was at that time that she had gone to live with her grandparents on Long Island, New York.

René wiped the tears from her eyes and then turned around to look up at the house again. She could remember looking out of the second story window late one night and seeing Captain Del standing on the end of the dock looking out over the lake. She had wondered what he was doing out there and what he was thinking about. Unfortunately, she had never gotten up the nerve to ask him. At this moment, she wished that she had asked him.

"Shall we go inside now?" Martin asked impatiently.

Once again he had disturbed her thoughts. He was getting on René's nerves. As she looked at him, she wondered what his big hurry was. From the very beginning it seemed that he didn't want her to spend too much time at the estate. It was almost as if he didn't want her to see the estate at all.

"Yes," she replied and walked toward the porch.

Once on the porch, she noticed the old porch swing at one end of the porch. She stopped and looked at it as she recalled sitting on it with Captain Del and listening to him read to her from books about sailors and the sea. He may have scared her when she first arrived, but during her stay they had become great pals.

The feel of a hand on her arm interrupted her thoughts, again. This was getting very annoying for her. She looked down at Martin's hand, then up at his face. She didn't say anything, but the expression on her face told him that she didn't want to be pushed, and she certainly didn't want him touching her. She just glared at him and waited for him to remove his hand from her arm.

Reluctantly, Martin let go of her. He could see that she was determined to take her time, and there was little he could do about it without making a scene.

As soon as he let go of her arm, René went inside. She could see that nothing had changed inside, either. The larger than life oil painting of Captain Del was still hanging above the stone fireplace, and the furniture was right where she remembered it to be. Stepping into this house was like stepping back into history a century or more.

"This is just as I remember it," René said more to herself than to Martin as she looked around.

"I thought you said you had never been here before?"

"No. I said that I didn't remember ever having been here before, but now I do," she said as she turned and looked at him.

There was a strange look on his face. He seemed somewhat disturbed. The expression on his face indicated that he might not like the fact that she could now remember having been in the old house.

"What's the matter?"

"Oh, nothing. I was just thinking."

"About what?" she asked politely.

"Nothing important," he said with a hint of disgust in his voice.

She didn't like the way his expression suddenly changed when she asked him questions, or the change in the tone of his voice. She got the feeling that he was keeping something from her, something that could be important for her to know. It was almost as if he were irritated by the fact that she was able to remember the place, but she could not understand what possible difference that could make to him.

"Good afternoon," a friendly female voice said.

René turned around to find a rather heavyset, yet pleasant looking woman standing in the doorway behind them.

"Good afternoon," René replied with a smile.

"Can I help you?" the woman asked, then she saw Martin standing off to the side. "Oh, Mr. Hanover. It is good to see you again."

René turned and looked at Martin. She wondered what was going on here. Martin had told her that he had not been there before, but it was obvious that he had lied to her.

"Good afternoon, Mildred," he said with a smile, but the smile quickly faded when his gaze returned to René and saw her looking at him.

"You must be Miss Richardson.

"Yes."

"Welcome. I have heard so much about you from the Captain."

"You knew him?"

"Oh, yes, my dear. I have been his housekeeper for the past fifteen years or so. I'm sorry that you didn't get a chance to see him before he passed away."

"So am I. I don't remember him very well, but I do remember him reading stories to me on the porch swing."

"He talked about you often. Oh, my. I guess I forgot my place. Would you like something to drink, coffee, perhaps?"

"I'm sorry, but we don't have time for that," Martin insisted. "We have to leave shortly so Miss Richardson can get back home before it gets too late."

René turned sharply and looked at him. She was puzzled by his continued insistence that they didn't have any time. She wondered why he was in such a hurry to get her out of there.

"Well, I, for one, would be very happy to have a cup of coffee. It's good weather for a warm cup to wrap your fingers around. Don't you agree?" René asked as she smiled at Mildred and waited for a response.

"Yes, Ma'am," Mildred replied with a smile and a nod, then turned to go to the kitchen.

René looked at Martin. She could see the tightness of his jaw and the stern look in his eyes. It was clear that he was angry with her for delaying their leaving.

"I don't think we have time for this," Martin said rather sharply.

"Maybe you don't, but I do. I have as much time as I want to take," she retorted.

"It is a long trip back to Utica," he reminded her.

"And just what makes you think that I'm going back to Utica tonight?" she countered sharply.

"Well, I thought, . . ."

"I don't care what you thought," she interjected. "I have until the end of the month to decide if I want my great uncle's home or not. I plan to take my time at making that decision. I'm sure that Mr. Cosgrove would expect nothing less, or do I need to call Mr. Cosgrove and ask him?"

René stood with her hands planted firmly on her hips as she looked at Martin. She didn't like being pushed, and she didn't like him. This was going to be a big decision for her to make, and she was going to take her time in making it.

Martin looked at her. His eyes showed his anger with her, but they also showed that he wasn't sure if she would carry out her threat to call Mr. Cosgrove. He looked into her eyes and decided not to press the issue any further. He had probably pressed it about as far as he could without causing problems for himself, and that was the last thing he wanted.

"That won't be necessary," Martin conceded as he stepped back closer to the door.

René took note of the look on his face when she hinted that she would be willing to call Mr. Cosgrove. She couldn't put her finger on it, but there was something about his change of attitude that made her wonder if there was something else going on here. She wondered if Mr. Cosgrove knew how pushy Martin was.

"If you don't wish to drive home in the dark, you are more than welcome to leave now," René said as she walked across the room and sat down in what looked to be a very comfortable high backed chair next to the fireplace. She crossed her arms in front of her, and crossed one leg over the other. She looked at him as if to dare him to continue to press her to leave.

Although René had the upper hand at the moment, she was not sure just how far she could go in objecting to Martin's demands. She could tell that he was getting more and more upset with her. The thought of being alone with him was beginning to make her feel a little apprehensive. She could hardly wait for Mildred to return. She would feel much better if she had someone with her to be a witness just in case things got a little out of hand.

Martin looked like he was about to say something, but remained silent when he saw Mildred come into the living room carrying a tray.

René watched him as Mildred set the tray on a coffee table. She noticed that Martin was watching Mildred rather closely. He had a disgusted look on his face. It was as if he wished she hadn't picked that exact moment to return.

"How do you like your coffee, Miss Richardson?" Mildred asked with a pleasant smile as she poured a cup.

"I like it black, but I would like you to call me René."

Mildred looked a little surprised by René's comment. She was not quite sure just how to respond to René's invitation to be less formal about their relationship.

"Please, sit down with me and have some coffee," René said.

Mildred looked as if she had been asked to do the unthinkable. She again looked at Mr. Hanover, then back at René.

"Oh, Ma'am," she said nervously. "I don't think I should."

"And why not?"

"It's not right. I'm a servant, Ma'am."

"I would like you to sit down with me. I wish to talk to you about the house, the grounds, and about my great uncle.

"Oh, I see. In that case, I would be most happy to join you for coffee," Mildred said with a smile as she started to pour herself a cup.

"I don't think it is necessary for you to discuss the property with the staff. I can provide you with all the information you will need about the property," Martin said with a stern tone to his voice.

Mildred looked at Mr. Hanover, then set her cup down. She seemed confused as to whom she should respond to.

"I will discus the 'property' with anyone I wish, and I wish to discuss it with Mildred. If you don't like it, you are more than welcome to leave," René said, the tone of her voice showing that she was determined not to be intimidated by Martin.

René looked at Martin as he looked at her. René could see the fire in his eyes and knew that he was mad as hell. She knew that he wanted to say something, but she got the impression that he didn't want to say it in front of any of "the staff", as he had so delicately put it. It was almost as if he didn't want any witnesses to what he said to her. René was glad that Mildred was there.

Mildred and René watched as Martin turned on his heels and stormed out the door.

"I'm terribly sorry, Miss Richardson. I didn't mean to cause any trouble," Mildred said.

"You didn't cause any trouble, Mildred. I have no idea what his problem is, but he has been pushy ever since I met him. Do you know who he is?"

"Yes, Ma'am. He is Mr. Cosgrove's personal assistant, at least that is what he told me the other day."

"Then he has been here before?"

"Oh, yes. Several times."

"When was the last time?"

"Let me think. I believe it was last Thursday. Yes, last Thursday."

"When was the first time you saw him here?"

"I believe that would have been just a few days before the Captain passed on. I don't think he saw me, though. I saw him again at the Captain's funeral."

René turned her head and looked up at the picture of the Captain that hung over the fireplace. The fact that Martin had shown up on the day of the funeral was not all that unusual. After all, he was Mr. Cosgrove's assistant. But what was he doing here before the Captain died?

"Did he talk to you at the funeral?"

"Oh, my, no. He would not talk to us. Come to think about it, I didn't see him talk to anyone. Wait, I did see him talking to one of the men at the funeral. I don't know who the man was. I'd never seen him before, but he did seem to know Mr. Hanover quite well. They went out on the dock near the boathouse and talked for some time."

"You never saw the man before?"

"No. And I've never seen him since."

René sipped at her coffee and wondered about Martin. He seemed to be in a hurry to get her away from the estate, but why? What was it that he didn't want her to see? Or was there something that he didn't want her to know about the estate?

"Is there anything else, Ma'am?"

Mildred's question startled René. She hadn't realized that she had been thinking so hard.

"Not right at the moment. I think I would like to take a look around outside before it gets dark. Maybe go down to the boathouse."

"Will you be staying for dinner?"

René thought for a minute before answering. She had no other plans, and she did want to look around some more. Why not stay for dinner? she thought.

"Yes, and I think I will be staying the night if it isn't too much trouble," René added.

"No trouble at all, Ma'am. I'll fix you a room upstairs."

"Would it be too much to ask if I could have the center room in the front? I had that room when I was here as a little girl."

"Oh, I'm sorry. That room has been used for storage ever since you were here. It will take me awhile to get it ready to use."

"That's all right. I'll use one of the other bedrooms."

"I'll prepare the room across the hall for you for tonight. Tomorrow I'll fix up the room in front for you."

"That would be fine, Mildred. Thank you so much. By the way, how many people work here?"

"Just my husband and I. My husband takes care of the grounds and does a little of the maintenance. I do, or did, all the cooking and cleaning inside the house for the Captain."

"If it would not be too much of an inconvenience, I would like to have dinner with you and your husband. That is, if you don't mind."

"Ma'am?"

"I want to have dinner with you and your husband."

"Yes, Ma'am," Mildred replied, not sure what to think.

"What time will dinner be ready?"

"Would six be all right?" Mildred asked.

"Six o'clock would be fine."

René went out on the front porch. She leaned against the railing and took a moment to look out at the lake. She thought about touring the house and looking into each and every room, but decided that there was plenty of time to do that tomorrow. It would be something that would keep her busy and something that she knew she would want to take her time at. Right now was a good time to just relax and remember the past.

She suddenly realized how cold it had become. It was still raining, possibly a little harder than when she arrived. René walked to the end of the porch. She sat down on the swing and reminisced about the time when she had been here as a little girl.

René sat swinging back and forth as she watched the rain fall on the lawn and in the lake. The gray skies seemed to reflect her thoughts as she remembered her father and mother. She wished that they could be with her now. Yet, maybe they were with her in a very special way. René was feeling very lonely at the moment.

* * * *

Time slipped by quickly for her. It didn't seem like she had been sitting on the porch very long when Mildred came out.

"Excuse me, Ma'am. Dinner is ready,"

"Thank you," René replied, then stood up and went inside.

René met Sam Catchum for the first time at dinner. Sam was in his late fifties or early sixties. He looked a little uncomfortable sitting at the dining room table. René was sure that he would have felt much more comfortable at a kitchen table. She considered suggesting it, but Mildred had already set the dining room table for the three of them. There was no need to change everything now.

It was a pleasant meal where they all sat around and had a chance to get acquainted while they ate. A good part of their discussion was about Captain Del, but later it turned to a discussion about the house and grounds.

René got the notion that Mildred and Sam seemed very secure in their positions. Yet, they must have known that there was a very real possibility that they would have to leave the estate.

During the conversation at the dinner table, René found out that Captain Del had some kind of a trust fund set up to insure that the property was kept in good repair. She also found out that the Catchums knew Mr. Cosgrove and spoke very fondly of him. They made it clear that they did not like Martin Hanover very much, although their reasons were a little unclear.

As soon as dinner was over, René thanked them for having dinner with her, then went upstairs to the room that Mildred had prepared for her. She sat on the edge of the bed to think.

René was convinced that something was not right here. Things that would certainly be important for her to know in making a decision on whether or not to accept this property had not been explained to her by Martin. Things like the fact that there was a trust fund set up to maintain the property. Maintenance of a place like this would be a major expense. Knowing that it was taken care of would relieve any worry about it. In fact, it seemed to her that Martin had intentionally not told her about the trust fund. If that was the case, then why was she not being told and what else was Martin keeping from her?

Martin didn't seem to want René to get a very good look at the estate. What was he trying to hide from her?

The Catchums had told her that Mr. Cosgrove had been ill, while Martin had told her that he had been "too busy" to show her the estate. If Mr. Cosgrove was ill, why hadn't Martin simply told her that he was ill? That seemed to René to be rather important bit of information.

When she had talked to Mr. Cosgrove on the phone, he hadn't said anything about being ill that she could remember. In fact, he had not indicated that he was ill at all. Who told the Catchums that Cosgrove was ill? Was it Martin?

René walked over to the window and leaned against the frame. She could see her car parked in front of the carriage house, although she was not really looking at it. Her mind was preoccupied with what she had learned about the estate over dinner.

She thought about what Sam had told her about the trust fund that was used to take care of the property. She wondered what other sort of arrangements Captain Del might have made before his death.

The more she thought about it, the more she was convinced that Captain Del would not have left anything to chance. He must have loved his estate very much to go to the trouble of making sure that it would be kept in good repair, even after his death. If he did that, he certainly would have made some kind of arrangements to make sure the taxes were paid so that the estate could be kept intact.

Suddenly, René realized that she had not seen the terms of the will or any other documents that might be important. In all the excitement at the prospect of inheriting Captain Del's estate, she had not thought to ask to see the will.

René decided that she would spend some time in the morning looking through Captain Del's desk and through his room in an effort to find anything that would help her discover all there was to know about the estate. She would also take some time to call Mr. Cosgrove and find out why she had not seen the will and its terms. It was getting late. Whatever René needed to do, it would have to wait until tomorrow.

After getting ready for bed, René laid down on the bed and curled up under the thick comforter. The bed was warm and comfortable. Although she had set her resolve to find out as much about the estate as she could, there was nothing more she could do tonight. She closed her eyes and tried to clear her mind. It had been a busy and exciting day for her. She was tired and it didn't take long before she was asleep.

CHAPTER FOUR

The sun was just starting to come up over the top of the trees when René woke. She slowly rolled over and sat up on the edge of the bed. She sat there looking around the room for a moment or two before she stood up beside the nice warm bed. René quickly found that the hardwood floor was cool under her bare feet. The slight chill in the room caused her to shiver.

René took the afghan off the foot of the bed and wrapped it around her shoulders then went down the hall to the bathroom and took a warm shower. When she was done, she dressed comfortably wearing jeans, a pullover shirt and comfortable shoes. It just seemed like the kind of a day to dress casually.

As soon as she was ready, she went downstairs to the kitchen and found Mildred busy baking. The aroma of fresh pies baking in the oven filled the air.

"Good morning, Mildred."

"Good morning, Ma'am. Did you sleep well?"

"Yes, I did," René commented as she looked at what Mildred was doing.

"Would you like a cup of coffee?"

"Yes, thank you."

Mildred retrieved a cup from the cupboard and filled it with hot black coffee.

"Thank you," René said as she wrapped her fingers around the warm cup and lifted it to her lips. She sipped the hot liquid as she watched Mildred roll out some dough.

"What are you making? It sure smells good."

"I have an apple pie in the oven, and I'm making breakfast rolls. They will be ready in about fifteen or twenty minutes."

"Sounds delicious. I think I will go and leave you to your work."

Mildred simply acknowledged René's comment with a slight nod of her head and a smiled.

René left the kitchen and went into Captain Del's den. As she entered the room, it suddenly struck her that she was entering a very private and personal part of the Captain's life. When she had visited here as a child, she had not been forbidden to enter his den, but she had been instructed not to touch anything.

The den was a large room with two of the walls covered with bookshelves full of old books. There was a fireplace made from large granite stones with a heavy oak mantel on another wall. Above the mantel was a large oil painting of a young Captain Del. René stood in the center of the room looking up at the picture, almost mesmerized by it.

"You were very handsome in your younger days," she commented quietly to herself.

It suddenly occurred to her that she did not really know him. All she knew about him was that he was her great uncle, that he had apparently liked her, and that he had lived here for a very long time. Other than that, he had been almost a stranger to her.

René let her eyes drift down from the picture to the mantel above the fireplace. She noticed several pictures and a few items that she was sure had been an important part of the Captain's life. She stepped up closer to the mantel to get a better look at the pictures.

The first picture she looked at was that of a young and very beautiful woman. She was dressed in a very nice summer dress and was wearing a hat that was typical of those worn in the mid-to-late thirties. It was clear from the background that the picture had been taken out in front of the house. René wondered who the woman was, but her thoughts were disturbed before she could get closer for a better look at the picture.

"Excuse me, Ma'am."

René swung around to find Mildred standing in the doorway holding a tray. On the tray was a pot of coffee, a plate with fresh breakfast rolls on it, and a small plate of butter.

"That's a picture of the first Mrs. Delcambra," Mildred volunteered as she walked across the room and set the tray down on the coffee table in front of an antique sofa.

"She was the love of the Captain's life, though she was a bit older than he was. It almost crushed him when she died."

"Do you know what was the cause of her death?" René asked as she stared at the picture.

"It is said that she died during childbirth. The Captain lost them both on that stormy night."

"I understand he remarried?"

"Yes, but he never got over the death of his first wife and son. His second wife was an old family friend. It was a marriage of convenience more than a marriage of love for both of them."

"Did he have any other children?" René asked as she turned and looked at Mildred.

"No, Ma'am. He spoke of you as if you were his own grandchild. He has a picture of you when you visited here. You must have been about six years old."

"Yes, I remember that visit. He seemed so big to me at the time," René said with a smile.

"He was a rather tall man. He told me one time that he often wished that you could have come to live with him after he found out that your parents had passed away. But by the time he found out about your mother dying, you were already living with your grandparents. He knew that he could not offer you what your own grandparents could, so he did not interfere with them."

"I never knew that," René replied, a quiver in her voice showing a note of sadness.

"I guess I better get back to the kitchen. If you need anything, just let me know."

"I will, and thank you."

As soon as Mildred left the room, René turned and looked up at the painting of Captain Del again. She wondered why he had not at least let her know that he cared about her. Why had he not tried to contact her?

René took another look around the room. There was a big rolltop desk arranged in such a way that anyone sitting at the desk would be able to look out over the lake. It was easy for her to see why he liked it here. The view of the lake was beautiful, and the room seemed so bright and airy.

René walked across the room and sat down at the desk. She just looked at it for several minutes before trying to lift the rolltop. She quickly found out that it was locked. She tried several of the drawers in the lower part of the desk, but they were locked as well. She wondered where the key to the desk might be.

She looked around the room looking for some place that the Captain might have hidden the key. She quickly realized that there must be a hundred or more places in the room alone where he could have hidden it, to say nothing of the rest of the house.

Once again her eyes fell upon the pictures on the mantel. Other than the pictures of the Captain's two wives, there were two pictures of her. It was the second picture of her that caught and held her attention making her forget about the key for the moment.

She stood up and walked over to the mantel to get a better look at the picture. It was one of her school pictures that had been taken when she lived on Long Island, New York, with her grandparents. She must have been about fourteen at the time.

She wondered who had sent the picture to him. Since she had been living with her grandparents at the time, it was only logical to assume that they must have sent it to him. But why hadn't they told her about him? Why was he such a well kept family secret?

When René picked up the picture to take a closer look at it, something fell to the floor with a metallic thud. She looked down and saw a small old style key lying on the floor. She bent down and picked it up.

Turning the picture over, she found a piece of tape hanging loosely on the felt-like paper backing on the picture. The tape apparently had not stuck very well and the weight of the key caused it to come loose when she moved the frame.

René set the picture back on the mantel. With the key in her hand, she returned to the desk. She slipped the key into the lock and turned it, unlocking the desk.

René hesitated to open the desk. It was almost as if she were afraid that she was trespassing into Captain Del's private world. She had to remind herself that what had once been his private world was now her world, or was it? Unlocking the desk reminded her that she had still not seen the will. Maybe none of this was really hers, she thought as she looked around the room.

She took a deep breath, then carefully lifted the rolltop. Inside she found the desk to be very orderly. Everything was neat and tidy. There were a couple of pens and an inkwell, but no papers laying on the desktop. Along one side were several long vertical slots that held writing paper and envelopes. There were several pigeonholes that held other small items, including wire-rimmed glasses. They were the same glasses she could remember Captain Del wearing when he read to her so many years ago.

She scooted back in the chair and pulled open the wide center drawer of the desk. In the drawer she found several old letters, some paper clips and rubber bands along with pencils and pens. She also found a file folder.

René pulled the file folder out of the drawer and laid it on top of the desk. She hesitated for just a moment before opening the folder.

Once she opened it, she found that it contained a number of legal papers. There was a photocopy of the Captain's birth certificate, a deed to the property, the titles to a boat and two cars, and two marriage licenses. The one thing that René was really hoping to find, his will or a copy of it, was not in the folder.

When she had finished looking through the papers in the folder, she set the folder aside and continued to look through the drawer. She came across an envelope with Mr. Cosgrove's name on it. It contained a letter from Mr. Cosgrove to Captain Del.

René hesitated to remove the letter from the envelope, but since it had already been opened she could see no reason not to read it. René removed the letter and unfolded it. The letter appeared to be more of a business letter than a personal letter. She began to read it.

Dear Del,

With regard to your question about leaving your estate to Miss Richardson, I feel that you will need to make the necessary arrangements that will insure that the property has sufficient funds to maintain the house and grounds.

Having completed a background check on her, I have determined that she would probably not be able to financially support the property on her own.

In order to provide the means to care for your estate after your death, might I suggest that we arrange a trust fund of sufficient size that it would provide for the maintenance, taxes and general care of the estate. It is not that difficult a process. It can be arranged through almost any bank. And it can be done in complete privacy, as you requested. I can assist you with this, if you wish.

Might I also suggest, old friend, that any trust funds you set up to maintain your estate be left to Miss Richardson should she decide not to accept the estate.

I look forward to hearing from you soon. Since you do not wish to have anyone know what your plans are, please continue to contact me at my home.

Your friend, Frank

The letter was signed simply, "Frank". It suddenly became clear to René that Mr. Cosgrove and the Captain might have had a much closer relationship than that of a lawyer and his client. She was now more convinced than ever that Mr. Cosgrove and the Captain were friends, but more importantly she was convinced that Martin was probably keeping important information from her. The only thing she did not understand was why he would do that?

After going through the desk and not finding anything that even resembled a will, René leaned backed and looked up at the picture of Captain Del. Someone had to know where Captain Del's important papers were hidden. Logic told her that Mr. Cosgrove would have a copy of the will. It was time to call him and find out just what belonged to her and what belonged to someone else.

Just as she was about to reach for the phone on the small table next to the desk, she heard the door to the den open. Startled by the sound of someone at the door, she quickly pushed the desk drawers shut before swinging around to see who was there. She found Mildred standing in the doorway with her hands clasped in front of her and a worried look on her face.

"Excuse me, Ma'am, but Mr. Hanover is here to see you," Mildred said, the tone of her voice indicating that she was a little upset or nervous about his being there.

"What does he want?" René asked abruptly.

Before Mildred could answer, Martin pushed his way through the door and stormed into the den. The way he barged into the room alarmed René. He seemed so forceful and direct, which frightened her. The nervousness that Mildred displayed didn't help René feel any safer with him in the room.

Martin stopped suddenly when he noticed that the desk was open. He seemed surprised that René had managed to get it open. It seemed to set him back a little causing him to stare at it. His eyes instantly went to the file folder lying on the desk. He quickly turned his eyes to René when he realized that he was staring at the file folder.

René felt that he was showing just a little too much interest in the file folder. Since the file folder was closed, she knew that he could not see what was in it, but that didn't seem to be enough for her. René quickly pulled the rolltop desk down, covering the file folder. If it was out of sight, he might not ask to see it. She quickly locked the desk before standing up and putting the key in her pocket.

"I want to see you," Martin blurred out, then his eyes drifted back to the closed desk.

René thought she could see a sudden change in his eyes, but she was not sure what it meant. Had the fact that she locked the desk conveyed her message to him that what was inside the desk was not something she wanted him to see? She certainly hoped so.

"Well, I see you are finding your way around," Martin said in his most pleasant voice as he once again looked at her before glancing back at the desk.

But it was more than the tone of his voice that caught René's attention. It was his eyes and the way he seemed to look right past her at the desk. It was clear to her that he was far more interested in what was in the desk, than in how well René was "finding her way around". It made her wonder if he already knew what was in the desk, or if he wished he knew what was in the desk.

"What can I do for you?" René asked as she straightened her shoulders in an effort to show him that she was in control of her new position as head of the house.

"I see you found the key to that old desk."

"Yes. What of it?"

"Oh, nothing."

"Are you upset because you couldn't find the key the last time you were here?"

"I don't know what you're talking about," Martin replied, the tone of his voice revealing a defensive stance.

"I know that yesterday was not the first time you were here. I happen to know that you were here on the day of Captain Del's funeral. That doesn't seem to match up with what you told me yesterday."

Martin didn't respond immediately. He was searching his mind for just the right thing to say without making a complete fool of himself.

René could see by the look on his face that he was trying to figure out a way to cover his tracks. She could also see in his eyes that it had made him angry that she had caught him in his own lie.

Just as he was about to speak, René noticed Mildred start to turn as if she was going to leave them alone in the den. René, for all her show of strength, was afraid of Martin and afraid of what he might do. The last thing she wanted was to be left alone with him.

"Mildred, please don't leave just yet."

Martin turned and glanced over his shoulder at Mildred, then turned back toward René. Mildred had stopped and stood silently at the door.

"Unless you have some business with me, I would suggest that you leave," René said.

"I'm afraid that you must have misunderstood me," Martin said with as much charm and composure as he could muster under the circumstances. "I have been here once before."

René just looked at him. She had no reason to believe him as Mildred had told her that he had been there at least twice before. René tended to believe Mildred over Martin, but it was not important how many times he had been there. All she wanted was for him to leave, and to leave now before her show of strength collapsed.

"I believe that we have no further business at this time. That being the case, I suggest that you leave," René said with as much authority as she could.

"I... I... I will be talking to Mr. Cosgrove very shortly. I'm sure that he will want me to have you sign some papers," he said, trying to think of what to say or do next.

René realized that he was stumbling for something important to say. She knew that she would have papers to sign. He didn't need to tell her that. She was just as sure that he had come here with a completely different agenda in mind, but that all seemed to have changed when he found out that she had gotten the desk open.

"In that case, you may leave until you have those papers. Mildred, will you please show Mr. Hanover to the door?"

Martin's eyes narrowed at the thought of this young woman dismissing him like he was some commoner. He glanced at the desk again, then turned on his heels and stormed out of the den, not waiting for Mildred to show him the way.

Mildred watched Martin as he stormed past her. As soon as he was gone, she turned and looked at René.

"I do believe that you upset him," Mildred said with a slight grin.

"I think I did more than that. I think I made him downright mad," René replied with a sigh, only too happy that he had gone.

After Mildred had left the den, René dropped down into the desk chair and let out a long sigh of relief. It had worked this time. Her show of strength had gotten rid of him for now, but she was sure that it was not the last time that she would have to deal with him. She knew that she would see him again, but she hoped that it would not be too soon.

As René sat staring at the front of the desk, she could still visualize the look on Martin's face when he saw that she had managed to find the key and get the desk open. Why was he so interested in the desk? What did he think was in there that would be important to him? There must be something in the desk that he wanted, and wanted very badly, but what? René knew that there was only one way to find out.

René opened the desk again and started going through every drawer, every pigeonhole and every space that could hold anything no matter how small. When she found three letters that were hand written to the Captain from Franklin Cosgrove, she leaned back in the desk chair and read each letter.

The letters turned out to be personal letters and had no significant meaning to René. Yet, they did point out one very important fact. Captain Del and Franklin Cosgrove were very close friends, and had probably been friends for a very long time.

One of the letters showed Franklin Cosgrove's concern for Captain Del's private papers by suggesting that the Captain get himself a safety deposit box at a bank and keep his personal papers in it. One paragraph in one of the letters even suggested that the Captain should be a little more cautious about discussing anything of a financial nature, especially with regard to his estate or the contents of his will with anyone. The letter gave no reason for Franklin's lack of trust, nor did it suggest whom it might be that he didn't trust.

René did find a key to a safety deposit box at a bank in Albany, New York. It assured her that the Captain had more than likely taken Mr. Cosgrove's advice. She slipped the key into her pocket.

During her search of the desk, René also found a small caliber automatic pistol in one of the drawers. Having been raised with a grandfather who was an avid hunter and sportsman, she had learned how to handle a gun. She checked it and found it to be loaded. She put it back in the desk, making a mental note of where she put it.

It was getting on toward noon when René finished her search of the desk. She had found nothing more that would help her in her quest for information about Captain Del's estate.

She sat back in the chair and looked around the room. It seemed strange, but she felt very comfortable there. It was almost as if she belonged there.

"Did you know what was going on around here before you died?" she asked out loud as she looked up at the painting of Captain Del. "More importantly, did you tell anyone?"

René thought about her last question. If Captain Del had known anything about what was going on, and if he had told anyone, the one person that he was most likely to have told would have been his closest friend, Franklin Cosgrove.

It was time to give Mr. Cosgrove a call. Maybe he could shed some light on what was going on here.

René looked up Franklin Cosgrove's home phone number, then placed the call. The phone rang only twice before it was answered.

"Hello?"

"Hello. Is this Mr. Franklin Cosgrove?"

"Yes."

"Mr. Cosgrove, this is René Richardson."

"Yes," he said, the tone of his voice indicating that he was happy to hear from her. "What can I do for you?"

"I would like to know if it would be possible to meet with you and discuss my great uncle's estate?

"Why certainly. Would it be possible for you to come to Albany and visit with me? I think I can probably answer any of your questions."

"Yes, I guess so," René replied.

"Good. You are welcome to stay the night at my home, if you wish. My wife would like very much to meet you, as would I. We have heard so much about you from Del."

"Okay. I'll leave shortly after lunch. I should be there late this afternoon, if that's all right with you?"

"Excellent. You can join my wife and I for dinner. I look forward to meeting you."

"Thank you," René replied, then hung up the phone.

René leaned back in the chair. Her eyes automatically went to the picture of Captain Del. She had to wonder if she was doing the right thing by going to Mr. Cosgrove's home. He had sounded friendly enough, but so had Martin when she talked to him on the phone.

She knew that if she was to get any answers to her questions, she was going to have to meet with Mr. Cosgrove. Something in the back of her mind told her that if he was such a good friend of Captain Del's, then it would probably be safe to visit with him. That thought reassured her that she had made the right decision.

CHAPTER FIVE

After completing her call to Mr. Cosgrove, René took a moment to make sure that the desk was locked and then left the den. As she entered the kitchen, she saw Mildred and Sam sitting at the kitchen table drinking coffee. She decided to join them. After getting a cup from the cupboard, she poured herself a cup of coffee and sat down across the table from them.

"Did you find what you were looking for, Ma'am?" Mildred asked.

"Not entirely. I did find out some very interesting information, though."

"Oh, really?" Sam said, his interest peaking.

"Yes. Have either of you ever met Mr. Cosgrove?"

"Oh, my, yes. He would often come here to go fishing with the Captain," Mildred declared.

"Yes," Sam agreed. "Mr. Cosgrove often stayed overnight in the very room you're staying in."

"Did you see the chess set in the den?" Mildred asked.

"Yes, I did."

"The Captain and Mr. Cosgrove would sit and play chess for hours. Sometimes until it was so late that Mr. Cosgrove would stay the night rather than drive back to Albany in the middle of the night. I have often thought that the Captain made the games last longer just so he could get his old friend to stay the night. I don't think Mr. Cosgrove minded very much, either. He always seemed to like to spend time here."

"Was Captain Del that lonely?"

"I don't know if he was lonely or not. He might have been, but I think it was more the fact that he liked Mr. Cosgrove's company," Sam explained.

"Oh, I almost forgot. I came into the kitchen to tell you that I won't be here for dinner tonight. In fact, I won't be staying overnight tonight."

"Oh," Mildred said as she looked from René to Sam, then back to René. "Are you going back home?"

"No. No, I'm not. I'm going into Albany to see Mr. Cosgrove. I'll be back, probably tomorrow afternoon. I would prefer that you not tell anyone where I have gone."

"What should we say to Mr. Hanover if he should come back and ask for you?" Mildred asked, the tone of her voice showing her concern.

"Tell him that I went to - - -, on second thought, don't tell him anything. As far as he is concerned, you have no idea where I went or when I will be back," René explained.

"Yes, Ma'am." Mildred nodded her head to assure René that she understood.

"I wouldn't be surprised if he comes back as soon as he discovers that I've gone. I get the feeling that he would prefer it if I was not here, anyway. But just in case he should come back, you can tell him that I will be contacting the police and filing harassment and trespassing charges against him if he doesn't leave immediately. Can you do that?" René asked.

"We sure can," Sam said with confidence. "I never liked that man very much. I never trusted him, either."

"Good," René replied with a smile. "If he gives you any trouble, call the police and have him removed from the property."

"Yes, Ma'am," Sam said with a grin.

"How about something to eat before you go?" Mildred suggested.

"That would be nice."

While Mildred prepared sandwiches, René went to her room and packed an overnight bag to take with her. When she returned to the kitchen, she found that lunch was ready. She sat down with Sam and Mildred at the kitchen table to eat.

After lunch, Mildred filled a small insulated cup with coffee for René to take with her. Sam and Mildred followed her out the back door.

"You be careful now. The road down to the highway is still pretty muddy and slippery," Sam said.

"I will."

* * * *

René got into her car and drove along the winding driveway. As she glanced over her shoulder, she saw Mildred and Sam still standing at the back door watching her as she drove away. She got the feeling that they really cared about her. They had already become almost like family to her, and that thought made her feel a little less lonely.

After turning out onto the dirt road, René headed back toward the highway that would take her east to the interstate. As she drove, her thoughts turned to Mr. Cosgrove and the reason that she was going to Albany. Her mind filled with questions that she wanted to ask him, but those questions would have to wait.

A quick glance into her rearview mirror revealed a car some distance behind her. At first she paid little attention to it. She had seen it pull out from under some trees onto the road, but it was too far back for her to identify. The only thing she could be sure of was that the car was dark colored such as a dark green or blue, maybe even black.

It suddenly occurred to her that if it was black, it could be Martin. A thought rushed through her mind. If it was Martin, he must have decided to follow her. But at this distance she couldn't be sure that it was him. Then again, if it was Martin, what did he have on his mind? Did he plan to follow her to see where she was going, or was he following her just to make sure she left before he returned to the estate?

With all that had happened up until now, she quickly became convinced that it was Martin. She could not think of anyone else that drove a dark colored car. René's mind was going a mile a minute trying to figure out what Martin was doing and what she should do about it.

It wasn't long before her imagination was producing all kinds of scenarios that caused her to become very frightened and nervous. She knew that there were a number of areas along the roads that she was taking that could be very lonely. There would be plenty of places where he would be able to catch up to her and even run her off the road, if he had a mind to, and no one would know. She knew that her little car would never be able to outrun his BMW.

Once again fear began to grip her chest making it hard for her to breathe. Her heart started to beat rapidly as panic was beginning to take control of her. She looked straight ahead in the hope of finding some place where there were people, or a place where she could stop so that she could try to regain some control of her emotions. She was afraid to look in the rearview mirror for fear of losing what little control of her emotions she still had.

When René finally worked up the courage to look in the rearview mirror again, she discovered that there was no one behind her. The dark colored car had simply disappeared as quickly as it had appeared. She wondered what had happened to it. Had it all been in her mind?

The disappearance of the dark colored car was almost as unnerving for her as seeing it behind her. She found it difficult to believe that it had been there one minute and was gone the next.

In her state of near panic, not knowing where the car had gone was almost more frightening for René than seeing it behind her. At least when it was behind her, she knew where it was.

René kept glancing in the rearview mirror as if she expected to see the dark colored car suddenly reappear. She gripped the steering wheel with both hands as if her life depended on it. René continued to drive along the twisting and turning road, her nerves on edge and her mind filled with fear.

In her current state of mind, René didn't realize that she had been gradually increasing her speed. It was only when she came upon a rather sharp curve that she suddenly realized that she was going much too fast. The tires began to squeal in protest as the car began to drift toward the edge of the road. René hit the brakes causing the wheels to lock up and for her to lose control. The tires continued to protest until the car skidded off the pavement and onto a grassy area where it finally skidded to a stop.

René closed her eyes and leaned over the steering wheel. She rested her forehead on her hands as she gasped for air. She had difficulty catching her breath and calming her frayed nerves. It took several minutes before she was able to regain any control of herself and several more before she felt that she could open her eyes again.

She slowly lifted her head from her hands and opened her eyes. She looked at where her car had come to rest. She could not believe that she had let her fears get so out of hand, and for the second time in as many days. She knew that she was an intelligent woman, but she was acting more like a scared, frightened teenager.

"Get control of yourself," she said angrily to herself.

René leaned back and took a couple more deep breaths before looking around. When she glanced up at the rearview mirror, her heart pounded and her breath caught. She could see the reflection of a black sedan in the rearview mirror. It had stopped along the side of the road several hundred feet away.

When the car didn't move, René took another deep breath as she gathered up what little courage she could muster. She reached over and opened the door. Slowly, she got out of her car and stood up in the hope of getting a better look at the black sedan. But as soon as she stood up along side her car, the black sedan hastily turned around in the middle of the road and sped away, quickly disappearing around a sharp curve.

Unfortunately, René had not been able to get a good look at the car, or its driver. It was too far away for her to read the license plate, but from the color and design she was sure that it was a New York State plate.

After the black sedan disappeared from sight, René's knees went weak. She had to sit down on the edge of the seat. Putting her head in her hands, she began crying uncontrollably.

It took her a long time before she stopped crying and felt like she could safely drive again. She swung her legs back into her car and started it, but she took a minute to dry her eyes before getting her car back on the road.

Once she was back on the highway and headed for Albany, she found herself continually glancing into her rearview mirror. She didn't see the car again all the way to the interstate.

Once on the interstate, René began to feel a little safer. There was a lot of traffic that moved along smoothly. The sun was up, the weather was clear and the roads were dry. But best of all, she had people all around her. Just the fact that there were cars around her made her feel as if she were out of danger, at least for the moment.

* * * *

It was almost four o'clock in the afternoon before René finally arrived in Albany. It took her another half an hour or so to find the residence of Mr. Franklin Cosgrove. The large house was located on a hill in a wooded area overlooking the Hudson River just outside the city limits of Albany.

As she stepped out of her car in front of the house, an elderly man stepped off the porch and came toward her. He had a pleasant smile and appeared to be in good health.

"Mr. Cosgrove?"

"Welcome, René. Please call me, Franklin. I would know you anywhere, my dear."

"How is that?"

"Del talked of you often, and there is a picture of you on the mantel above the fireplace in his den," Franklin explained.

"Oh, yes. I forgot."

"Come. Please, come inside," he insisted.

Mr. Cosgrove seemed very pleasant. He led her into the house. Inside, René met a nice looking woman who appeared to be much younger than Mr. Cosgrove.

"René, this is my wife, Kathleen. Kathleen, this is René Richardson."

"It is so nice to meet you. I have heard so much about you from Del," Kathleen said with a welcoming smile.

René wondered what was going on. How would they hear about her from Captain Del unless someone had been keeping him informed on where she was and what she was doing?

"It's nice to meet you, Mrs. Cosgrove."

"Oh please, call me, Kathleen."

"You look a little confused," Franklin said, his concern for her showing in the expression on his face.

"Franklin! She has come a long way to see us and we are strangers to her. I'm sure that she would like to freshen up a little before we sit down to get to know each other."

"No! I - - - I mean, I'm sorry, but I am a little confused. You seem to know all about me, yet I know very little about you."

"I'm the one who should be sorry. I'm sure you must have a million questions. Why don't you get settled in, then we will have a nice long talk over coffee. You do drink coffee?" Franklin asked with a smile.

"Yes, of course," she replied.

"I promise to answer each and every one of your questions as best I can."

"Thank you."

"Kathleen, would you show her to the guest room?"

"Yes, dear," Kathleen replied with a smile. "Come along, dear."

Kathleen motioned for René to follow her. René followed her up the long spiral staircase to the second floor.

"How was your trip?' Kathleen asked.

René noticed that Kathleen had not turned to face her when she spoke. At first it seemed like a strange question, but as she followed Kathleen she realized that it was not really all that strange a question. René decided that it must have been her frazzled nerves that made her think that.

"It was all right," René answered.

René had decided not to say anything about her trip or the black car. Other than the fact that she could not prove that any of it was intentional, she didn't want to upset anyone.

"That's nice," Kathleen replied as she stopped and opened the door to a room, then turned to René. René stepped to the door and looked in. It was a comfortable looking room.

"This will be your room for as long as you would like to stay," Kathleen said. "This is the room that Del often used when he would come to visit."

"Did he come very often?"

"Yes. Yes, he did," Kathleen replied. "When you are ready, please come down. We will be in the den. It's to the left at the bottom of the stairs."

"Thank you," René replied, then watched as Kathleen turned and left the room.

René took a minute to look around the room. It was a very pleasant room, light and airy, and it seemed warm. She was sure it was the kind of room Captain Del would have liked.

After refreshing herself, René wandered downstairs. She hoped that they could shed some light on what was going on at the estate. She was also positive that Mr. Cosgrove could explain the terms of Captain Del's will.

"Come in, please," Franklin said when he saw her at the door to the den.

"Would you like a cup of coffee, dear?" Kathleen asked.

"Yes, please."

"I'm sure you have a lot of questions to ask me. I'm ready to answer all of them as best I can," Franklin said with a smile.

"I would appreciate that," she said as she took the cup of coffee that was offered her by Kathleen.

After making sure that René was comfortable, Kathleen turned and left the room leaving her with Franklin. Franklin began by telling René about his lifetime relationship with Captain Del.

"Del and I grew up together until the mid-thirties. He joined a group of soldiers of fortune and went off to fight in China against the Japanese. He was the captain on a submarine that sank a large number of Japanese freighters carrying supplies to the Japanese forces that had invaded China. It was all sort of hush-hush at the time.

"He never liked to talk about it, but after he came home he was never the same. He tried to join the Navy at the outbreak of World War II, but because of his health they would not let him join. His family had a great deal of money, which he inherited. He bought the property on the lake and built that big house for his bride."

"So he was really a ship's captain?" René asked.

"Oh, yes. He never served in the U.S. Navy, but he did his part in slowing the expansion of the Japanese Empire just before the outbreak of World War II. He was as much a war hero as anyone."

"Why didn't he try to get in touch with me after my parents died?"

"That I'm afraid I can't answer. In the last few years he had become very weak and couldn't do much. I would go to his house and play chess with him as often as I could. He liked to play chess, and it was the one thing that he could still do well even after he became very ill."

"Why did he want to leave the estate to me? He hardly knew me."

"Keeping the estate intact was the one thing that Del wanted more than anything else, other than for you to have it. I think he knew that you would like the place. And he felt that you were the one person who would do whatever it took to keep the estate intact."

"Well, I am considering doing just that."

"Great. Nothing would have pleased him more."

"I'm not sure that I am going to live there."

"Oh, but I thought you said you were going to keep the estate?"

"I am. I just don't know if I can afford to live there all year round. I would certainly like to, but I have to make a living."

Franklin looked at her with a surprised look on his face. As he looked at her, his eyes narrowed as he thought about what she had said. He had a feeling that she must not have seen the will.

"Would it be correct for me to assume that you have not read Del's will?" he asked, the expression on his face indicating that she should have read it.

"No, I haven't."

"Didn't Martin go over the will with you and give you your copy of it?"

"No."

"That's strange. I gave him a copy of the will with instructions to give it to you."

"If you gave it to him, he never gave it to me. That's why I came to you. I want to find out what was actually in the will," René said.

"Do you happen to know where Martin is now?" Franklin asked, the expression on his face showing a great deal of concern.

"No. I have no idea where he is. All I know is that as soon as we got to the estate, he seemed to be in a big hurry to get me away from it. He acted like he didn't want me to spend any time there. I got the impression that he would have preferred that I didn't see the estate at all."

"That's strange," Franklin said. "He was supposed to give you all the time you needed to look over the estate and to study the terms of the will."

René was positive from the tone of Franklin's voice and by the look on his face that he was as confused as anyone over Martin's actions.

"What's going on?" René asked as she looked at Franklin for answers.

"I don't know, but I wish I did. When Martin called and said that you had called about the letter, he asked me if I would mind if he showed you the property."

"He told me that you told him to show me the property. He said that you were too busy to show it to me."

"I would never be too busy to show you Del's estate. But - - - in a sense, I guess maybe I did," Franklin said thoughtfully. "But it was not because I was too busy. It was because he asked me if he could show it to you."

"That's interesting. Why would he want to show me the property, then try to get me away from it as soon as he could?"

"I have no idea, unless - - -," Franklin replied, then hesitated as he looked across his desk at René.

"Unless what?"

"Unless he doesn't want you to claim the estate," Franklin said as he rubbed his chin thoughtfully.

"What difference would it make to him if I claim the estate or not?" René asked.

"Now that I don't know, but there has to be a reason. I've never known Martin to do anything without a reason."

The thought that Martin might be trying to get control of Captain Del's estate passed through René's mind once again. It was easy to see that it was a valuable piece of real estate. She could think of no other reason for him to act the way he did.

"If you and Captain Del were such good friends, why didn't you go to his funeral?"

"I haven't heard him called 'Captain Del' in years," he said with a smile.

"Mildred said that you had not been feeling well since you had a heart attack just before Captain Del died. Is that why you didn't go?"

"I've never had a heart attack," he replied with surprise. "I don't know where she got that idea. But to answer your question, I was in England when he passed away. I wasn't told about his death until after I returned some three weeks after the funeral. If I had known about it, I would have come home immediately to attend his funeral."

"Did your office know where you were?"

"Yes, of course. They knew how to get in touch with me."

"Did you know that Martin attended Captain Del's funeral?"

"No. As a matter of fact, I didn't. Why would he attend the funeral?"

"That's a good question. I wish I knew the answer," René said.

"I'll tell you what. I have a copy of Del's will here. I'll give it to you after dinner. You are more than welcome to look it over here in my den. If you have any questions, I'll be right here to answer them," he said in a reassuring voice.

"Thank you," René replied.

The look on Franklin's face was enough to tell René that he was as concerned about what was going on as much she was. He seemed honestly puzzled by Martin's actions.

There was a light tap on the door. René looked toward the door in time to see Kathleen step into the room.

"I hate to interrupt, but dinner is ready," Kathleen said with a smile.

René stood up and followed Kathleen into the dining room with Franklin close behind. The aroma of the dinner filled the room. René had not realized just how hungry she was until she was in the dining room.

"Please, sit down," Franklin said as he gestured toward a chair.

René sat down across from Kathleen, while Franklin sat at the head of the table. The conversation during dinner was mostly about Captain Del. René became aware of how much a part of the Cosgroves' life the Captain had been, especially Franklin's. It was clear that they loved him and enjoyed his company, and how much they missed him now that he was gone.

Franklin spoke fondly of the times he had spent at the lake with Captain Del. He spent most of their time at the table talking about fishing trips, and hunting trips into the woods on the estate, and of course, chess games he and the Captain had enjoyed together.

Kathleen talked about how hard it had been for the Captain when his first wife passed away. It seemed that the Captain had spent the better part of a year in Albany with the Cosgroves after her death, as he could not bear to return to the empty house on the lake.

"Del finally accepted the death of his wife, but it took him more than a year," Kathleen said.

"She must have been someone very special," René said.

"She was very special. She loved Del's estate almost as much as he did. She was beautiful and intelligent. Very much like you, dear," Kathleen said with a smile.

René was a little embarrassed by Kathleen's comment. She had never considered herself beautiful.

"I think it is time for René and I to retire to the den," Franklin said as he pushed back from the table.

"Yes. I would like to read the will."

René noticed a sudden change in the expression on Kathleen's face at the mention of Captain Del's will. However, Kathleen quickly forced a smile when she noticed that René was watching her.

"I'll bring you some coffee in a little while," Kathleen said as she stood up from the table.

* * * *

Franklin and René returned to the den. René sat down and watched Franklin as he unlocked his desk. He took a blue folder out of his desk and handed it to René.

Reluctantly, René took the folder and looked at it. She was almost afraid to open it. She looked up at Franklin.

"Go ahead. It's all right. You'll even find a letter addressed to you in there," Franklin said, his voice soft with a hint of understanding at what René was going through.

René opened the folder and took out the will. Franklin was right, there was a letter inside. She set the will on the edge of the desk and carefully opened the letter. After looking at Franklin, she looked back at the letter and began reading it to herself.

Dear Missy,

I write you this letter not to make you sad, but to let you know that I have gone to a better place. I know that it is hard for you to understand, but it is true.

I have made all the necessary arrangements for you to have my estate on the lake. I have done all I can to assure

78

that you will not be financially burdened by it. I can only hope that you will treasure it as much as I did.

Please do not hesitate to ask Franklin for any guidance that you may need. He has been my very close friend for many years.

Should you decide that you do not wish to have my estate, do not feel that you are letting me down.

I only wish that I could have gotten to know you. Your grandparents kept me well informed as you grew to womanhood. I wish you nothing but happiness all the days of your life.

With Love, Captain Del

René sat in the chair and stared at the letter. Tears filled her eyes as she thought about what it had said. She only wished that her grandparents had let her know about Captain Del. If she had known about his interest in her, she would have taken the time to visit him in an effort to get to know him.

"I remember him calling me, Missy," she said as her voice trembled and tears rolled down her cheeks.

Franklin looked at her for a moment, then walked around the desk. He handed her a tissue then put his arms around her to comfort her.

As he tried to comfort her, he wondered why Martin had not given her a copy of the will and a copy of the letter. What was his interest in Captain Del's estate? What was Martin up to?

There was no question in Franklin's mind that Martin was not working in his or René's best interest. Martin had probably used the law firm to get inside information on Captain Del's estate, but why? What was he planning? The thought also crossed Frankin's mind as to what other inside information had he gotten while working in the law firm?

"I'm sorry," René said as she looked up at Franklin and wiped the tears from her eyes.

Her comment interrupted Franklin's thoughts. He stepped back and looked at her. He wanted her to know that she would not have any problems with Martin, but he could not promise her that. He couldn't even fire Martin without the other partners agreeing to it. And to get them to agree, he would have to have some very solid proof that Martin was doing something illegal, or at the least unethical.

"I've been wondering what Martin's interest in Del's estate could be," Franklin said.

"Do you suppose that he is trying to get the estate for himself?"

"I don't know, but I'm going to find out."

"I'm sorry, but I'm kind of tired. If you don't mind, I think I would like to get some rest before I read the will."

"I understand. I'm sure it has been a long day for you. We can talk again in the morning," Franklin assured her.

"Thank you for understanding," René said as she stood up.

René left Franklin in the den with her copy of the will, but she kept the letter. Once inside her room, she sat down on the edge of the bed and stared at the letter as she thought about what it had said. She was tired and knew that she would not be able to make any sense out of anything if she didn't get some rest.

She put the letter down on the bedside table, then got ready for bed. Once she crawled in between the fresh sheets and laid her head down on the pillow, she found it easy to close her eyes. But it was not so easy for her to get her mind to relax. She could not stop thinking about the letter and about how guilty she felt for not making an effort to get to know Captain Del. If only her grandparents had told her about him, if only. Interesting how life was full of "if only", she thought.

She was tired from the long day and the emotional ups and downs, yet it still took her some time before she finally drifted off into what could only be described as a rather restless sleep. René tossed and turned, waking from time to time and drifting in and out of sleep. It was a long night with little real rest for her.

CHAPTER SIX

René woke with the morning sunlight shining in around the edges of the curtains that covered the long narrow windows. The light cast a pleasant glow over the entire room, giving it a warm comfortable air. She wasn't sure what it was that woke her, but she thought that she had heard something that sounded like the closing of a car door outside her window. She swung her feet out of bed and stood up. She slipped into her robe as she went over to the window to look outside. Drawing the curtains back a little, she looked out.

Out in back, near the far corner of the yard, was a small grove of trees. Hidden in among the trees was a small house. It looked like it might have been servant quarters at one time, or possibly a studio of some kind.

René caught a glimpse of some sort of movement behind the house. Although it had caught her attention, it was hard for her to see what it was. Whatever was behind the small house was almost completely hidden by the surrounding trees and the house itself. It wasn't until it moved out from behind the trees and into the open that René realized what she was seeing.

Her breath caught and her heart raced as she tried to understand what she was seeing. René could hardly believe her eyes. It couldn't be, not here, she thought. She leaned closer to the window and strained in the effort to get a better look.

What she saw was what appeared to be a black car backing away from the back of the small house. It then quickly disappeared down the alley behind the trees as it drove off. René was sure that she had gotten a pretty good look at the rear of the car. The fact that the back of the car was dirty immediately made her think that it might have been Martin's BMW.

She began to wonder what Martin was doing there. Why was he sneaking around in back? It only seemed logical that if he were here to see Franklin, he would have come to the front of the house. Her mind was filled with confusion.

Suddenly, her attention was drawn to the front of the small house. Someone was coming out of it, but it was hard for her to see who it might be with all the trees blocking her view.

As she watched, Kathleen stepped out from behind the cover of the trees. She stopped near the edge of the trees as she finished buttoning her blouse. As she tucked her blouse into her slacks, she looked up toward the house. There was a rather pleasant smile on Kathleen's face as if she had just done something that she had really enjoyed.

René quickly ducked back away from the window to avoid being seen. She didn't think Kathleen had seen her, at least she hoped that she had not been seen.

As René leaned back against the wall, she began to speculate on what Kathleen and Martin might have been doing out there. It didn't take her long to realize that it was obvious by Kathleen's actions what they had been doing. At first, René found it hard to believe that Kathleen could have anything to do with the likes of Martin. She seemed so devoted to Franklin, and Martin was such an arrogant, self-centered male.

Yet, Kathleen was an attractive woman, although some years older than Martin. And René had to admit that Martin was a handsome man, even if she did not like him.

René walked across the room and sat down on the edge of the bed. No matter how hard she tried, she could not get what she had seen out of her mind. The more she thought about it, the more she was convinced that Martin and

Kathleen were having an affair right under Franklin's nose. How could she do that to Franklin, she wondered?

As René thought about it, she began to realize that if Kathleen was having an affair, it was none of her business. She had enough of her own problems to be wasting time thinking about anyone else's. She decided that it was best to say nothing about it.

Although René had decided to say nothing, she found it far more difficult to get her thoughts of Martin and Kathleen out of her mind. It didn't take René long to begin to put two and two together. She began to think that Kathleen's involvement with Martin might be more than just an affair. She even began to wonder if Kathleen might be involved with Martin for other than romantic reasons.

While René finished dressing, her thoughts about Kathleen and Martin continued to disturb her. She didn't know what to do about it. It quickly became clear that there was really nothing she could do about it. She decided that her best course of action at this time would be to get the estate settled and get out of there as quickly as possible.

As soon as she had gotten herself together, she went downstairs. Her mind was somewhere else as she walked down the long curved staircase into the foyer. She suddenly found herself standing right in front of Kathleen at the bottom of the stairs. René noticed that there was something about the look on Kathleen's face that made her feel uneasy.

"Are you all right, my dear?" Kathleen asked as she looked into Rene's eyes.

"Yes. Yes, I'm fine," René replied nervously.

"You look a little startled. I'm sorry if it was my fault."

"No. No. I guess I had something on my mind," René replied unable to think of anything else to say at the moment.

Although Kathleen gave her a pleasant smile that indicated that she understood, René was not convinced that it was a smile with any degree of sincerity behind it. With what she had seen in the backyard, there was no doubt in her mind that Kathleen's apparent relationship with Martin was reason enough for her to be suspicious. There was no question in René's mind that she would have to be extremely careful about what she said and did around Kathleen.

"Franklin is waiting for you in the den, my dear. Would you like something to eat before you read the will?" Kathleen asked disturbing René's thoughts again.

"No. No, thank you."

"You should have something," Kathleen insisted.

"Maybe just a cup of coffee," René conceded.

"I'll bring it into the den for you," Kathleen said, then turned and walked away.

René watched Kathleen as she left the foyer and walked toward the kitchen. She wondered if Kathleen might have seen her looking out the window, but again she didn't think so.

René turned and looked at the door to the den. She was reluctant to face the task that was before her. She hesitated, but after taking a deep breath, she knocked on the door.

"Come in."

When René entered the den, she saw Franklin sitting at his desk. As she walked across the room, he looked up at her and smiled.

"Good morning," Franklin said as he stood up to greet her.

"Good morning."

"I trust that you slept well?" he asked as he gestured toward a chair in front of his desk.

"Yes, I did. Thank you," she said not wanting him to think that she didn't really get very much rest.

"Are you ready to take a look at Del's will?"

"Yes, I think so," she replied softly as she sat down.

She was not entirely convinced that she was ready to read it, but she was going to have to sooner or later. Besides, reading it might answer a few of the questions that haunted her mind.

"I am sure this is not easy for you. If you would prefer, I could leave you alone while you read it?"

"No. I think I would prefer that you stay here with me. If you don't mind."

"Not at all," Franklin replied as if he understood what she must have been going through.

Franklin handed René the blue folder that contained Del's will. René removed the document from inside the folder and opened it. It looked so legal, so formal, she thought.

It was at that very moment that Kathleen came into the den carrying a tray. On the tray were a pot of coffee and a couple of cups.

"I thought you might like some coffee, Franklin. René said she would," Kathleen said sweetly.

René watched Kathleen as she walked across the room and set the tray on a table. She couldn't help but notice how sweet Kathleen sounded when she spoke to Franklin.

"Thank you, dear," Franklin said with a smile. "That was very thoughtful of you."

René didn't say anything as she watched Kathleen pour coffee into the cups. Without consciously thinking about it, René refolded the document as if she was trying to hide its contents from prying eyes. When she realized what she had done, she looked down at the document. She had hidden it from Kathleen's view, but why? What reason could she have to keep Kathleen from seeing what was in it? After all, she had been a friend of Captain Del's, too.

"I'll leave you to your business," Kathleen said to Franklin, then glanced over toward René.

The coy smile on Kathleen's face disappeared as she glanced down at the folded document that René held tightly in her hands. After a moment, she looked up at René's face, then turned to leave the room.

For just a split second René got the feeling that Kathleen was angry that she had Captain Del's will. It caused René to question if Kathleen knew what was in the will. The more she thought about it, the more convinced she became that Kathleen probably knew its contents, at least part of it. It only seemed natural that she would know what was in the will. On the other hand, if she knew the contents, then why did she seem so interested in it?

After Kathleen left the room, René turned her attention back to the document. She unfolded it and began reading it. Many of the terms in the will were legal terms, but René was able to read and understand them. Having worked in a law office at one time helped.

After René had finished reading the will, she sat quietly looking at it and thinking. Captain Del had left to her his entire estate, including complete control of all the assets with the exception of a trust fund that had been set up to cover the expenses of maintaining the property in good repair.

There was also a trust fund that provided a lifetime income to René. Everything had been taken care of. There was nothing she would have to do. Captain Del had set her up for the rest of her life. She could hardly believe it.

"Are you finished?" Franklin asked, interrupting René's thoughts.

"I - - - I think so," she finally replied.

"Is there anything in the will that you do not understand?"

"No. I think it is pretty clear."

"Good," he replied with a smile.

"Mr. Cosgrove?"

"Please, Franklin."

"Franklin, did my great uncle have any other living relatives?"

"No, not that I know of. As far as I know, you are his only living relative. Why?"

"I was just wondering if there was anyone out there who could challenge the will?"

"A will can always be challenged, but I doubt that would happen here. There is no one who would have grounds to challenge it. Del made it clear in the will that no other person or persons are entitled to any part of his estate."

René sat there looking across the desk at Franklin. She could hardly believe that it was that simple. One minute she was a workingwoman, the next, she was a woman of wealth. Nothing could be that simple. She had learned a long time ago that if something seemed too good to be true, then it probably was not true.

Slowly the terms of the will began to soak in. Now that she was about to be a woman of means, there was no reason for her not to move to the estate and enjoy it as Captain Del had. It belonged to her now, or would as soon as all the titles could be transferred over to her. Everything had been taken care of.

"I guess I'm ready to sign the necessary papers," René said as she looked at Franklin and smiled a shy, sheepish smile.

"Now that you have been provided for, do you think that you will live on the estate?"

"Yes. Yes I will," she replied with a wide grin.

"Great. I know that Captain Del, as you call him, would be so pleased to know that you will be living there."

"How long before I can take possession of the estate?"

"As soon as you sign the papers, it is yours."

René could hardly believe that in the next couple of days she would be the new owner of Captain Del's estate.

"Are you all right?" Franklin asked.

"I guess this is a little overwhelming."

"I'm sure it is, but you need to remember one thing. If you need any help, any help at all, you can always come to me."

"Thank you," she replied.

René folded the will and put it back in the blue envelope. Clutching the will tightly in her hand, she walked to the door. Franklin followed her out of the den and into the foyer.

As they entered the foyer, they found Kathleen near the door to the den. She seemed surprised at their sudden appearance. René was almost certain that Kathleen had been listening at the door.

"Oh, Kathleen. René has decided that she will live on Del's estate."

"Oh, how nice. I know that Del would have been pleased," Kathleen replied.

Although her words gave the indication that she was pleased with René's decision, the tone of her voice did not seem to convey the same message. Even the smile on Kathleen's face lost its sincerity when René looked into her eyes.

"I'll take René to the bank to sign over Del's property to her tomorrow morning," Franklin said, the tone of his voice showing how pleased he was with René's decision to live there.

René was not sure what to say. She had a lot on her mind. One thing she knew that she wanted was to get away from Kathleen and to be alone for a little while.

"I thought I would take a walk outside for a little while, that is if you don't mind," René said.

"Of course, my dear. I'm sure that you have a lot to think over," Franklin said.

"Yes. Excuse me," René said then turned and went outside.

* * * *

As René turned off the porch onto the well-kept lawn, she glanced back over her shoulder. She could see Kathleen and Franklin talking just inside the door. Franklin seemed sincerely happy for her. However, René was not so sure about Kathleen. There was something about her that left René a little apprehensive.

As René walked around the large yard, she could not get the look in Kathleen's eyes out of her mind. Although Kathleen had said that she was pleased with René's decision to live at Del's estate, the look in her eyes indicated that she was upset about it. It seemed as if she didn't want René anywhere near the estate. René could not think of a single reason why Kathleen should be upset. What difference could it make to her? Was it possible that she had wanted the estate for herself and was jealous of René? Why would she want the estate?

That last thought caused René to shake her head. She couldn't believe that Kathleen would want the estate for herself. After all, she already had one of the most beautiful mansions in the Albany area.

The more she thought about it, the more confused she became. Even though René had nothing to go on except her feelings, there was this underlying feeling that both Kathleen and Martin didn't want her to take possession of the estate.

René began to wonder if moving onto the estate was the right thing for her to do. If this was a dream come true, then why was she so full of misgivings about it? Why was she wondering if she was doing the right thing? The strange actions of Martin, the looks from Kathleen, and the near "accidents" caused René to question her decision to live there. What if this was all a big mistake? What could she do if it turned out to be a mistake?

This was rapidly becoming a very difficult time for René. Her mind was filled with suspicions, doubts, and fears. She needed answers to some very distressing questions, but she did not seem to be getting them. It had reached a point where she did not know who she could trust any more. She was not even sure that she could trust Mr. Cosgrove, but at this point what choice did she have.

Just before lunch, René called Mildred to tell her that she would be staying with the Cosgrove's another night, as she didn't want them to worry about her. She did not tell them that she would soon be the new owner of Del's estate.

René spent the rest of the day trying to relax by spending some time trying to read in the guest room. She also spent some time just looking around the grounds of Mr. Cosgrove's home. Nothing seemed to help her relax. There were too many things running through her head to allow her mind a single moment's peace.

Shortly after dinner, René excused herself and went to her room. Once again she spent the night tossing and turning, and not getting any rest. The thought that she was going to be a very wealthy woman in the morning should have made her feel bubbly and happy, but it didn't. René was just trying to understand what it all really meant to her, and how it would change her life.

* * * *

When it was finally time to get up, she was still wondering if she was really ready for such a drastic change in her life. She had to wonder if she was taking on more than she could handle.

After getting dressed, René went downstairs to the kitchen. She found herself watching every move that Kathleen made during breakfast. She had convinced herself that Kathleen had some secret interest in Del's estate. It was clear to her that Kathleen was not pleased with her decision to live on the estate, but why? Was there something at the estate that Kathleen could not get hold of if René was living there?

René began to think that maybe her suspicions were just getting the best of her, and it was all her imagination. There was nothing in anything that had been said, or in anything that Kathleen had done that would support René's suspicions. The only thing was Kathleen's apparent involvement with Martin, and there was no real proof of anything there that pertained to René's inheritance of the estate.

No matter how much René tried to dismiss her suspicions and her worries from her mind, she could not. It just seemed that too much had happened in such a short time. Even though there was no proof, she still would be distrustful of Kathleen if for no other reason than to be cautious.

* * * *

René and Franklin spent a good part of the morning at the bank getting papers signed, transferring the property to René and reviewing the documents in Captain Del's safety deposit box. When they were done, they returned to Mr. Cosgrove's home. René gathered her things and thanked the Cosgroves for their hospitality. She then got in her car and started down the driveway.

As she drove down the driveway, she glanced in her rearview mirror. Although Franklin was smiling and waving goodbye, Kathleen was just standing there staring at her as she drove away. Once again she could not get the idea out of her head that Kathleen had something to do with what had been happening to her.

René had told the Cosgroves that she was returning to Utica to pack, but decided to return to the estate first. Once out on the interstate and cruising along with the rest of the traffic, René's thoughts again returned to Kathleen.

Kathleen had seemed pleasant enough, but the look in her eyes often seemed to reveal something very different, something more sinister. It bothered René to think that there might be two sides to Kathleen. One that could be pleasant and very nice, but another that could be cunning and unscrupulous. And the thought that Kathleen was involved with Martin only helped convince René that Kathleen might be involved in the events that had occurred recently.

As René drove along the interstate, she slowly began to convince herself that everything would get better. After all, everything on the estate now belonged to her. The property was no longer in limbo, no longer vulnerable to other claims, if there were any.

The further René got away from the Cosgrove's home, the more her mind turned toward other things. Before long her mind was filled with a million thoughts all racing around in her head at the same time. The one thought that seemed to capture and hold her attention the longest was the thought that her entire life was rapidly changing and that she had no one to share it with. There didn't seem to be anyone she could trust with her thoughts, her ideas, her feelings, her concerns and even her suspicions.

Suddenly, she began to feel very lonely. She was already twenty-six years old and there was no man in her life. René let out a sigh as she thought about how nice it would be if she had someone special to share in her good fortune. Someone who would be there for her. Someone to help her make the decisions that she knew she would have to make. Someone who could hold her and make her feel safe and secure when things frightened her. Someone who could make her feel loved and make her feel like a desirable woman.

Even though René had a lot on her mind, she made it a point to pay attention to her driving this time. She had not forgotten what had happened to her on the road through the Adirondack Mountains. She had no desire to meet another truck head-on or to be chased along some winding and twisting road by some crazy person.

Thinking about being chased by some crazy person brought thoughts of Martin to her mind again. Just the thought of him was enough to make her look around. She had become suspicious of just about everyone, especially those in black cars. She knew it would not be long before she would have to turn off the heavily traveled interstate onto the much less traveled two-lane road through the mountains. That thought did nothing to make her feel safe and secure.

Shortly after she turned off the interstate onto the highway that would take her toward Blue Mountain Lake and back to Del's estate, she noticed a black car coming up behind her at a rather high rate of speed. The closer the car got to her, the more frightened she became. She lost sight of it for a minute or so when she rounded a curve, but it quickly reappeared.

René grew very nervous. Her heart began to race and her chest tightened as panic began to well up inside her. She looked desperately for some place where she could pull off and get help. The thought of being caught out there all alone added to her fears.

In no time at all, the car was very close behind her. She saw that the driver was a man, but she could not make out his features with the sun and shadows reflecting off the windshield. As they rounded a curve, the car was only a few feet from her rear bumper. She wanted to get out of his way, but there was no place for her to go. To slow down would mean that he might run into her from behind. If that happened, she might lose control of her car and crash.

She gripped the steering wheel tightly with both hands as she prayed for a place to get help. When the road straightened out for a short distance, the big black sports sedan darted out from behind her and roared passed. It passed her on a yellow line and quickly disappeared around a sharp curve. She tried to see who was driving it when it passed, but the windows were tinted very dark and she was too busy trying to keep her own car under control. She never got a chance to see who was driving the black sedan.

As she came around a curve, she caught a glimpse of the car again before it disappeared around another curve. It was too far ahead for her to get a good look at the license plate. René let her car slow down in the hope that the black sedan would continue on and she would not see it again.

When she came around the next corner and found the car was already far enough away to be out of sight, she let out a long, slow sigh of relief. She began to breathe a little easier as she followed the twisting, winding road toward Blue Mountain Lake. She could not help but think about how nervous she had become.

After she had traveled several miles without seeing another black sedan, she began to feel more comfortable, more relaxed. She even began to scold herself for acting like a child, until she glanced into the rearview mirror again.

Once again her heart was in her throat and her breath caught at the sight of the same black sedan. It was suddenly behind her again. She could feel her heart race and panic began to take control of her again. Where had he come from? How did he get behind her again? What was he trying to do?

Once again the black sedan roared up close behind her, but there was no place for her to get out of its way. The car would back off a little and flash his lights as if he wanted to pass, but there were few places where the car could pass. Even when it could pass, the driver would just pull up to within a few inches of the back of René's car and honked the horn impatiently as if he wanted her to get out of the way so he could pass.

René's little car could not outrun the big, powerful sedan, nor could she take the sharp corners as fast. At one point, the car bumped her as if he wanted to push her off the road and out of his way. René didn't know what to do. She was going as fast as she dared. Every nerve in her body was tense and sweat began to roll down her face. Even her hands were clammy and sticky as she gripped the steering wheel. She was scared to death, but there was nothing she could do but try to keep her car on the road. The black car was forcing her to drive way too fast to pull off the road and stop.

Suddenly, the black car backed off and gradually dropped back behind her until it disappeared behind a curve. René didn't know what to think as she looked in her rearview mirror.

When she looked ahead again, terror gripped her. There was a very sharp turn in the road just ahead. She slammed on the brakes. Her car shuddered as the tires squealed on the asphalt pavement as she tried to stop her car. Gravel flew as her car skidded across the road and off the pavement onto the gravel shoulder of the road. René closed her eyes as she prepared herself for the crash that she knew was coming.

René's car finally skidded to a stop at the very edge of the road. The front wheel stopped just inches from going over the embankment. There was a ten-foot rocky drop off into the stream below. Her car had narrowly avoided going over the edge.

René sat holding her breath for what seemed like a lifetime before she was able to breathe again. She slowly opened her eyes and looked out the side window of her car down at the stream below. There was no doubt in her mind that if she had gone over the edge she would have ended upside down in the stream. If that had happened, she might very well have drowned.

"He was trying to kill me," she cried hysterically. She could hardly breathe as her chest was so gripped with fear.

René had been too caught up in trying to keep her car under control to think about anything else. But for the first time it was clear that someone was actually trying to kill her. It was no accident. The fact that the sedan never did go past her simply reinforced what she already knew. It also became clear to her that the other "near accidents" might not have been accidents, either.

As soon as René was able to regain her composure, she started her car again. She looked both ways, not just for oncoming traffic, but for the black sedan. When she saw nothing, she pulled back out onto the road and continued her drive back to the estate, but she drove much slower. She decided that if she saw the black sedan again, she would immediately pull over to the side of the road as best she could and stop before he had a chance to make her drive so fast that she couldn't stop. He would not force her to crash her car to make it look like an accident. She would not help the driver of the black car kill herself just because she was scared.

René arrived back at the estate without further incident. However, she found herself very tired and worn out. The tension of driving the roads through the mountains, half expecting to see another black sedan pop up at any moment or at every turn, had drained her both physically and emotionally of her energy.

CHAPTER SEVEN

René parked her car in front of the carriage house. It took her a moment or two before she could get herself together and to be ready to talk to Mildred. As soon as she felt that she was composed enough, she opened the door and got out of the car. She walked around the car and started toward the back porch. She was hoping that she could keep herself composed when Mildred asked her about her trip to Albany.

Mildred had come out onto the back porch and watched René as she walked toward the house. René let out a sigh, as she knew that Mildred would want to know everything that had happened and what she had decided to do. One thing René had already decided was that she would not tell Mildred every little detail, and she would definitely not tell her about the car that had tried to run her off the road.

"You look tired," Mildred said, her concern showing on her face.

"I am tired. I'm afraid that I don't sleep very well in a strange bed," she said as a way of explaining her tiredness.

"How did things go otherwise?" Mildred asked as she wiped her hands on a towel while she impatiently waited for René to step up on the porch.

"They went well, very well indeed," René replied with a smile.

"Good. Come in and tell me all about it," Mildred said as she held the door for René.

Mildred followed René into the kitchen. While René sat down at the table, Mildred poured a cup of coffee for each of them. After setting the coffee on the table, Mildred sat down across the table from René. She could hardly wait to hear what René had to say.

"Tell me, how is Mr. Cosgrove?"

"Mr. Cosgrove is fine," René replied as she wrapped her fingers around the warm cup and lifted it to her lips.

"But Mr. Hanover said that he was ill," Mildred explained, the look on her face indicating that she was confused.

"Well, he's not ill at all. Mr. Hanover has said a lot of things that were not true."

"Why would he do that?"

"I don't know. The one thing I do know and can tell you is that all of this is now mine," René said with a grin as she took a quick look around the room.

"That's great. Captain Del would have been so pleased to hear that. He wanted so much for you to have his home."

"I know," René said with a hint of sadness.

"What are your plans now? I mean now that the estate is yours, what do you plan to do?" Mildred asked.

René thought she could see a bit of worry on Mildred's face. She didn't want Mildred to worry any longer than necessary.

"You don't have anything to worry about, Mildred. I plan to be moving in as soon as I can. I would like you and Sam to stay on, that is if you don't have other plans."

"We would love to stay on," Mildred said with a smile.

"I'm so glad."

"Oh, by the way, Mr. Hanover came by just shortly after you left. Sam told him that he was not welcome here and that he had been instructed to call the police and have him removed if he didn't leave immediately."

"I'll bet that frosted him," René said with a bit of a chuckle in her voice. "What did he do?

"He got really upset, but he did leave," Mildred said with a grin. "He tore out of here as if his tail was on fire. Oh, he was very mad."

"Good. Maybe, he will stay away."

Even though Martin had left as instructed, René had a deep-seated feeling that she had not seen the last of him. He wanted something. She had no idea what it was, but she was sure that he was not about to give up until he got it.

"I have a couple of things I need to do before I move in," René explained. "I will be going back to Utica in the morning. I have some things to take care of there."

"I understand, Ma'am. What time would you like to have dinner?"

"Six o'clock will be fine."

"Yes, Ma'am. Oh, I got your room upstairs ready for you, the one in front."

"Thank you, Mildred," she replied as she picked up her cup of coffee and carried it to the kitchen sink.

René went directly to the den and sat down at the old rolltop desk. She swung the chair around, leaned back, and looked up at the painting of Captain Del that hung above the fireplace.

"I hope you knew what you were doing when you decided to leave all this to me," she said as she looked up at the painting.

It was quiet in the den. The only sound was the ticking of the old clock on the mantel above the fireplace. René turned back around and looked at the rolltop desk. She just sat there and allowed her mind to wander. For the first time she was really looking at the rolltop desk, but she was not looking for anything in particular.

It was at that moment she remembered she had inherited two cars. One was an old antique car, while the other was a fairly new Cadillac. The idea of owning a Cadillac had kind of appealed to her. René could not help but think about how strange the turn of events that were changing her life had come about. It crossed her mind that she had never even ridden in a Cadillac and now she owned one.

She remembered that she had found the titles to the cars when she went through the desk the other day, but she had not found the keys to anything. If the keys were not in the desk, maybe they were in Captain Del's bedroom, she thought.

René stood up and left the den. She went upstairs to Captain Del's bedroom. When she got to the door, she reached out and took hold of the doorknob but didn't turn it. Although she knew that everything in the house was now hers, it gave her a strange feeling to be standing in front of his bedroom door. She had not been allowed to go into his bedroom when she was there as a child. It was as if she was about to invade Captain Del's private quarters.

She had to mentally shake herself and remind herself that it was her house now. There was no place in the house that was off limits to her anymore.

René pushed the door open. She could see that the drapes were pulled closed. They were heavy drapes that shut out almost all of the light from the outside making the room rather dark and giving sort of an eerie look to the room.

She made her way across the room to one of the large windows and drew back the drapes letting the evening sun shine into the room. René then turned around to get a good look at Captain Del's bedroom. She stood frozen at the sight of the room.

A soft smile came over her face as she slowly looked around the room. René had never seen anything like it. It looked like the captain's cabin from a movie set of an old Hollywood pirate movie. There was a large four-poster bed with the canopy draped with fishnet. The walls had old paintings of Clipper ships and Schooners on them.

On top of a small desk were a sextant, a scale and a ruler that were used by sailors for plotting a course at sea. There was also a large brass and glass compass on a shiny brass base near one of the windows. It was the kind of compass that one might find on the bridge of an old sailing ship.

In front of one of the other windows was a shiny brass telescope on a tall stand. It was pointed out toward the lake. Above the small fireplace was a pair of crossed cutlasses. Against one wall was a bookshelf that had a number of books about the sea and sailing ships.

René just stood there in amazement as she looked around the room, taking in everything. She had never seen a bedroom decorated quite like this one before. If she had not just walked into the room, she would have sworn that she had just stepped into the Captain's Quarters of a real sailing ship, complete with kerosene lanterns and old maps of the seas.

After several minutes of looking around, René began to move about the room. She had always known that Captain Del loved the sea; but as she examined some of the old artifacts in the room, she began to understand just how much he loved the sea.

While looking around the room, René found a small treasure chest on top of the dresser. She reached out and opened the chest. Inside, on the top tray, she found two sets of keys. One set of keys had a GM car key on it, along with what looked like a door key and a padlock key. The other set of keys had a strange looking key, a door key, and another padlock key on that ring. She guessed that the second set of keys probably belonged to the antique car.

She picked up the set of keys with the GM car key and slipped them into her pocket. She lifted the small tray in the chest to see what might lie underneath. There she found a third set of keys. They didn't look like any of the others. There was a small tag on the key ring that read "Chris Craft". She smiled as she thought of the old wooden powerboat. She could remember the rides she had had in it when she was a little girl. The thought of actually driving it excited her, but that would have to wait until another time.

René left the keys to the boat and the keys to the antique car in the bottom of the treasure chest and replaced the tray. She left the room closing the door behind her.

Mildred had set just one place at the dining room table for René. René did not mind eating alone tonight. She was tired and felt that she would not be very good company.

After a quiet dinner alone, René went out the backdoor to the garage. All three doors had padlocks on them. She wondered which padlock the key she had in her hand would fit. A quick glance at the key indicated that the padlock might be fairly new, as the key was not tarnished with age. She took a quick look at the padlocks and noticed that one of the padlocks looked newer then the others. She tried the key and the lock snapped open.

René pulled open the garage door and looked inside. She could hardly believe her eyes. Parked in the garage was a bright red Cadillac convertible. It had the top down and was the most beautiful car she had ever seen. She walked up along side it and looked in. It was showroom perfect. It looked so nice that she was almost afraid to touch it.

"Go ahead. Open the door and get in."

René was startled by the sudden sound of Sam's voice. She had not heard him come into the garage.

"Go ahead. Get in," Sam insisted with a smile. "It's your car now."

René smiled back at him, then reached out and opened the car door. She hesitated for a second, then slid in behind the steering wheel. She slid her hands over the steering wheel, almost caressing it as she looked over the inside.

"I've always wanted a red Cadillac," she said in almost a whisper.

"Well, you have one now, Missy," Sam said with a grin as he watched her look over the car.

René quickly turned and looked up at Sam. Tears came to her eyes. Sam was confused by her reaction. He didn't know what to think. René could see the confused look on his face and felt an explanation was in order.

"I'm sorry, Sam, but it has been a long time since I've been called Missy. Captain Del used to call me that."

"I'm sorry. I shouldn't have called you that, Ma'am," Sam said.

"No, it's all right. I sort of like it. I hope that you and Mildred and I can become more like family."

"We would like that," Sam said with a slight grin. "Have you seen the other car?"

"No, not yet."

"You should see it. Captain Del bought it for his first wife. It has been sitting in the garage ever since her death. I've kept it in good running order just in case he wanted to drive it some day, but he never did," Sam said with a note of sadness in his voice.

"If you don't mind, would you be so kind as to show it to me later. It's getting late and I'm pretty tired. I should try to get some rest. I have to return to Utica tomorrow and pack."

"Sure. I understand," Sam replied.

René sat in the car and watched as Sam turned and left her alone. She was almost sorry that she didn't take the time to let him show her the old car. She was sure that she had disappointed him. Maybe she would have him show it to her in the morning when she was rested.

René got out of the car and locked up the garage. She returned to the house and went directly to the bedroom that Mildred had prepared for her. As she stepped into the room, she looked around. It was just as she remembered it. The curtains that covered the windows were colorful and bright. The matching comforter on the bed seemed to invite her to climb under it and get a good night's sleep.

As soon as she was ready for bed, she climbed in under the covers. The bed was as comfortable as it looked. It did not take long before she was sound asleep.

* * * *

For the first time in several nights, René finally got some much needed rest. She wasn't sure why, but it may have been because she felt safe here with Sam and Mildred close by. It may have been simply that she was so tired. Whatever the reason, she liked waking up to the sound of birds singing just outside her window. It was not hard for her to understand why Captain Del liked it here so much.

After getting dressed and having a light breakfast, she was ready to drive back to Utica. She took the time to have Sam show her the old car, a 1936 Packard Convertible Victoria 907. It looked as if it was brand new. It seemed to please Sam that she took the time to let him show it to her.

René briefly thought about taking the Cadillac to Utica, but decided to take her Dodge instead. She reasoned that she would have plenty of time to enjoy the Cadillac after she moved here. Besides, she didn't like the idea of having to park the Cadillac on the street in front of her apartment because she didn't have a garage in Utica to park it in.

René got into her car and started back to Utica. The drive was uneventful, although she kept an eye out for black sedans and any large trucks.

* * * *

She arrived at her apartment shortly before noon, but the stress of the drive had made her weary. As she entered her apartment and looked around, a strange feeling came over her and seemed to haunt her senses. It was as if someone had been in her apartment without her knowledge.

She stood in the middle of her living room and slowly looked around as she tried to find some evidence to support her feelings. There was nothing out of place as far as she could tell. Yet, it still didn't feel right. She let out a long sigh. She had a lot to do, and standing here letting her imagination run away with her was not getting it done.

She had not been sorting and getting things organized for very long when the phone rang. As she walked across the room to answer the phone, she wondered who might be calling her.

"Hello?"

"Is this Miss René Richardson?"

"Yes."

"This is Martin Hanover."

René's breath caught as a chill raced through her. She knew that she would hear from him, but she had not expected it to be so soon. She certainly had not expected to hear from him here.

"How did you get my number?" she asked, almost instantly realizing that she had given it to him when she called about the letter.

"That's not important."

"What do you want?" René replied with a sharp tone in her voice.

"I want you to know that I'm sorry about the way I treated you at the estate. I would like to make it up to you."

Although he sounded sincere, René could not help but feel that he had some ulterior motive for calling her other than to apologize to her. She wanted nothing to do with him. Even hearing his voice frightened her and made her nervous. The last thing she wanted to do was to meet with him.

"I don't think that will be necessary. As you probably already know I have signed all the papers, and have taken possession of the estate. It is now mine," she said with a slight emphasize on the word "mine".

René listened for some sort of response from him, but he said nothing. She could hear him breathing. It gave her a feeling of satisfaction to think that the fact that she was now the sole owner of the estate caught him off guard and probably irritated him.

"I didn't know that," he blurted out, then paused to take another breath.

René could sense the frustration in his voice. She smiled to herself, enjoying the fact that she now had control of whatever it was that he wanted.

"Well, I guess congratulations are in order. Would it be too much to assume that you will be moving to the estate soon?" he asked trying very hard to keep the sound of his voice under strict control.

"As a matter of fact, you can. I will be moving to the estate as soon as possible," she said, immediately wishing she hadn't told him her plans.

"Well, I guess you have taken care of everything."

"Yes, I guess I have."

"In that case, would you consider having dinner with me as a way of celebrating your new life?"

"I don't think so."

"I see," he said, his voice showing his disappointment. "In that case, I guess I will say goodbye."

"Goodbye," René replied, then quickly hung up the phone before he could say anything more.

She smiled to herself as she looked down at the phone. She was a bit satisfied with herself, but the smile on her face soon faded away as she thought of him. Something in the back of her mind told her that she had not heard the last of him. She was sure that whatever it was he wanted, he was not the type to give up so easily.

René looked around the room. She quickly realized that she had not gotten very much done so she returned to packing again.

* * * *

As time went by, she became so engrossed in her work that she forgot about Martin, at least for the moment. When she finally stopped to take a break, she realized that it was getting late. She walked over to the window, drew back the curtains and looked down at the street.

A sudden chill ran down her spine causing her to shiver, and her breath caught. She could feel her heart race within her chest. Parked across the street and down a house, was a black BMW. The first thought that ran through her mind was that Martin was out there somewhere. He was watching her apartment, which meant that he was watching her.

She looked up and down the street, but didn't see anyone. When René turned and looked back at the car, she began to stare at it. She was straining in an effort to see if Martin was sitting inside the car watching her, but she could not see anyone in the car. The longer she looked at the car, the more apprehensive she became.

As logic began to seep into her head, she started to think more rationally. It even occurred to her that it might not be Martin's car, but she was familiar with most of the cars that belonged in the neighborhood. That car did not belong here. The more she looked at it, the more she was convinced that it was Martin's car. If it was his car, where was he? What was he doing?

The thought that Martin might be right outside her door caused a sense of fear to fill her head. She rushed across the room and locked the door. René set the dead bolt and put the chain on the door. She then stepped back and looked at the bolted door almost as if she expected Martin to try to break in. She could feel her heart pounding. Her breath was coming is short rapid breaths.

She waited, but when nothing happened. Her racing heart and her breathing gradually returned to something close to normal. She walked over to the sofa, flopped down on it, tipped her head back and closed her eyes as she tried to regain her composure. She began to scold herself for acting like a scared child.

She opened her eyes and looked across the room at the boxes that she had filled and stacked against the wall near the door. For the first time she was beginning to realize just how tired and hungry she was getting. She decided that she might not be so paranoid if she would just take a few minutes to relax and then get herself something to eat.

She went to the kitchen, but a brief look in the cupboards and refrigerator reminded René that she had not gone to the store. She had forgotten all about it with all that had happened over the last couple of days.

The thought of going out sent another cold chill through her. If it was Martin's car across the street, then he was close by, maybe just outside her door in the hallway. She certainly didn't want to go out in the dark with him hanging around. She decided that she would take another look in the kitchen for something to eat rather than to chance a meeting with him by going out. She was sure she could find enough to eat.

After looking around, René found a couple of slices of bread, some crackers, and a can of soup. She made the soup, then sat down at the table to eat. When she was done, she cleaned up the kitchen, then packed it away.

René found it difficult to put Martin out of her mind. Every once in a while, she would go over to the window and peek out from behind the curtains to see if the car was still there.

It was past midnight when René finished packing and flopped down on the sofa. It had been a long tiring day for her. The thought that Martin had been watching her apartment all day didn't help make her feel any better. She had no real reason to be afraid of him, but she was just the same.

Thinking of him caused her to look toward the window again. She realized that it had been awhile since she had looked out to see if the BMW was still there. She pushed herself up and walked across the room to the window. Carefully pushing the curtain aside, she peeked out. She looked up and down the street, but the car was nowhere in sight. She should have been relieved to see that the car gone, but she wasn't.

René dropped the curtain and leaned back against the wall next to the window. Her breath caught again causing her chest to tighten.

"Come on, girl, get it together," she scolded herself out loud.

It was getting late and she was tired. She took a deep breath and went into her bedroom. After taking off her clothes, she went into the bathroom for a long warm shower. The shower seemed to help her feel more relaxed, which allowed her to think more clearly.

She slipped into a terry cloth robe and wrapped her hair in a towel. Stopping in the doorway to the living room, she looked over what she had accomplished. Stacked in the living room were the boxes that she had filled with her belongings. She smiled to herself, feeling satisfied with all she had achieved in one short day.

As she looked around the room, her eyes drifted to the front door and stopped. The smile of satisfaction slowly faded from her face and she clutched the front of her robe, holding it tightly closed.

The door to her apartment was no longer chained, and the dead bolt looked as if it was no longer locked. She was sure that she had locked and chained the door earlier.

The thought that someone had opened it caused her heart to pound. Her chest tightened as panic began to wrap its cold fingers around her and squeeze the breath out of her.

With a great deal of urgency, she looked around the room. She slowly stepped back into her bedroom and closed the door. She tried to think of what to do, but her mind was cluttered with random thoughts of what could happen to her if someone was in her apartment. She closed her eyes, took a deep breath and tried to get a grip on herself. If someone had come into her apartment, where could he be hiding? How did he get in? Maybe through a window?

Her eyes moved slowly around the room until they came to the closet. She stood silently staring at the closet doors.

The doors to her closet were shut, but she could not remember if she had closed them or not. Was someone hiding in the closet?

She looked around the room for something strong and heavy, just in case. Quietly, she slowly moved closer to her bed. She bent down next to her bedside table and unplugged the lamp, never once taking her eyes off the closet doors.

She picked up the heavy brass table lamp and slowly moved toward the closet. Raising the lamp high above her head with one hand, she reached out and took hold of the closet door with her other. After taking a deep breath, she jerked the door open. There was nothing in her closet that didn't belong there.

She let out a sigh of relief as she lowered the lamp to her side. Almost immediately she realized that there were other places in her apartment where a person could hide. Still gripping the lamp tightly in her hand, she went back to the door to the living room. After slowly opening the door, she paused and looked around before going into the living room.

She walked quietly across the room toward the front door closet. Again, she prepared herself for a confrontation with an intruder, but there was no one there.

She turned and looked around again. When her eyes fell on the kitchen door, she realized that was the only room left where anyone could hide. She slowly approached the door to the kitchen. As she got closer to the door, she slowed down. She was hesitant to enter the kitchen and glanced over at the telephone. The idea of calling the police passed through her mind, but she felt she would look like a fool if the police came and found nothing.

She turned back toward the kitchen. After raising the lamp high and taking a deep breath, she slowly pushed the swinging door open. She reached around the corner and quickly switched on the light. Light filled the kitchen showing her that there was no one there.

She lowered the lamp to her side as she let out a sigh of relief. Slowly, she turned back around and looked at the front door again.

Staring at the door, she was no longer convinced that she had locked and chained it. She was not sure of anything right now. She was so confused that she felt like sitting down and having a good old-fashioned cry.

Tears began to fill her eyes as she realized how tired she was. It had been a long day with her emotions going up and down like a roller coaster. Her whole life was changing so fast. Maybe a little too fast, she thought.

René set the lamp down and went to the front door. She set the dead bolt and hooked the chain. Once she was satisfied that the door was properly locked and secured, she checked all the windows and made sure that they were locked as well. She found two windows that had been closed but not locked. If anyone had been in her apartment, it was most likely that was how he got in. If whoever had been in her apartment left, he left through the front door which would explain why it was unlocked.

René then picked up the lamp and returned to her bedroom. Normally René liked to sleep in the nude, but tonight she wanted to be wrapped up. She tied her robe tightly around her waist as if it would protect her like a suit of armor. She pulled the covers back, then crawled into bed pulling the covers over her. She looked at the clock. It was already past one in the morning.

As she laid back, she realized that she had not shut off the ceiling light in her bedroom. She started to get out of bed to turn it off, but stopped. She looked up at the light, then laid back down and pulled the covers up over her again. With all that had happened in the last couple of days, she decided that she would leave the light on. She figured that she was tired enough that leaving the light on would not keep her awake. In fact, it might actually help her sleep.

Resting her head on the pillow, she closed her eyes and tried to clear her mind. It wasn't long before she was asleep, but it was not a very restful sleep. She spent a good part of the night tossing and turning, unable to prevent her mind from thinking of all that had happened, and all that could have happened if someone had been in her apartment.

CHAPTER EIGHT

When morning arrived, it did so with the spirit and clamor of the Fourth of July. The flash of the lightning and the crash of thunder woke René with a start from one of her few moments of sound sleep that she had been able to get. It caused her to sit straight up in bed. The thunder was so close that it sounded as if the lightning may have hit just outside her bedroom window.

It took a moment or two for her to understand what was going on, and for her to catch her breath. When she recovered from the sudden shock of her awakening, she looked around the room and listened. She could hear the rain as it pelted against her bedroom window.

"More rain. Just what I need," René said to herself with a disgusted tone in her voice as she fell back on the bed and stared up at the ceiling.

It was still very early and she was feeling almost as tired as when she had gone to bed. Leaving the ceiling light on had done little to make her feel safe and secure in her own apartment.

She thought about trying to sleep a little more, but she knew that it would be of no use. Plus, there was too much to do for her to stay in bed any longer. She doubted if she would actually get any more rest, anyway.

René reluctantly got up and pulled her robe tightly around her. As she walked into the living room, her eyes immediately went to the chain on the door. The chain was still securely in place as was the dead bolt. She looked toward the window as she remembered seeing the BMW parked across the street last night. She crossed the room, then slowly pulled back the curtain to peek out.

Her heart caught in her throat and her chest tightened. Down on the street directly in front of her apartment building was the same black BMW that she had seen last night. It looked just like the one Martin owned and was parked right behind her car. She could see that there was someone in the car, but she could not see who it was because of the glare on the windshield.

She closed the curtains and leaned back against the wall next to the window. Her mind was racing in an effort to decide what she should do. She was not sure that she could handle a face-to-face encounter with Martin right now. Her nerves were wound so tightly that she was convinced in her own mind that she would not be able keep her composure.

Even though she wasn't sure what she should do, she was beginning to realize one very important fact. She was going to have to confront him whether she wanted to or not. There didn't appear to be any way out of it. She had too much to do to stay cooped up in her apartment just to avoid him. And to avoid him would simply delay the inevitable.

René went to her bedroom and got dressed. As soon as she was ready, she straightened her shoulders and went back into the living room. Looking toward the window, she took a deep breath. She gathered up what strength she could muster, then picked her keys up off the table. She took a deep breath and walked up to the door.

With a new resolve to face Martin and not let him intimidate or frighten her, she unlocked the door and opened it. She peered out into the hall. In spite of her newfound courage, she was thankful that the hall was empty.

Closing the door and locking it behind her, she started down the stairs. She was convinced that each step she took was taking her closer and closer to an encounter with Martin. It was a thought that caused her to want to turn around and run, not walk, back to her apartment. She knew she couldn't do that. She knew that she would have to face him sooner or later, and sooner seemed to be the right thing to do.

As she opened the door to the street, she noticed that the rain had let up a little, and the wind was no longer blowing so hard. She stopped in the doorway out of the rain and looked at the black BMW. With the rain and the glare on the windshield, she still could not see who was in the car, but she was sure that it was Martin. She took a deep breath and mentally prepared herself to confront him. She thought about going over to the car, knocking on the window and confronting him head on, once and for all. She would tell him to leave her alone and stop following her, or she would call the police and file charges of stalking.

Before she had gathered up the will and the courage to carry out her thoughts, the car door opened and Martin stepped out. He ran around to the sidewalk and up the steps, stopping under the canopy over the front door. He stood only a few feet in front of her.

"Don't look so surprised," Martin said with a devilish grin.

Surprised was hardly the word René would have used to describe how she was feeling at that moment. Her breath caught and her heart seemed to be pounding so hard she could feel it. He frightened her, but she didn't know why. He had actually never threatened her. At least that she could prove.

"What are you doing here?" René asked as soon as she was able to speak.

"Aren't you going to invite me in?" he asked with his pearly white teeth shining as he smiled at her.

It took a moment for René to get control of herself before she could form a decent response.

"I hadn't planned to," she said nervously.

"I apologized last evening on the phone. I didn't think it would be necessary for me to apologize again."

"You're absolutely right," she replied after taking a deep breath. "It is not necessary for you to apologize again. And since you apologized last night, our need to talk to each other is over. I do not wish to talk to you, or even see you again. I would appreciate it if you would go away and leave me alone."

"Is that any way to be?"

"As a matter of fact, yes," she said defiantly, only slightly able to retain her composure.

"I was hoping that you could forgive and forget," he said as he smiled at her.

"Forgive and forget? You've almost gotten me killed, twice. Leave me alone before I call the police and have you charged with stalking," she threatened, but the crack in her voice gave away the fact that she was not as strong as she would have liked him to believe.

"I don't know what you are talking about. All I want to do is to get to know you better."

"Let's just say that I forgive you. I'll forget you if you will just leave me alone and get out of my life."

She could feel her resolve slowly giving way to her fears.

"My, aren't we being unfriendly?" he said without any indication that he was afraid that she might make good on her threat to call the police.

"Yes. Leave me alone," she said without hesitation.

Martin stood looking into her eyes for just a moment.

René thought she could see a small hint of satisfaction on his face and in his eyes. He knew that she was afraid of him, she was sure of it. She was also sure that was what he wanted.

There was no doubt in his mind that he had her right where he wanted her. But he began to think that if he pushed her too far here in town she might make good on her threat to call the police. He didn't need that kind of hassle.

Martin smiled slightly and gave her a little nod of his head. He then turned and ran back through the rain to his car and got in.

René let out a deep sigh of relief as she watched him get into his car and drive away. He may be gone, but something told her that he still had not gotten what he wanted. He was not out of her life, not yet anyway.

René returned to her apartment and spent the rest of the day cleaning and packing. She took several breaks to get a snack and to check out the window to see if Martin might have returned. She didn't see his car again for the rest of the day.

* * * *

It had been raining on and off most of the day. It was getting late when René realized that she had not had a proper meal all day. Everything was done that could be done. There was nothing left to do except wait for the movers. René decided to walk down the street to a nearby café for a relaxing dinner.

René locked her apartment and started along the wet sidewalk toward the café. She found herself continually looking around as she hurried along the sidewalk. Her eyes were in constant motion as she observed her surroundings.

Within a few minutes she was in the café. She sat down at a booth next to a window. From there she could see out onto the street. She found herself continually looking up and down the street for Martin's BMW.

The surroundings in the café were pleasant and she had been able to have a leisurely dinner. It was quiet and she felt comfortable and reasonably safe in the café, but that might have been due to the fact that there were people around. It was also the first time in the past several days that she felt like she could relax and let her guard down.

By the time she was finished eating and had paid for her meal, it had grown dark outside. As she approached the door of the café to leave, she hesitated to go outside into the darkness. She had no idea what might be waiting for her out there.

"Are you all right?" the waitress asked.

Her question startled René. She swung around and looked at the waitress. The expression of the waitress's face showed that she was concerned.

"Yes. Yes, I'm fine," René replied.

"Is there anything that I can get you?"

"No. I'll be going."

The woman nodded as if she understood, then returned to the counter. René looked out into the darkness again. She knew that she had no choice but to walk back home. She took a deep breath, then started for the door.

After stepping outside, she stood on the front porch of the café and looked around. There was no one on the sidewalks, and the street was almost deserted. The dampness gave a chill to the air, and a chill to René. She could not remember a time when she had felt so much alone and so vulnerable. It was as if she was just waiting for something terrible to happen to her.

René began walking toward her apartment building. She moved along at a rather brisk pace. It seemed that every sound she heard was strange to her, and every sound caused her nerves to jump. The sounds of the night caused her to hurry even more. By the time she got to the block her apartment building was on, she was running as if her life depended on it.

She ran up the stairs and quickly entered the building, slamming the door behind her. She leaned back against it as if trying to hold it shut against some invisible demon that had been chasing her. René was breathing hard, and her heart was racing.

It took her several minutes to get herself under control again. When she finally felt that she could continue to her apartment, she straightened up, turned around and looked through the glass door back toward the street. There was nothing out there. There was no Martin, no black car, no nothing. There was just an empty quiet street.

René began to think that her fears were unwarranted. She felt a little embarrassed by her actions and looked around to make sure that no one had seen her acting like a frightened child. She tried to convince herself that everything that had happened she had managed to blow way out of proportion, but she could not dismiss everything. There were just too many "accidents" to dismiss all of them as part of an overactive imagination.

The one thing she knew was that she was tired and needed to get some rest so she could deal with her emotions. She went directly to her apartment. After going through her apartment, room-by-room to make sure that she was alone, she secured the door and then got ready for bed. Once again she decided to sleep with a light on, only this time she left the smaller bedside lamp on. Since she was totally exhausted, it didn't take her long before she was asleep.

* * * *

The morning started out much different than the previous morning. René could see the sun trying to peek in around the edges of the curtains. For the first time, she even felt rested and ready to take on whatever the day might bring.

She rolled over and looked at the clock on the bedside table. It reminded her that she needed to call her boss and let her know that she was going to terminate her employment.

Telling Mrs. Westall that she was going to quit was not going to be easy, but she knew that to wait was just going to delay the inevitable.

René picked up the phone and spent the next twenty minutes or so talking with Mrs. Westall. She explained why she was terminating her employment. Although Mrs. Westall seemed to understand, it was clear that she would miss René.

After completing the phone call, René took a warm shower and dressed in a nice pair of slacks and a colorful blouse. The next thing that she had to do was to contact the

120

movers and confirm the time. Once that was done, she would go get some breakfast.

Since the movers would not be able to get there until one o'clock, she decided that she would walk down the street to the corner café for breakfast.

* * * *

As René left her apartment building, she stopped on the front porch to look up and down the street. The air smelled fresh. It was as if the rain had washed everything clean, including those things that had been troubling her. The fact that there was no black BMW on the street didn't hurt any, either.

After taking a deep breath of the fresh air, René started down the street toward the café. It was such a nice morning that her thoughts turned to what she might be doing if she was already at the estate. It occurred to her that she might even be having her breakfast out on the porch in the morning sun. The thought of having breakfast on an open porch overlooking the lake made her smile. It was one of the things that she would not even have thought about a week ago.

Before she realized it, she was at the café. Just as she was about to open the door, she saw the reflection of a man coming up behind her. She immediately thought of Martin, which caused her heart to skip a beat and her chest to tighten. She froze with fear, as she had not expected him to be right behind her.

"Excuse me, please," the man said.

The pleasant sound of a man's voice caused her to turn quickly and look at him. The man was tall and rather handsome, but he had a very worried look on his face. More importantly, it was not Martin.

"Are you all right, Miss?" he asked, the tone of his voice showing his concern for her well-being.

"Yes," she replied after taking a moment to catch her breath.

The man smiled as he reached around in front of her and opened the door. He watched her as he held the door and waited for her to go inside.

René quickly gathered herself together and stepped into the café. Once inside, she quickly stepped aside and allowed the man to move on past her. As she took a moment to regain her composure, she watched as the hostess led the man to a table.

"May I help you?"

The sound of another strange voice startled her again. She looked at the waitress for a second or two before she could answer.

"Yes. I would like a booth in non-smoking if you have one available, please."

"Right this way."

René followed the waitress to a booth in the back corner. As she slid into the booth, the waitress set a menu on the table in front of her.

"Can I get you something to drink?"

"Yes. Coffee, black, please."

René watched as the waitress turned and walked away. She was still a little shaken by the man at the door. Martin had managed to make her very jumpy. It seemed that every little noise and every little movement rattled her nerves.

As she sat waiting for her coffee, she let her eyes slowly wonder around the room. She stopped when she saw the man who had held the door for her. He happened to be sitting at a table halfway across the room, facing her. She noticed that he was alone, and he was looking back at her. He smiled and gave a slight nod of his head.

Embarrassed that he had caught her looking at him, she quickly picked up the menu and held it in front of her so he could not see how embarrassed she must have looked. She took a deep breath, then looked at the menu.

As she looked at the menu, she could hardly keep from thinking about the man. He had a pleasant smile. He looked like he had a good tan. She wondered if he was the outdoor type, he certainly looked like it.

She was so busy thinking about the man, that she had not selected anything to eat when the waitress returned with her coffee. She quickly gave the waitress an order, then reached for the coffee. It might have looked a little ridiculous, but René almost wished that the waitress had not taken the menu away.

As René sipped the hot liquid, she looked over the rim of the cup and found the man still looking back at her. It was a little unnerving for her to have him watching her, especially with all that had happened to her over the past few days. She tipped her eyes down in the hope that he would not look at her anymore, but she found that she could not keep from looking back at him.

René suddenly became very nervous when she glanced over toward him and saw him stand up. She watched him as he walked across the room toward her, carrying his coffee cup.

"I'm sorry if I'm disturbing you, but I really hate to eat alone, and you look as if you could use a little company. Would you mind if I join you?" the man asked as he stood next to her booth and looked down at her.

René just looked up at him. His voice was pleasant to the ear and he looked sincere in his request. It didn't seem to her that he wanted anything except to provide her with some company. She could see no harm in letting him join her in the booth. Besides, she was thinking that company might be kind of nice right about now.

A quick look around the café confirmed her decision to let him join her. After all, it was a public place and there were lots of people around just in case she needed some kind of help.

"I know it's probably a line you have heard a hundred times before, but I really don't like to eat alone," the man said with kind of a shy smile as he patiently waited for an answer.

"I guess it would be all right," she replied as she gestured toward the bench on the other side of the booth.

"My name is Jeff Dailey," he said as he reached a hand across the table.

"René Richardson," she replied with a smile and lightly shook his hand.

"Nice to meet you, René Richardson. I hope that I am not intruding?"

"No, not at all. Have you ordered yet?"

"Yes. We have the same waitress. I'm sure she will bring my meal over here."

"I'm sure she will," René replied. "I don't remember seeing you around here before. Do you live in this neighborhood?"

"No. I live up near Blue Mountain Lake. That's a little town in the Adirondack Mountains."

"Really?" she asked, a little surprised by his answer.

"Yes, really. Why? Do you know someone who lives around there?"

"Yes. As a matter of fact I do."

"Who is it? Maybe I know them."

"I live near Blue Mountain Lake," she replied with a smile.

"You're kidding. I don't remember seeing you before, and I'm sure I would have remembered you."

"Actually, I don't live there yet. I just inherited my great uncle's estate near Essex Lakes."

"Your great uncle? Could that be William Delcambra's estate? I don't know of anyone else who has died around there recently."

"Yes. It is his place. How do you know that?" she asked suddenly a little afraid that he might be here to spy on her.

"I'm the wildlife manager for that area. I live just a little way from your place. In fact, I live just across the lake. I was really sorry to hear about his death."

"Did you know Captain Del?"

"I've known him from the time I was assigned to that area, a little over five years ago. He was a great guy. We used to sit on that big front porch and talk about the wildlife in the area for hours. He knew a lot about the area. He gave me permission to hunt on his land, but I guess I'll have to come over and visit you some time so I can ask you about hunting on your land," he said with a smile.

"I guess you will," she replied with a shy smile.

Just then their orders came. As René sat back to make room for the waitress to set the plates down, she looked at him. She thought about this chance meeting and wondered if it was really a chance meeting. Was it possible that he had planned to meet her? Was it his purpose to meet her here, or did he really have some other reason for being here. It seemed to be too much of a coincidence for her to accept this chance meeting at face value, especially with all that had happened over the past couple of days.

"It sure is a small world," he said as he smiled at her.

"Yes, it is," René said as she looked at him over the rim of her coffee cup. "What brings you to Utica?"

"I came to spend the weekend with my sister and her family," he said after taking a bite of his eggs.

"I was about to drive back, but decided to stop in here for breakfast first. I'm glad I did," he said as he looked across the table and smiled at her.

"Your sister lives near here?" René asked as she spread jelly on her toast.

"My sister lives about a block from here, over on Walnut."

"When will you be going back?"

"In a little while."

At least he picked a street that was close by. He seemed very sincere in what he said. He didn't have to stop and think about his answers, and he answered her questions without hesitation. Maybe he was what he appeared to be, René thought.

"When will you be moving to your great uncle's estate?"

"Probably late this afternoon. I have to wait for the movers to come."

They talked about the area around the Essex Lakes and what the lake was like. René found him easy to talk with. It was mostly small talk, but the more they talked the more she found him to be very interesting. The more they talked the more comfortable and believable he seemed to her. The fact that he was handsome and pleasant to spend time with didn't hurt.

By the time they were finished eating, she found that she liked him. He seemed to know the area around the Essex Lakes very well. From what he said, he apparently knew Captain Del. This helped to assure her that he was who he said he was. By then, she was hoping that after she got moved in at the estate he would come to visit her.

When they were done eating, Jeff leaned back in the booth. He looked across the table at René as she took a sip of coffee.

"I wish I could stay longer and talk, but I must be going. I have to get back. There are a couple of things I have to check out on my way back before I can call it a day."

"I enjoyed your company, thank you," René found herself saying.

"The pleasure was mine, I assure you. I hope that I'm not being too forward, but would it be all right if I call on you after you get settled in?"

René's heart skipped a beat. The look in his eyes seemed to ask the same question. Just the thought that he might want to see her again excited her.

"Yes. That would be nice," she said with a smile. "Besides, you will have to ask me if you can hunt on my property.

"Right," he said with a smile. "Well, I'd better go. I'll see you in a couple of days."

René couldn't say anything. She nodded her approval while she sat there and watched him as he stood up. He dropped a tip on the table, then turned and walked away. Before she realized it, he was gone.

This had been an unusual morning for her. She certainly had not expected to meet a man that she liked. Here she was only a couple of blocks from her apartment in Utica, meeting a man who lived just across the lake from where she was moving. What a coincidence, she thought.

René sat and sipped her coffee for several minutes as she thought about her chance meeting with Jeff Daily. It had been the first pleasant thing to happen to her for some time. She had a deep feeling that she would like to get to know him better.

After finishing her coffee, René decided that she should get back to her apartment and make sure that she was ready for the movers. The walk back to her apartment was far more pleasant than it had been the other night. She was convinced it was due to the fact that she had met someone that she felt might prove to be pleasant company.

Shortly after noon, the moving truck arrived with two strong-looking men. They loaded her belongings into the truck and were ready to take them to the estate. René suggested that they follow her to the estate, but gave them directions just in case they got separated. She knew that she would feel safer if she traveled with the moving truck rather than alone. It seemed to her that her "accidents" only occurred when she was alone on the highway.

CHAPTER NINE

It was close to dinnertime when the movers finally left the estate. Most of René's things had been carefully stored in the garage with the exception of her personal papers that she had taken into the den. She felt she would have plenty of time to sort things out after she got settled in.

As soon as the movers had gone, René stepped out onto the front porch and looked out across the lake. One chapter of her life had come to a close, and another chapter was just beginning. Although her mind was filled with doubts about the future, the one thing that she had no doubt about was that she would love this place as much as Captain Del had loved it. It was beautiful and quiet here, and it gave her a sense of peace.

As she looked out over the lake, her thoughts turned to Jeff. She strained to see if she could see where he lived, but it was a large lake and the forest that surrounded it was thick. She remembered that he had said that he lived directly across the lake, but she could not see any kind of a house or cabin on the other side of the lake. All she could see were trees, lots and lots of trees.

"Excuse me, Ma'am. Dinner is ready," Mildred said from the doorway.

"Thank you, Mildred."

René turned to go into the house, but stopped long enough to take one more look across the lake. She still had not seen anything that even came close to resembling a house or a cabin.

With all that had happened over the past few days, René found it difficult to believe that there was a house or cabin on the other side of the lake. She began to wonder if Jeff was for real, or if he was just someone that had been hired to get close to her. That thought was a little depressing for her. She once again began to question if there was anyone she could truly believe and trust anymore.

With a long sigh, René went into the house. She ate in the dining room alone that evening. She had decided not to invite the Cathums to join her for dinner, although she half expected that they would. Tonight it didn't bother her to eat alone. She was feeling a little down and preferred to be by herself. She wasn't sure if it was because of her thoughts of Jeff, or if it was something else. Whatever the reason, she felt that she would not be very good company tonight.

Immediately after dinner, René retired to the den. Mildred had fixed her a pot of coffee. Then with René's permission, Mildred retired to her quarters above the garage for the evening.

René sat at the rolltop desk and read the papers that she had found in the desk. It gave her a good deal of insight into Captain Del and why he loved the estate so much.

Time passed by quickly and before she realized it, it had gotten rather late. René went to the window and looked out. As she stood at the window, she could see that it was starting to rain lightly.

She found herself automatically looking across the lake, but this time she could see a dim light. It seemed to be almost hidden back in the trees. Not sure what it was, her first thought was that it could be a light in the window of a cabin. Her heart skipped a beat. Maybe Jeff really did live across the lake after all, she thought. If his cabin was set back in the forest a little, it would not be easy to see even in the daytime. That would certainly explain why she could not see it from the porch.

As she stared at the dim light, she started to think about Jeff again with a more positive attitude. She began to wonder what kind of a house he lived in, if he had any pets, and what he liked to do. She knew he liked to hunt, but she didn't know what kind of hunting he enjoyed.

She found it easy to picture him living in a rustic log cabin with a big stone fireplace and a gun or two hanging above the mantel. She could even picture storm lanterns on the table, and maybe a bearskin rug on the floor in front of the fireplace and the head of a big deer hanging on the wall.

Her daydream seemed so romantic, yet so real. It was so real to her that she could almost feel the warmth of the fire. She could even picture herself lying on the rug in front of the fireplace, wrapped in Jeff's strong arms.

Lost in her romantic fantasy, the bright flash of lightning and the sudden crack of thunder startled her. It quickly brought her out of her dream world and back to reality. She had not noticed that the light rain had turned into a downpour. It was now raining so hard that she could no longer see the dim light on the other side of the lake. In fact, she was unable to see the other side of the lake at all.

René let out a sigh as she turned away from the window. She was once again feeling very much alone and very tired. It had been a busy day for her and it was getting late.

René looked around the room. As she glanced at the clock on the fireplace mantel, she hadn't realized just how late it was getting. There were hundreds of books to look over, rooms to check out and acres to explore. She now had all the time in the world to do those things. Right now it was time for her to get some rest.

She closed the desk, locked it and then went upstairs to her room. After getting ready for bed, she climbed into bed and pulled the covers over her. She lay on her back and listened to the rain as it pelted against the window. The wind had come up. Every once in while she could hear the sound of thunder and see a flash of lightning as it lit up her bedroom, even with the curtains closed.

The sound of the storm outside her window kept her from falling asleep. As she listened, she realized that it did not seem to be letting up. She slid out from under the covers and wrapped the afghan around her shoulders. Mildred had left the afghan on the end of the bed for her. She walked over to the window.

Just as she drew the curtain back, lightning flashed briefly lighting up the surrounding landscape. It was almost immediately followed by the loud crash of thunder indicating that the lightning was very close. The wind blew in off the lake, and the rain seemed to come down in sheets. The light on the side of the boathouse cast a dim glow over part of the dock and over the water nearby. In the faint light, René could see white caps on the water as the waves dashed against the shore under the light. She could also see Sam's small fishing boat roll and toss as it banged against the dock as if it was trying to free itself. This was not a night to be out in the elements, René thought.

Just as René was about to close the curtains, she thought she saw something move on the dock near to the boathouse. She moved closer to the window and strained to see what it was. She could see the faint outline of the figure of a man in a heavy raincoat. At first she thought that it might be Sam going out to make sure that his boat was secure. But as the figure passed under the boathouse light, she realized it was not Sam. With the rain on her window and the darkness outside, she could not tell who it might be, but she was positive that it was not Sam.

Under the light, René could make out the figure a little better. Whoever it was appeared to be a much taller man than Sam and probably much younger by the way he moved. He was dressed in a wide brimmed hat that cast a shadow over his face, not that it mattered much. She would not have been able to see his face from her bedroom anyway. The black rain slicker he wore was shiny from being wet, and it covered the man's form making it difficult for her to get any idea as to who it might be.

The figure suddenly disappeared. Looking through her rain streaked window made it impossible for her to see where the man had gone. The only place that seemed logical to her was that he most have gone into the boathouse.

What would anyone be doing at the boathouse on a night like this, she wondered? Was he looking for shelter from the weather? That was certainly a possibility, but he seemed to be dressed for being out in the rain. Was he trying to steal her boat? That didn't make much sense. It was an old classic boat that would quickly be recognized if anyone tried to use it or sell it.

René continued to watch. It wasn't long before the man reappeared on the dock next to the boathouse door. René watched him as he looked around as if he were trying to make sure that he had not been seen. Then he looked up toward the house. He was standing under the light, but with the rain pouring down so heavily, René still could not make out any facial features. Suddenly, he turned and ran off into the night, disappearing into the darkness.

Her first thought was that he might have seen her standing in the window watching him. With the way he ran off, it was possible that he knew that he had been seen. René immediately dropped that thought. With no lights on in her bedroom and the heavy rain, it would have been almost impossible for anyone to see her in the window.

Secure in the thought that the man was gone, René closed the curtains and leaned back against the wall. Her mind was filled with thoughts of what the man was doing in her boathouse. She thought about going down to the boathouse to look around, but with the stormy weather that idea passed quickly. It would have to wait until morning, she quickly convinced herself.

The idea of a strange man stalking around outside concerned René. She wondered if the man might sneak around and try to get into the house. She tried to remember if Mildred had locked all the doors before she retired for the evening.

Not convinced in her own mind that the house had been locked up for the night, René left her room and went into Captain Del's bedroom. She took one of the cutlasses off the wall, then started downstairs. She started with the front door, then went to each room to make sure that all the windows were closed and locked, as well as the doors.

Once she was satisfied that the house was secure, she returned to her bedroom. As she leaned the cutlass up against her nightstand next to the bed, she smiled. She began to feel a little foolish having carried the cutlass around the house as if she knew how to use it. She was just glad that she hadn't run into anyone.

René returned to her bed. She lay in her bed trying to think of what anyone could possibly want in the boathouse. It occurred to her that she had not been in the boathouse, yet. Other than her boat, she had no idea what else might be in there.

René's mind was filled with questions that she knew would have to wait to get answered. It took her a long time before she was able to clear her mind enough to get some sleep.

* * * *

When morning arrived, the sun was shining and the birds were singing outside her window. Upon waking, her first thoughts were of the man who had been in her boathouse last night. She once again began to wonder what he was doing in there. Since she had not been in the boathouse, she decided that she would check it out this morning for herself.

She got up and dressed. As she walked into the kitchen, the smell of freshly baked bread filled her senses. It made her realize just how hungry she was. She took time to sit down at the table and enjoy a hot cup of coffee and a couple of slices of toasted fresh bread.

After her light breakfast, she went outside. She looked across the lake toward where she had seen the light last night as she walked across the lawn toward the boathouse. She could not see anything, but she was sure that there was a cabin or house of some kind hidden back in the woods.

As she stepped onto the dock and walked toward the boathouse, she noticed that the door into the boathouse was ajar. She hesitated slightly before walking up to the door.

René stopped at the door and slowly pushed it open, then looked in. Inside was the old Chris Craft boat that had been Captain Del's. It was suspended above the water on web straps that hung on a steel frame.

René stepped inside and took a moment to look around the boathouse. A deck surrounded the boat on three sides. It would allow a person to get into the boat from either side when the boat was in the water. Along the front of the boathouse was a long workbench with some tools and what looked like extra boat parts. The more she looked around, the more she wondered what anyone would want in here. The only answer she could come up with was the boat.

"You going to put it in the water?"

René swung around to find Sam behind her in the doorway. It took a moment for her to catch her breath as he had startled her.

"I was thinking about it," she said as she turned back around to look at the boat again.

The sun shining in the window reflected off the shiny polished wooden hull of the boat. The chrome trim of the boat sparkled. It was a beautiful boat just waiting for someone to take it out on the lake for a spin. René could remember the roar of the big engine when her father had taken her for a ride in it.

"Would you like me to put it in the water for you?"

"Yes, please."

René stepped back and watched as Sam pushed the button on the wall that lowered the boat into the water. After the boat was in the water, Sam tied the bow of the boat to a post, then pushed another button that opened the garage-type door.

"There you are, Missy. All ready for a spin on the lake," Sam said with a grin.

"Sam, do you know a man by the name of Jeff Dailey?"

"Sure. He's the wildlife manager around here. He lives on the other side of the lake."

"What's he like?"

"A nice fellow. He used to spend a lot of time fishing with the Captain. Why?"

René was glad to hear that Sam knew Jeff and thought well of him.

"Sam, I thought I saw someone sneaking around down here last night."

"You mean here, in the boathouse?"

"Yes."

"I doubt that Jeff would come around without coming up to the house first."

"I wasn't suggesting that it was Jeff."

"No one in their right mind would have been out in the storm we had last night."

"I'm sure you're right. I must have been mistaken," she said not sure what to say now.

"Maybe I'd better look around, just to be sure that nothing is missing."

"Thank you. I have to go up to the house and get the key for the boat. I'll be right back."

Sam nodded, and then René left the boathouse.

While René returned to the house for the boat key, Sam looked around the boathouse and in the boat. Something didn't set right with him. There was something wrong, but he could not put his finger on it for a couple of minutes.

Suddenly it came to him. He could smell the faint odor of gasoline. He looked around, but didn't see any signs of gasoline on the floor of the boathouse or around the workbench. The closer he got to the boat, the stronger the smell became. He realized that it was coming from inside the boat.

Sam climbed into the boat and took the cover off the engine compartment. He immediately realized that gasoline was leaking inside the engine compartment. He also knew that if the engine was started with the compartment full of gasoline fumes that it would most likely explode and burn the boathouse down, as well as kill anyone in the boat.

He examined the fuel lines inside the engine compartment and discovered that one of the lines was leaking. It appeared as if it had been leaking very slowly for some time. Time enough to fill the compartment with fumes making the boat a potential fiery bomb.

Sam shut off the flow of fuel to the engine, then examined the fuel line closely. It was clear to him that it had been cut with something very sharp, probably a knife. It had been done very carefully so that it would not leak too much, and would not be easy to find. Seeing the cut fuel line simply assured Sam that René was right. Someone had been in the boathouse.

René returned while Sam was still removing the damaged fuel line so he could replace it. He heard her come in and turned to look at her. He could see the worried look on her face. He was a little worried himself. If she had started the boat, she could have been killed. Close calls tended to make Sam nervous.

"It's a good thing you didn't try to start the boat, Missy," Sam said as he held up the damaged fuel line for René to see.

"What is that?"

"It's a cut fuel line. It looks like it was cut on purpose. You were right. Someone was in the boathouse last night. Do you know who it was?"

"No," she replied weakly as she stood paralyzed while staring at the cut fuel line.

René began to mentally put all the strange or unusual things that had happened together. In just the past few days she had been run off the road twice, someone had been in her apartment, and now someone had tampered with her boat in an apparent attempt to kill her.

She could feel her chest tighten, and her heart pound inside her chest. If she had had the key to the boat when she first came down to the boathouse, she might very well have died in a fiery explosion.

Suddenly, her attention was drawn to the sound of a boat motor. René turned and stepped out of the boathouse onto the dock. She could see a small boat coming toward the dock. Still unsettled by another near "accident", she stepped back inside the boathouse and watched as the boat came closer.

René let out a sigh of relief when she realized that it was Jeff Dailey in the boat. Although she had not expected to see him so soon, she was glad that he had come to visit her.

He waved to her as she stepped back out onto the dock. She found herself waving back at him, but not with the same enthusiasm as he was showing. As he approached the dock, she walked out toward the end of the dock and waited for him to come up along side.

"Hi," he said with a smile as he reached out and grabbed hold of the dock, but his smile faded quickly when he saw the look on René's face.

"What's the matter?" Jeff asked as he tied his boat to the dock.

René could hear the sound of concern in his voice. She was hesitant to tell him, but he seemed worried about her.

"Someone cut the fuel line on my boat."

"What?" he said sharply as he stepped out of his boat.

"Sam's working on it now."

"Are you sure it was cut?"

"Sam seems to think so."

"Where's Sam now?" he said as he reached out and took hold of her hand.

Jeff didn't wait for a response. He started toward the boathouse with René in tow.

"He's in the boathouse trying to fix the fuel line."

Jeff let go of her hand at the door to the boathouse. She watched him as he went inside while she stood at the door to listen.

"What yah got, Sam?"

"Hi, Jeff. Looks like a cut fuel line."

"You sure?"

"Yeah. It was intentional, too. There's nothing anywhere near the fuel line that could cut it like that. It's a nice clean cut."

"I think we should call the Sheriff. He should know about this," Jeff suggested.

"You're probably right. There won't be any finger prints on the hose with all that fuel, but he should know that something is going on out here."

René stood at the door and listened as the two men talked. How was she going to explain everything that had happened over the past few days and have anyone believe her? She had no proof, and there were no witnesses. The cut fuel line was the only evidence to indicate that there was something going on. She doubted that it would be enough to convince the sheriff.

"You want to call the Sheriff?" Sam asked.

"Sure," Jeff replied.

"He'll probably send someone out to take a report, but that's about all he will be able to do," Sam said.

"I'm sure you're right, but I still think we should call him," Jeff added.

Jeff turned and looked at René standing by the door. He could see that it had frightened her, but then it should have. He wanted to get her away from there, but that would have to wait until after they talked to the Sheriff.

Jeff decided that it would be a good idea if he took René up to the house. He wanted to get her away from the boathouse and the boat in the hope of relieving some of her fears.

"Let's go up to the house," Jeff suggested. "Sam will get the boat fixed."

"Okay," she agreed, just glad to have him there to hang on to.

Jeff took hold of her hand and they began walking toward the house. He didn't mind at all that René was holding his hand tightly.

Just as they stepped up on the first step of the porch, they heard a loud explosion. It startled them. They quickly turned in time to see a big ball of fire and smoke rising from where there had once been a boathouse. Pieces of the boathouse and the boat were falling on the lawn and into the lake.

"Oh, my God," René cried as she put her hands over her mouth and stared at what was left of her boathouse.

"Get in the house," Jeff ordered as he pushed René up the steps toward the door.

Reluctantly, she stepped inside the house, but she didn't close the door. Instead, she stood in the doorway and watched as Jeff took off running toward the boathouse.

Jeff raced across the lawn even though he knew there was little chance of anyone surviving such an explosion. He still had to see if he could find Sam.

René could not believe what she was seeing. The last thing she could remember was Sam working on her boat inside the boathouse. It was clear to her that the gasoline must have caused the explosion. There was no doubt in René's mind that anyone inside the boathouse would not be able to survive such a fiery blast.

As René watched Jeff standing near the burning remains of the boathouse, she walked out to the edge of the porch.

She heard something behind her and turned to see Mildred coming out the front door to see what had happened.

"Oh, God," Mildred cried as she saw the smoke and flames.

"I'm sorry," René said softly, not knowing what else to say.

Mildred looked at René, then looked toward the boathouse. After a moment, she started looking around. When Mildred didn't see Sam, she put her hands over her mouth. Tears began to roll down her cheeks.

René immediately went to Mildred's side and put her arm around her. Together, they walked down to where Jeff was standing, just a little way away from the burning boathouse.

Jeff turned and looked at Mildred and René. He could see the tears on Mildred's face. He wanted to say something that would console her, but he didn't know what to say.

"What the hell happened?"

Everyone turned to see Sam coming toward them. Mildred ran to him and threw her arms around his neck, almost knocking him down. She hugged him hard as she buried her face in his shoulder and cried openly.

After the shock of seeing Sam unhurt had passed, Jeff and René walked over to him. It was hard to believe that he had not been killed.

"What happened?" Jeff asked.

"Darned if I know. I went over to the storage shed to get a new fuel line when I heard the explosion. Something must have fallen in front of the door to the storage shed. I had a hell of a time getting the door open."

"We thought you were still in there," René said.

"I left the doors open to air out the gas fumes while I went to the storage shed. That place never should have exploded," Sam said as he turned to watch the remains of the boathouse burn.

"But it did, and I can still smell the gas," Jeff replied.

"Yeah, and I smell something else," Sam added.

"You're right, Sam," Jeff agreed as he took another smell of the air. "It smells a little like gun powder."

"Yeah. Someone blow it up. I think they thought that the gasoline would cover up the smell of the gun powder," Sam said.

"You might be right, but why?"

"That I can't tell you."

"Any idea why someone would want to harm René?"

"No," Sam replied.

"I think we need to find a safe place for her," Jeff said.

"Good idea."

"Let's all go up to the house. I'm not sure what might happen next," Jeff said.

"Yeah. Once we get René safely in the house, we need to call the Sheriff," Sam said as he reached out a hand to Mildred.

Mildred took Sam's hand and held on tightly as they walked to the house. Jeff put his arm around René and guided her back toward the house, searching the area as they went. He didn't know what he was looking for, but he didn't want any more surprises. He wasn't sure if the person who had caused the boathouse to explode was still in the area and still a threat to René.

CHAPTER TEN

René stood at the window in the den and looked out at the boathouse as the remains of it continued to burn. She stood with her arms folded across her chest. Her eyes were fixed on the flames, but she was not really seeing them. René was not thinking about the fire spreading as the boathouse was over the water. She was not thinking about the loss of the building or even the loss of her classic powerboat.

The fact that the boathouse had exploded and could have killed her was what was racing through her mind. At this point, she was thinking about her own mortality and the fact that someone apparently wanted her dead.

Jeff stood beside the rolltop desk. He was on the phone talking to Sheriff Stone. As he explained what had happened, he looked over at René just to check on her and make sure she was all right. The look on her face showed the strain on her nerves.

After hanging up the phone, Jeff walked over to René. Standing behind her, he reached out and wrapped her in his arms, gently pulling her back against him. He looked over her shoulder and watched as the remains of the boathouse continued to smolder. If there had been any doubt in his mind about what René was thinking, it became clear to him at that moment. He could feel her entire body shiver.

René didn't look at him. She simply closed her eyes and leaned back against him. She let him hold her in his strong arms. For the first time since the explosion she began to feel at least a little safer.

"Sheriff Stone will be out in a little while. I think they will be sending someone from the state police to investigate the explosion in the boathouse, too," Jeff whispered in her ear.

René didn't say anything. She could not keep from shaking. All she wanted was for him to hold her and make her feel safe and secure.

Jeff turned his head and looked over toward Mildred and Sam. They were sitting on the sofa very close together and holding hands. The explosion had been a real shock to Mildred as well. She had been so sure that Sam had been in the boathouse when it went up in a fireball.

"Jeff?" René whispered without turning around to face him.

"Yes?"

"Do you think someone is trying to kill me?"

Jeff could tell by the sound of her voice that she was scared, which was certainly understandable. He didn't know just what to say, but to lie to her would not help matters, either. But to tell her what he really thought might scare her even more.

"I'm not sure. Whoever blew up the boathouse may have just wanted to scare you."

"What about the cut fuel line? That would certainly have killed me if Sam hadn't found it," René added as she turned around in his arms and looked up at him.

Jeff looked into her pleading eyes. She wanted answers, but he didn't have any to give her. He didn't know what to say to her that would make her feel more secure.

"Jeff?"

René and Jeff turned and looked toward Sam. Even Mildred was wondering what Sam had on his mind.

"I don't think René is safe here."

Sam didn't want to scare René any more than she already was, but it was clear to him that someone was willing to do anything, including murder, to get their hands on the estate.

Jeff glanced at René, then turned back to Sam before he answered.

"I have to agree. We need to get her away from here. Someplace where she will be safe."

René looked up at Jeff. This was her home, like it or not. She had no place else to go.

"As I see it, it might be best to offer the place for sale and get out. It's not worth losing a life over," Sam said as he looked at René for some kind of reaction.

"Sam!" Mildred said, surprised that he would even suggest such a thing.

"I won't sell," René insisted nervously as she pushed herself away from Jeff and stood straight. "You can leave if you want to, but I'm not leaving. Captain Del would have put up a fight. I will do nothing less."

"That a girl. I needed to know just how committed you are to this place," Sam said, obviously pleased with her response.

"Okay, that's settled," Jeff said as he smiled at René for her show of courage.

"We have to form a plan. A way to keep everyone as safe as possible and still let them know that we are not leaving," Sam said.

"Maybe if we make no effort to show that we are leaving, they will get the message that René is going to stay right here," Mildred added.

"I don't think that will work. Someone wants this place bad enough to kill for it. I think things will get worse before they get better," Jeff said.

René looked up at him. The look in his eyes convinced her that he was probably right.

"What do we do?" she asked.

"We first talk to Sheriff Stone. Maybe he has some ideas that will help. Meanwhile, I think we should get some coffee and begin making plans."

"Come with me," Mildred said looking at René. "You can help me fix the coffee."

René looked up at Jeff, then let go of him. She turned and left the room with Mildred. Jeff walked over to the window and looked out toward the lake.

"I'm worried about that girl," Sam said as he walked over next to Jeff.

Jeff didn't move or look at Sam. He continued to look out the window at the smoldering remains of the boathouse, a constant reminder of what could have happened.

"I am, too," he finally replied.

"Got any ideas of how we can protect her?"

"I've got one."

"What's that?" Sam asked.

"I need to take her someplace where I can protect her. This place is too big, too open. It's too hard to protect her here," Jeff said as he looked around the room.

"Take her to your place. It's small, it's well hidden in the trees, and you know the woods better than anyone does. If you run into trouble, you can hide her in the woods until things cool down or help arrives."

"Do you think she will go with me?"

"You'll never know unless you ask her," Sam replied.

"I'll do that. I'll have to figure out a way to sneak her out of here so no one will know that she's gone. We need to make it look as if she is still here."

"Good idea," Sam agreed.

"What about you and Mildred?" Jeff asked.

"What about us?"

"I don't think it is all that safe for the two of you, either."

"Whoever is trying to get this place is not interested in us. We don't have any rights to it. René is the one. The fact that they almost got me, I think was an accident."

"You might be right, but I don't think they care who they kill to get to René," Jeff said after giving it a few moments of thought.

"You might be right about that," Sam agreed.

Sam and Jeff turned around to see René and Mildred come back into the den. They were carrying mugs of coffee.

"We were just speculating about the fire," Sam said as he took a mug of coffee from Mildred.

René walked across the room to Jeff and handed him a mug. She then sat down in a chair next to her desk.

Jeff sipped at the hot liquid and looked over the rim of the cup at René. She had put up a good front so far, but he wondered if she would be able to keep it up if things got any worse. The explosion of the boathouse had shaken her pretty badly, yet she had shown a determination to keep the estate.

"The sheriff is here," Sam announced.

They all turned and saw Sheriff Stone's car coming down the driveway toward the house. A state patrol car was right behind it.

"They didn't waste any time getting here," Jeff said as he set his mug on the table. "I think you should wait here."

René did not respond other than to nod in agreement. She watched as Sam and Jeff left the room and went out to meet the sheriff and the state patrolman.

Mildred crossed the room to stand beside René. They watched from the den window as the men introduced themselves to each other and shook hands. They could not hear what was being said, but it was clear that the men were talking about what had happened. They watched as Sam and the two law officers started toward the burned out boathouse, while Jeff came back toward the house.

"Sheriff Stone will want to talk to you in a little while," Jeff said as he walked into the den.

"What are they doing?" René asked.

"They're just looking over the boathouse and talking to Sam about what he did and saw this morning."

146

"They don't think Sam caused the explosion?"

"No, Mildred. They just want to talk to him because he was the last one in the boathouse before it exploded. He can tell them what he saw, what he smelled and what was done to the boat before the explosion."

"Oh," she replied feeling a little foolish.

"What will happen now?" René asked.

"That depends on what they find and what you tell them, I guess."

René turned and walked toward the window. She could see the three men standing near the remains of the boathouse and dock. Although it was still smoldering, the state patrol officer bent down and picked up something while the Sheriff seemed to be just walking around looking at the ground. She noticed that Sam just stood where he was and seemed to be watching and waiting for them to finish whatever it was they were doing.

"They're looking for clues," Jeff said as he stepped up behind René and wrapped his arms around her.

René held his arms around her as she leaned back against him. Although she had made an effort to show her strength, she wasn't as sure of herself as she had tried to appear. She seemed to draw strength from Jeff. Just his touch helped her confidence and eased her fears, at least a little.

Jeff could feel her lean back against him. He liked holding her and hoped that she liked having him hold her. She seemed to be able to cope better, and didn't seem so afraid.

"Jeff?"

"Yes?"

"Do you really think someone is willing to kill me to get my home?" René asked in a whisper.

Jeff didn't want to tell her what he really thought, but to do otherwise would be endangering her even more.

"Yes," he replied as he held her a little tighter.

René could feel a chill run through her entire body. She was sure that Jeff felt it, too. She wanted to run away, but she knew that would not settle anything. It was already clear to her that whoever was trying to get the estate would be able to find her, no matter where she might go. After all, Martin had found her apartment in less time than it had taken her to get there from the estate.

She also remembered that someone had gotten into her apartment even when the doors were locked. Even while she was there taking a shower.

The more she remembered the things that had happened over the past couple of days, the more she began to realize just how vulnerable she really was.

"Jeff?"

"Yes?"

"I don't want to stay here tonight," she whispered.

"I'll stay with you, if you want me to."

"No. I mean, I want you to stay with me. It's just that I don't want to stay in this house. Not tonight."

"Would you feel safer staying at my place?"

René didn't have to think about what he had suggested. She knew that any place with him would make her feel safer than here.

"Yes."

"Then you can stay with me."

René let out a sigh of relief. Just the thought of having him close to her made her feel better. She closed her eyes and leaned back against him. She could feel him breathe as he held her close. This was the first time in a very long time that she felt she didn't have to carry all the weight of this burden by herself.

René opened her eyes when she heard the door to the den open. Jeff let go of her as she turned around to see who had come in.

"Miss Richardson, I'm Sheriff Stone. This is State Trooper Busack. We would like to have a word with you, if we may."

"Certainly. Would you like some coffee?"

"No, thank you. We would like to talk with you alone."

René nodded and sat down. She watched as Sam and Mildred left the room. When Jeff started to leave, René reached out and took hold of his hand.

"Do you mind if he stays?" she asked, her eyes pleading for him to let Jeff stay.

Sheriff Stone looked at Jeff. He had worked with Jeff on several occasions during the hunting season and knew Jeff well. He also trusted Jeff and respected him. He could see no reason not to grant René's request.

"No, of course not."

Jeff stood behind René with his hand resting lightly on her shoulder as Sheriff Stone and Trooper Busack sat down on the sofa.

"We understand that you came up to the house to get the key to the boat after Mr. Catchum discovered the cut fuel line. Is that correct?"

"No. He discovered the cut fuel line while I was getting the keys to the boat."

"Where were you when the boathouse exploded?"

"I was with Jeff. We were on our way here to call you about the cut fuel line."

"Where was Mr. Catchum?"

"When we left, Sam was in the boathouse fixing the fuel line on the boat."

"It had been cut. Is that correct?"

"Yes."

"Why would anyone want to cut the fuel line on your boat?"

"I don't know."

"Do you have any idea?"

René looked up at Jeff as if looking for help. Jeff simply nodded as if to tell her that he was there for her and that she should tell them everything she knew. She then looked back toward the Sheriff and began explaining everything she knew or thought she knew.

René told them about someone being in her apartment in Utica, and about the car that had run her off the road on her way back from Albany. She told them about the man hanging around the boathouse last night during the storm. She even told them about the truck that had nearly hit her head-on when she was on her way to meet Mr. Hanover in Blue Mountain Lake.

She realized that she had no evidence to back up what she was telling them except for the destroyed boathouse. Yet, it was certainly a good indication that something was going on.

Sheriff Stone and Trooper Busack listened very carefully to what René had to tell them. Several times Stone would look at Busack as if to see if Busack was getting the same feelings about this that he was.

When René finished, she looked at Sheriff Stone and Trooper Busack in an effort to get some indication as to whether or not they believed her. When she didn't get any kind of a response or reaction from them, she looked up at Jeff. Her eyes pleaded with him to believe her.

"Well, Miss Richardson, that's very interesting. Do you believe that all these things are tied together somehow?"

"I really don't know. What I told you is the truth. If they are tied together, as you put it, I would think you'd be interested in talking to Mr. Martin Hanover."

"It's not that we don't believe you, Miss Richardson," Trooper Busack said. "It's just that we don't have any proof."

"What do you call that?" she blurted out in frustration as she pointed toward the remains of what had been a beautiful boathouse with the classic speedboat inside less than two hours ago.

"We understand your feelings," Trooper Busack said.

"Do you?"

"Yes, we do," Sheriff Stone interjected. "But we have to have proof. We can't just go around accusing people without some kind of proof that they were involved."

"I plan to pay a visit to several of the homeowners along the road where you said you were run off the road. Maybe someone saw that black car speeding along the road about that time. I have to tell you that it's a very slim shot, but it could prove helpful. If we are really lucky, we might even find a witness," Trooper Busack explained, giving René only minimal hope.

"Thank you," René said with a sigh of relief.

She felt Jeff gently squeeze her shoulder. It was important for her to know that Jeff believed her.

"I can't spare a man full-time to watch your place, but I'll keep a man in the area. Hopefully, we will find the black sedan and get a chance to question the driver. I have to tell you that we don't have a lot to go on here."

"What about Martin Hanover?" René asked.

"We can't just question him without something to go on," Sheriff Stone replied.

"I doubt that he cut the fuel line or set the explosives in the boathouse. If he is the kind of man you say he is, he would have someone else do his dirty work while he was in a public place miles from here for an alibi," Trooper Busack added.

"Does that mean you are not going to question him?"

"Well, not at the moment. I think the first thing we have to do is to make sure that you are safe," Sheriff Stone said. "I would like to take you back to town with me. I have a policewoman that can stay with you at a safe house."

"No. I won't leave my home," René insisted.

"But, Ma'am. It's for your own protection," Trooper Busack said.

"I won't be run off to someplace where I can not see my home," she insisted.

"If Miss Richardson does not mind, I will take some time off and stay with her," Jeff suggested.

René turned and looked up at him. She squeezed his hand as a way of letting him know that she liked the fact that he was being discreet.

Sheriff Stone and Trooper Busack looked at Jeff. They both knew him to be reliable and very good with a gun should it be needed. They also knew that he knew his way around the woods. He would know where to look for trouble, and where to hide René if trouble came.

"Is that all right with you, Miss Richardson?" Trooper Busack asked.

René turned back around and replied, "Yes."

"In that case, I think we have all we need for the moment. I will have someone in the area as much as possible," Sheriff Stone reminded her.

"I will, too," Trooper Busack added.

"Thank you."

René held onto Jeff's hand as she watched the sheriff and the trooper stand and leave the room. Knowing that Jeff would be with her and there would be a law officer in the area made her feel a little more secure.

"Thank you," René said as the sheriff and the state trooper left the room.

Jeff, still holding her hand, waited for her to stand up. He then walked with her to the kitchen where Sam and Mildred were waiting for them.

"Well, how did it go?" Sam asked.

"Okay," René replied, her voice showing that she seemed a little disappointed.

"They're going to try to keep an officer in the area," Jeff added obviously disappointed, too.

"That doesn't seem like much help." Mildred said.

"No, it doesn't," René agreed.

"I'm going to sneak René out of here after dark. We'll go across the lake to my place for the night."

"That sounds like a good idea," Mildred said.

"We could all have dinner together tonight," René said as she sat down at the kitchen table.

"Good idea. We need to take some time to make this place as secure as possible," Jeff agreed.

"Yeah. We also need to make it look as if René is still here," Sam added. "We have no idea who might be watching us."

After a brief discussion on what they should do, Jeff and René returned to the den. While Jeff stayed with René, Sam began preparing the house to make it more secure from outside intruders. He checked the door locks and secured windows.

It had been a hard day and René was feeling drained. She dropped down on the sofa and looked up at Jeff.

"Would you mind if I lie down on the sofa and rest for a little while?"

"No, not at all. I'll sit over here," Jeff said as he walked toward a comfortable looking chair.

Jeff sat down and picked up a magazine that was on the table next to the chair. He began thumbing through it, but found himself glancing over at René every few minutes just to be sure that she was okay.

It wasn't long before René was sound asleep. This had been a very hard day on her. Jeff was worried about her and how she would do if things got worse. He was sure that it would get worse.

It wasn't long before he had tipped his head back and dozed off. It was a quiet afternoon, a good time to rest.

CHAPTER ELEVEN

Jeff woke from a light sleep shortly before it was time for dinner. He looked over at René and saw that she was still sleeping on the sofa. He knew that she was tired and that this day had been very difficult for her. He could see no reason to wake her at this time and decided to let her sleep a little while longer. He watched her sleep for a couple of minutes, then tipped his head back and closed his eyes again.

The sun was just beginning to set when René finally opened her eyes. She slowly turned her head and looked toward Jeff. She found that he was still sitting in the chair, but he had dozed off. Even though he was sleeping, she still felt protected. Just the fact that he had stayed with her was enough to make her feel secure.

René took the opportunity to look at him. The sun had tanned his skin. His dark brown hair was slightly messed, yet it somehow managed to look good. It seemed to give him a rugged, outdoor appearance, which she found to be rather sexy. His arms were muscular and strong, and his broad chest filled out his knit shirt very nicely. There was no question that Jeff was handsome. That, along with being nice, made him just what she liked in a man.

"Hi," Jeff said softly disturbing René's thoughts.

"Hi," she replied shyly, a little embarrassed by the fact that he had caught her looking at him.

"Did you sleep well?" he asked.

"Yes."

"Good."

"When are we going to your place?" she asked, her eyes almost pleading with him to take her away from there now, at least for the tonight.

154

"Any time you're ready."

"Could we go soon?" René asked as she sat up on the sofa.

"Sure."

"I'll go get ready."

Jeff stood up and watched her as she left the room. As soon as she was gone, he let his eyes drift around the room. As his eyes came to the painting of Captain Del, he stopped and looked up at it. It seemed to him that the captain was looking down at him.

"I'll take care of her," he whispered.

Suddenly his thoughts were interrupted by a hair-raising scream coming from upstairs. He turned and ran from the den and up the stairs, taking the steps two or three at a time.

"René!" he called out as he reached the top of the stairs and looked down the hall.

Before he got an answer from her, he saw her slowly backing out of one of the rooms. She had her hands over her mouth and her eyes were as big as saucers. Something in the room had scared her half to death.

"What is it?" Jeff asked as he rushed to her and took hold of her arm and pulled her close to him.

René turned and looked at him. She couldn't speak, she was shaking terribly and she could hardly breathe.

Jeff pulled her up against him as he turned his head and looked into the room. His eyes narrowed as anger welled up inside him. He turned René away so she would not have to look into the room.

Someone had killed a rabbit and deliberately laid it on the floor next to the bed. The poor creature had had its throat cut. There was no doubt in Jeff's mind that it was obviously a message to René. A message telling her to give up her claim to the estate before something worse happened.

René buried her face in Jeff's shoulder. He looked past her into the room again. He could not see anything else from the doorway. Jeff turned and started to lead René down the hall just as Sam came running up the steps.

"What happened? We heard a scream," Sam asked as he got to the top of the stairs.

"Call the Sheriff back out here."

Sam didn't say anything, nor did he hesitate. He quickly turned around and went back downstairs. Jeff followed him down the stairs, his arms around René as he led her back to the den.

Once in the den, Jeff sat down on the sofa with René. He did not let go of her. He couldn't have even if he wanted to. She was holding onto him for dear life.

"It's okay," he whispered, but he didn't believe a word he was saying. Someone out there was going to stop at nothing to get control of René's estate.

"It's not okay," she cried out in frustration. "Someone came into my house and none of us knew he was here. He just strolled in here, did what he wanted, then left without anyone knowing."

Jeff continued to hold her. He could understand her frustration, her fear and her anger. He wondered how anyone got in without them knowing, but he was more interested in knowing who was doing this to her.

Just then, Sam came into the den with Mildred right behind him.

"The Sheriff is on his way. What happened?"

"Some real sick son of a . . ., sorry," Jeff said as he stopped to take a breath. "Someone left a dead rabbit in René's room on the floor next to her bed."

"Who?"

"That's what I'd like to know."

"I'll go clean it up."

"No," Jeff blurted out.

"But," Sam replied, then quickly realized the importance of leaving the evidence untouched.

"I want the Sheriff to see it just as it is. Don't disturb anything in the room until after the sheriff has been here," Jeff insisted.

"Of course," Sam agreed.

Mildred was visibly shaken by what she heard. It frightened her to think that someone could do such a thing and not be seen. She stepped up to Sam and took hold of his hand.

Sam looked at Mildred. He then led her out of the den, leaving Jeff and René alone.

Jeff held René tightly. He could feel her body quiver as it responded to her fears.

"Who's doing this to me?" René cried as she pleaded for answers, but the answers were not there.

"I don't know, but I'm going to find out," Jeff said, his voice indicating his strong determination to find out who was at the bottom of what had happened.

René buried her face back in Jeff's shoulder. It took a while, but she finally was able to get control of her emotions and regain some semblance of normal breathing. Just having Jeff with her and holding her seemed to be enough for the moment.

* * * *

The sheriff arrived and immediately examined the room for any evidence that might help him figure out who had been in René's room. After the sheriff had finished his investigation of the room and gathered what evidence he could find. He then went to the den and sat down to have a talk with everyone.

"Miss Richardson, when was the last time you were in your room?" Sheriff Stone asked.

"This morning, I guess," she said after giving it a moment's thought.

"You haven't been in your room since?"

"No, I don't think so."

"What about when you came in the house to get the keys to the boat?" Jeff asked.

"The keys were in Captain Del's bedroom," she replied. "I didn't go into my bedroom."

"She's been with me all the rest the time," Jeff added.

"Well, from the looks of it, the rabbit has been there for some time. It was probably put there while all of you were outside looking at the boathouse right after the explosion," Sheriff Stone explained.

"Sam, you didn't see it when you were securing the house?" Jeff asked.

Sam looked at Jeff, then at Mildred. Everyone was looking at him and waiting for an explanation. He seemed confused and baffled by Jeff's question. Suddenly, an almost shocked look came over his face.

"Oh God, I didn't even look in her room," he said feeling rather dumb for his oversight.

"Sam!" Mildred said, surprised that Sam would overlook René's room when he was checking out the house to make sure it was secure.

"Well, I guess I didn't think I needed to check her room. It's on the second floor and there's no way to get up there from outside the house without a ladder," Sam offered as an explanation.

"Whoever did this was probably already in the house. He probably triggered the explosion by remote control, then came in the back door while all of you were out in front watching the boathouse burn," Sheriff Stone explained. "Then he made his escape by going out the back of the house, around behind the garage and disappearing into the woods. With everyone out in front, no one would have seen him make his escape."

"You mean this was all done this morning?" Sam asked.

"Yes, I believe so. I think Miss Richardson was supposed to find the dead rabbit this morning."

When Sheriff Stone had finished talking with all of them, he left to return to his office to sort it all out. Sam and Mildred left the den, leaving Jeff and René alone.

Jeff sat next to René on the sofa holding her hand. They didn't say much, but it was clear that neither of them wanted to be separated from the other.

"I want to get out of here," René said, her voice showing the urgency she was feeling.

"I'll get your things."

"Let's just go. I don't want to stay here one minute longer," she insisted.

"Okay," Jeff replied, then stood up.

Jeff took René's hand and started to leave the room with her. As he did, he shut off the lights in the den and turned toward the stairs.

"Where are we going? I thought we were leaving," she asked when Jeff turned her and led her toward the stairs.

"We're going to make it look like we are going upstairs to bed. If we're being watched, we want whoever is watching us to think we are staying right here."

René said nothing more. She didn't want to go upstairs, but she didn't want to let go of Jeff's hand, either. She simply followed him as he led her up the stairs, shutting off the lights as they went. He took her into one of the empty bedrooms, turning on the light as they entered. He led her across the room to the windows. With her standing near him so that they could be seen by anyone watching from outside, he closed the drapes.

"There. If anyone is watching us, they might think that we are going to bed. And if they are watching, hopefully they will think that I am staying with you."

After a few minutes, Jeff shut off the lights in the bedroom. He again took René by the hand and led her back through the dark house. When they entered the den, Jeff did not turn on a light. Instead, he led her over to a dark corner of the room.

"Wait here," he said, then let go of her hand.

René didn't want to let go of his hand, but did as he instructed. She watched him as he moved closer to the windows. She waited while he looked outside in an effort to see if anyone might be out there.

"See anything?" René asked in a whisper.

"No. I think it's clear to go. We'll go down to the dock and get my boat, then row across the lake."

He motioned for her to come to him, then waited at the window for her to join him. As soon as she was at his side, he opened the patio doors just far enough for him to slip through, then stepped out onto the porch. He looked around to make sure that it was clear. As soon as he was satisfied that there was no one around, he motioned for her to join him. She stepped out the door onto the porch.

As soon as they were outside, Jeff closed and locked the door as quietly as he could. He then took René's hand and led her to the end of the porch. Again he looked around for any signs that someone might be nearby. When he felt that it was clear, he led René down to the beach.

With half of the dock destroyed by the explosion, Jeff had to wade out to the end of the dock where he had tied his boat before the boathouse had exploded. He pulled the boat up closer to the beach and helped René get in. She moved to the back of the boat as Jeff climbed in. He quietly put the oars into the water and began slowly rowing the boat away from the beach. He turned the boat around and pointed it toward the other side of the lake and began rowing.

René looked back over her shoulder at the house. The house was silhouetted against the glow of the yard light at the back of the house. There was no light in front of the house. The porch lights had been left off. There had been a yard light on the boathouse, but it was gone now.

René turned back and watched Jeff as he silently rowed the boat across the lake. She didn't say anything. She knew that voices tend to carry in the silence of the night, especially when out on a lake.

Jeff kept the silhouette of the house in a direct line over René's shoulder. He watched her as he rowed. He was worried about her. After all, she had had a lot to deal with over the past few days. He was a little surprised that she had held up as well as she had under the emotional stress.

* * * *

It seemed to take a long time to get to Jeff's dock. When they arrived at the dock, they were met by a large black dog with a white patch on his chest. The dog seemed very excited to see Jeff. He was jumping up and down.

"Easy, Jake," Jeff commanded, his voice firm, yet soft. The dog immediately settled down.

"Is he friendly?" René asked.

"Most of the time. He's a good watch dog."

René looked at the dog and smiled. She slowly reached out the back of her hand to the dog and let him sniff her hand. After a moment or two, the big dog let her pat him on the head.

"Good boy," she said.

Once the boat was tied to the dock, Jeff helped René out and led her to his cabin. The dog followed along behind them. Jeff left the dog outside while they went inside.

"You know that you are going to have to return to your house sooner or later," Jeff said softly as he turned on a small table lamp.

"Yes, but I just can't be there now. I just need a little time away to get my thoughts together," she replied as she watched him move around the room closing the curtains on the windows.

"I understand. You can stay here as long as you want," Jeff assured her.

While Jeff was making sure that his cabin was secure and changed into dry clothes, René took the opportunity to look around. It was a rustic cabin made of large logs. It had an open beam ceiling and a stone fireplace. Above the fireplace was a gun rack with two guns on it. One was a rifle, the other a shotgun. The walls had several wildlife pictures on them. She liked his cabin, it seemed to fit him. It was also just what she had expected.

"It's quiet out tonight. Hardly a breeze," he said, interrupting her thoughts.

"Yes, it is," René replied.

"Jake will let us know if anyone comes around," Jeff said in the hope of reassuring her that she was safe there.

René didn't say anything, she just turned and looked at him. She could not help but think about how romantic his cabin could be under different circumstances, but right now she was not feeling very romantic.

"Would you like me to build a fire, it's kind of cool tonight?"

"That would be nice."

René stood back and watched as Jeff built a fire in the fireplace. As the flames began to flicker, they cast a warm glow over the entire room.

Jeff turned and looked up at her. He noticed how she was standing. She had her arms folded across her chest as she stared into the fire. The look on her face showed how deep in thought she was.

"Are you all right?" he asked as he stood up and stepped in front of her.

"Yes," she replied as she turned slightly and looked at him. "Just being with you makes me feel safe."

René hesitated a moment then stepped up in front of him. She reached out, put her hands on his shoulders and looked up at his face.

Jeff slipped his arms around her and drew her up against him. He looked down into her beautiful brown eyes. Slowly, he leaned down until their lips met. It was a soft, gentle kiss. It was a kiss that was loving, but cautious.

Jeff pulled back slightly. He didn't want to push himself on her. With all that had happened to her, he was convinced that she was more than a little vulnerable. She would need time and a little space before she could think about him.

"You know, we didn't have any dinner. Are you hungry?" he asked.

"A little," she replied softly as she took her hands from his shoulders and stepped back.

"Would you like to help me fix something to eat? You'll have to put up with what I have," he warned her.

"I'm sure we can find enough," she said with a smile.

Jeff took her hand and led her to the kitchen. Together, they prepared a meal and sat down in front of the fire to eat.

After dinner, Jeff took the dirty dishes to the kitchen. When he returned, he found René sitting on the floor in front of the sofa gazing at the fire. He wondered what she was thinking about, but decided not to ask. If she wanted him to know, she would tell him.

René looked up at him and smiled.

"Comfortable?" Jeff asked.

"Yes. I've always liked to sit on the floor in front of a fire."

"In that case, I'll join you, if you don't mind?"

"I don't mind at all," she replied, looking up at him.

Jeff sat down beside her on the floor. As he settled in, she leaned up against him. He reached over her and put his arm behind her, tucking her up against his side while she rested her head on his shoulder.

They sat quietly for some time just watching the flicker of the flames. René almost wished that Jeff would just turn out the one table lamp that was on and let the flames of the fire light the room.

As the evening wore on, René began to feel the tension of the day slowly fade away. As it did, she began to realize just how much energy it had taken from her and how tired she had become. In Jeff's arms, she felt safe and able to relax a little. She suddenly yawned.

"Tired?"

"Yes. I guess I am."

"It's been a difficult day for you. If you would like to go to bed, you can use my bed. It's pretty comfortable."

René yawned again. She was rather tired, and a good night's rest would probably help her deal with her situation better. Right now she was too tired to think clearly.

"I guess I will go to bed, if you don't mind."

"I don't mind," Jeff said as he stood up and helped her to her feet.

Once she was standing in front of him, he didn't want to let go of her. He reached out and put his hands on her narrow waist. As he looked into her eyes, he gently pulled her to him and slipped his arms around her.

René reached up and put her hands on his shoulders again. As she tipped her head back and waited for his lips to meet hers, she let her arms slide around behind his neck and drew him closer. The warmth of his lips felt good against hers. She liked the way he held her and the feel of his strong arms holding her tightly against his strong muscular body. His kiss was tender, too. It had been a long time since she had been held in the arms of a man. She had never felt a kiss like the one Jeff was giving her. She wanted more, but at the same time she was afraid.

Jeff was reluctant to release her, as he liked the feel of her firm body pressed against his. When Jeff finally let go of her, she stepped back and looked up at him.

Without a word, she stepped around him and hurried into his bedroom. His kiss had radiated through her entire body sending a tingling sensation that affected her like nothing she had known before. In fact, it scared her.

Jeff watched her as she walked away from him. He wanted her to stay with him. From the feel of her body against his, he was sure that she wanted to stay with him, too. But he knew that logic and caution must prevail. It was not a good idea for them to get too emotionally involved until certain things were cleared up. The biggest one was to find out who was trying to kill her and get control of her estate.

Once inside Jeff's bedroom, René took a deep breath. A thought passed through her mind that maybe coming here with him was a mistake. She quickly let that notion pass when she realized that she had not brought anything with her.

"Jeff," René called from the bedroom.

"Yes?"

"I don't have anything to wear to bed. I guess I wasn't thinking very clearly before we left."

"I'm sorry, but I don't have any pajamas. There's a shirt in the closet that you could wear as a nightshirt if you like," he suggested.

"I guess that will have to do," she said as she looked toward the closet.

René walked over to his closet and opened the door. She found a long-sleeved light blue shirt right where he said it would be. She took it off the rod and looked at it. It looked like it was big enough for two of her. A smile came over her face as she thought about scenes in movies that she had seen where the girl wore just a man's shirt. She wondered if she would look that sexy to Jeff in the morning, but she dismissed that thought when she decided that Jeff would not see her in just his shirt.

René removed her clothes and laid them over a chair in the corner. She slipped into the shirt and buttoned the front. As she rolled the sleeves up, she turned around and caught sight of her reflection in the mirror above the dresser. The sight of her reflection surprised her. For some reason she had expected to look silly in his shirt, but she discovered that she did look rather sexy.

While René was getting ready for bed, Jeff went to the kitchen and fixed dinner for Jake. When he was done, he set it outside the backdoor. While Jake ate, Jeff returned to the living room and began to arrange the pillows and afghan on the sofa for a bed. He could hear René moving around in his bedroom. Jeff's thoughts quickly turned to her and how it had felt to hold her in his arms. He smiled as he tried to picture René wearing one of his shirts to bed.

"I hope you think I look sexy," she whispered to herself as she turned and looked at herself in the mirror again.

"Did you say something," Jeff asked from the living room.

"Ah, no, not really" she replied as she looked toward the door.

It was then that she realized that the fireplace was two sided. She wondered if he could see her as well as hear her. More importantly, she wondered if he had seen her get undressed.

"As soon as you're ready and in bed, I'll fix the fire for the night."

Looking at the fireplace, she was sure that he had not seen her. In fact, she was sure that he had not tried to peek in on her. He is a gentleman, she thought to herself.

René walked over to the bed and pulled back the covers. The bed was big and looked very inviting. She climbed into the bed and pulled the covers up over her.

"I'm ready," she called out.

She half expected Jeff to come into the room, but he didn't. She could hear him as he stacked the wood on the fire so that it would burn slowly and provide heat all night long. She sat up and watched him. It was hard to see him, but she did get glimpses of him from time to time as he added logs to the fire. He was not wearing a shirt. The glow of the fire accented his muscular chest and strong arms.

It didn't take Jeff long to stack the fire. When he was finished, he sat back and looked at the fire. He knew that it would keep the cabin warm all night.

"Goodnight," he said.

"Goodnight," she replied.

Jeff went to the back door and called Jake. He brought the dog inside and got him settled down next to the sofa for the night.

René closed her eyes and tried to sleep, but her mind was too cluttered for her to fall asleep immediately. She could hear Jeff as he settled down on the sofa. She lay quietly on her back as thoughts of Jeff and how sexy he looked with the glow of the fire on his bare chest filled her mind.

She began to remember the times when he had held her and comforted her that day. He had done everything he could to make her feel safe and secure. Although she was sure that he wouldn't come into the room, she sort of wished he would. She knew that if he came into his room and wanted to lie next to her, she would not refuse him.

The more she thought about him, the more she wanted to know about him. It suddenly occurred to her that she really didn't know very much about him. Was he really everything that she thought him to be? Was he just being nice to her, or did he care for her as much as she hoped he did? He seemed very kind and considerate, but did he love her?

The thought of love made her wonder if she loved him. Was it love that she felt for him, or was it just the fact that he was showing a good deal of attention and kindness toward her during a trying time?

René had no answers for her questions, and there would be no answers that night. There was nothing she could do but try to get some sleep. She took a deep breath and tried to doze off.

Jeff lay on the sofa with his hands behind his head as he thought about the woman in the next room lying in his bed. There was no doubt in his mind that she was beautiful, but he had known a number of beautiful women. Some of them were very nice, while some were not so nice. But he was sure that René was different. He took a minute to review what he knew about her as if to measure her against some idea of what he thought the ideal woman should be like.

She was scared, but then she had every right to be after all that had happened to her. She was rich, or at least well off, but that was not important to him. He had all the money he needed to live the way he wanted. She seemed very nice and had a very nice personality. That was important to him. She seemed to like the outdoors, and that was very important to him, too.

Jeff remembered holding her and liked the way she felt in his arms. He had to smile to himself at that thought. The way her body felt pressed against him and the warmth of her kiss was all any man could want, he thought.

It was that last thought that made it easy for him to close his eyes and to drift off into a pleasant sleep. Except for an occasional crackle of the fire, or a shifting of Jake as he slept on the floor next to his master, the cabin was quiet and peaceful.

CHAPTER TWELVE

René woke to an unfamiliar sound coming from somewhere outside of the bedroom. At first, she didn't know what it was, but soon realized that it was Jeff's dog, Jake. What she was hearing was a low soft growl coming from deep inside the big dog's chest. She looked around in an effort to see where Jake might be, but she could not see anything except for the slight glow of the embers in the fireplace. The black dog was invisible in the darkness of the cabin.

Just as she was about to toss the covers off and go out into the living room to wake Jeff, she felt a hand quickly cover her mouth and a strong arm wrap around her. She could feel herself being held against someone, but was not sure who it was. Her heart raced and her breath caught as she tried to break free and to call out for Jeff, but to no avail.

"Ssssssh," Jeff whispered in her ear in an effort to settle her down. "Someone's out there."

As soon as Jeff felt René relax a little, he took his hand off her mouth and let go of her. She breathed a sigh of relief as Jeff quietly stood up and backed away toward the end of the bed. Even in the darkness, she could see the glow of the embers reflected off a gun that Jeff held in his hand. He stood at the foot of the bed and listened for any sound, any sound that would help him understand Jake's nervousness.

"Slide off the side of the bed and get down on the floor," Jeff whispered, but he didn't take his eyes off the window.

René didn't need to be told twice, nor did she hesitate. The sight of Jeff's gun told her that he was serious, and that he was prepared for trouble. She quickly slid off the bed and sat down on the floor. She watched Jeff as he looked around, then moved closer to her.

"Where's Jake?" she asked in a low soft whisper.

"At the front door," Jeff replied in a whisper.

Jeff motioned for René to lie flat on the floor. As she did what he wanted, he flipped the comforter off the bed and onto the floor, covering her with it.

Jeff moved up next to the window and very carefully pushed the curtain back. He peered out into the darkness from the edge of the window.

Jeff could see a light back in the trees. It looked like it might be the headlights from a car or pickup, but it was too far down the road for him to be sure which. His first thoughts were that someone had discovered that he had brought René there, but he found that hard to believe. After all, if anyone had been watching the house, they would have seen them in the upstairs bedroom. He was sure that he had been careful enough not to be seen when they left, or had he?

The one thing that didn't make any sense was the vehicle with the headlights on. If it was someone coming to get René, they would certainly have shut off the lights much further down the road where they could not be seen from the cabin.

Just then he saw something cross in front of the lights. It was not one of the animals that lived in the forest that surrounded the lake. It was hard to make out what it was, but it looked like it might be a man. Then he saw a man running toward the vehicle. The lights began to move away as the vehicle backed on further down the road. In a short time the lights were gone and it was dark again. It was possible that it was just someone who had pulled off the road for a short break, but Jeff didn't believe that for one minute.

The more he thought about it, the more he began to figure out what was going on. It was more likely that someone had been checking out the cabin and discovered the boat at the dock. When they realized that Jeff must be at the cabin, they tried to leave as fast as they could, hopefully before they were discovered.

Jeff dropped the curtain, turned around and walked over to the side of the bed where René was still hiding. He reached down and lifted the comforter off her.

"They're gone," he said as he turned and put a log on the fire.

As he sat down on the edge of the bed, the log burst into flames filling the room with a soft yellow glow.

"Who was it?" René asked as she stood up.

"I don't know," he replied as he let his eyes drift over her. "I didn't get a good look at them."

René looked at Jeff. She wasn't sure if he was keeping something from her or not. However, even in the dim glow of the room she could tell that he was looking at her. It was then that she remembered that she was wearing just his shirt. She was a little embarrassed at first; but when she realized that he was not wearing anything but briefs, she sat down on the bed next to him.

"It was someone after me, wasn't it?" she asked, her eyes pleading for the truth.

"I don't know. It could have been someone who was going to check out my cabin in case we came here. He probably discovered that we were already here and split."

"How would he know that?"

"My boat. We left it tied at the dock. If we were still at your house, my boat would have been over there, on the other side of the lake."

"Oh," she replied feeling a little foolish. "What do we do now?"

"We try to get some more sleep. In the morning, we go back to your place."

"Do you think they might come back?"

"I doubt they will come back tonight. It's almost four in the morning. By the time they report that we are here and get back, it will be light. I don't think they will try anything now. They don't want us to know who they are. That puts daylight on our side."

"Just who are 'they'?" René asked knowing full well that neither of them knew the answer to that question.

Jeff realized that René had asked the question out of frustration more than anything. He didn't bother to try to answer her.

"I think you should get back to bed and try to get a little more sleep," Jeff said as he stood up. "I'll have Jake sleep in here at the foot of the bed."

René looked at Jeff. She didn't really want him to go. She would rather have him sleep with her than to have Jake sleep at the foot of the bed. She knew that she would feel much safer with him there, but she decided not to ask him to stay.

Jeff turned around and picked the comforter up off the floor while René climbed back into bed. When she was settled in again and had the sheet pulled up over her, he spread the comforter out over her.

As he tucked her in, he leaned down and kissed her lightly on the forehead. He then called Jake into the bedroom. The big dog came into the room and laid down at the foot of the bed at Jeff's command.

René looked at Jeff's face. She was about to ask him to stay with her when he looked down at her and smiled.

"I'll be just on the other side of the fireplace. If you need me, just call."

René smiled up at him. Even though she wanted him to stay with her, it was probably better if he went back to the living room. With all that had been happening, she didn't know if her feelings for him were real, or out of a desire to be protected.

Before he returned to the living room, Jeff put another log on the fire. The hot coals quickly ignited the bark and gave the room a little more light.

As Jeff stood up, he looked around the room before walking over to the window. He adjusted the curtain to make sure that the light from the fire couldn't be seen from outside.

René watched him as he walked back across the room to the door. She couldn't help but look at him. In just his briefs, he looked very sexy. His body was muscular and athletic.

Jeff stopped at the door and looked back over his shoulder at René.

"Try to get some sleep," he said softly, then left the room.

As soon as he left the room, René closed her eyes. In her mind she could see him still standing near the fire. He was so good looking, and he was nice, too, she thought. Why had she not met someone like him before?

She could hear him as he settled back on the sofa to sleep. The cabin was once again quiet except for the occasional crackling of the fire, and the snoring of Jake at the foot of the bed. It was not long before she was able to doze off again.

* * * *

The next thing René heard was the sound of birds in the trees outside the bedroom window. When she opened her eyes, she could see the sun shining against the curtains. It gave her new hope that today would be better than yesterday.

There was another sound that she heard, but she couldn't place it. It was coming from the other side of the fireplace. She immediately wondered if Jeff was up.

René tossed the covers off to the side and swung her feet off the edge of the bed. She stretched, then stood up. She walked to the bedroom door and looked out into the living room. She noticed that Jeff was not there.

She looked toward the kitchen where the sound seemed to be coming from. There was Jeff standing in front of the stove. He was wearing pants but no shoes or shirt. She smiled to herself as she watched him fixing breakfast.

Jeff turned and saw René watching him. He took a minute to look her over. Although his shirt was much too big for her, it still made her look very desirable. In fact, it made her look downright sexy.

"You look very sexy," he said with a smile as he looked back at her face.

"You really think so?" she replied smiling back at him. "I've never looked that good in that shirt."

René liked the way he looked at her, and the way he looked without a shirt. She walked across the room toward him. Jeff had turned back to tend to the eggs he had cooking on the stove. René walked up beside him and put her hand on his bare shoulder. His skin was soft and warm. As she leaned against him, she looked down at the frying pan on the stove.

"It looks good, and smells good, too. How soon before it will be ready?"

"It's ready now. Sit down."

René sat down at the table and watched Jeff as he put the eggs and bacon on plates. After setting the plates on the table, he poured coffee for both of them, then sat down.

René found it hard not to watch him as he ate. This morning felt strange to her. It seemed so natural for her to be sitting across the table from him wearing just his shirt, and having him sitting across the table from her without a shirt.

"What are you thinking about?" Jeff asked as he interrupted her thoughts.

"Oh, I was thinking about us," she admitted, a little concerned about what he might think.

"What about us?"

"Us sitting here like this is a little like one of those romance movies," she said, not really sure that he would understand what she was trying to say.

"How is that?"

"Well," she said a little hesitant to try to explain. "You know, the girl ends up wearing the guy's shirt in the morning."

René felt a little embarrassed. She knew what the movies tried to make the patrons think. It had not happened for her, although she sort of wished that it had.

"Oh," he said with a smile.

"You're teasing me."

"Yes, I am," he admitted with a big grin. "But you do look very sexy in my shirt."

René smiled. She liked the idea that she looked sexy to him, but it also embarrassed her just a little as she knew so little about him.

Jeff stood up and began clearing the table. René tried to help, but the kitchen in the cabin was a little small. Jeff accidentally ran into her a couple of times. They laughed at the effort they were both making to try to keep things on a friendly basis. It was clear that they were fast becoming more than just friends.

"I think I'd better go get dressed," René said softly.

"I think that would be a good idea, but could I ask you something first?"

"Sure," she replied as she looked up at him and wondered what was on his mind.

"May I kiss you?" he asked in a low soft voice.

René looked into his eyes, as the smile faded from her face.

"Yes," she replied softly.

She couldn't take her eyes off his face as he moved closer to her. When he reached out and put his hands on her narrow waist, she reached up and put her hands on his bare shoulders. The feel of his bare skin caused her heart to race with excitement and her nerves tingled with desire. She continued to look into his eyes as he leaned closer to her.

As he drew her up against him and their lips met, she could feel the warmth of his body through the thin material of his shirt. She pressed her body against him as the passion of their kiss grew like wild fire. The feel of his hands as he slid them down her back and over her shapely bottom made her want more of him.

René returned the passion of his kiss with a passion of her own. The warmth of his strong chest pressing hard against her breasts sent a wave of wanton passion rushing through her like she had never felt before, causing her to melt in his arms.

Jeff liked the feel of her body against him. He also liked the feel of her body under his hands. After a few moments, he took his hands off her bottom, pulled back a little and looked down at her. He was breathing rather hard as he looked into her eyes.

René was breathing hard, too. His kiss, and the feel of his hands on her body, had been more stimulating than she had expected. He had been warm and passionate, yet loving. And the feel of his body against hers through his shirt deepened her desire for him. It made her want him to take her back into the bedroom and make love to her, but at the same time it scared her. She felt as if she was losing control of herself, a feeling that frightened her even more.

"I think you better get dressed," Jeff suggested as he reluctantly loosened his hold on her.

"Yes," she replied softly as she slid her hands off his bare shoulders.

René reluctantly stepped back away from him. She found it hard to take her eyes off him as she slowly turned away from him.

Jeff watched her as she turned and walked toward the bedroom. The sight of the gentle sway of her hips as she walked away from him, her long shapely legs and her bare feet made him want to follow her into the bedroom. He could not remember a time when a woman had had such an affect on him as she had at this moment. He didn't want her to go, but he knew it was best to let things cool down between them a little before they went too far.

As soon as René had returned to the bedroom, Jeff went into the living room and put on his shirt. He could not get the feel of her body out of his mind any more than he could get the picture of her out of his mind. She looked so sexy and desirable in his shirt that he smiled as he remembered her comment about the romantic scenes in movies.

René went into the bedroom, shut the door behind her and leaned back against it. She let out a long sigh as she tried to get control of her desires. She wasn't sure if she was leaning against the door to keep Jeff out, or to keep herself from running back into his arms. She could not remember when she had been so shaken by a kiss. It took a few minutes for her to catch her breath and get her heart rate back to something close to normal.

When she heard Jeff moving around in the living room, she moved over next to the bed and took off his shirt. She quickly dressed and looked in the mirror. She certainly didn't look as sexy as she had in Jeff's shirt, but decided that she didn't look too bad for someone who had not come prepared to stay overnight.

René decided that she was ready to rejoin Jeff. She took a deep breath and walked out into the living room. Much to her surprise, Jeff was not there. She wondered where he might have gone.

After a quick look around, she decided that he must have gone outside. She went to the door and looked outside. She found Jeff kneeling on the ground with his dog beside him. At first it looked as if he was just spending some time playing with his dog, but René soon realized that he was looking at something on the ground. Whatever he had found, he seemed to be studying very carefully.

"What are you looking at?" René asked as she walked up behind him.

"Tracks. There were two men here last night. One stood over there by that tree. The other came up to the house, then took off rather quickly."

"You can tell all that from a few tracks?"

"You can if you know what to look for. I think the one at the tree was kind of a backup or lookout for the one who came up to the house. He took off rather quickly, too."

"What do you think they were doing?"

"My best guess is that they were checking out my cabin."

"What for?"

"That I'm not sure of," he said, not wanting to frighten her.

Jeff had a pretty good idea why they had come to his cabin. He was sure that they had been casing it just in case he brought René here. Jeff figured that either Jake had scared them off with his growling, or they discovered the boat. From the tracks, it was probably the boat tied at the dock.

"Why did they leave so quickly?"

"I don't think they expected to find anyone here. When they discovered the boat tied to the dock, they knew someone was around. I doubt that they wanted us to know that they had been here."

"What do we do now?"

"We go back to your place."

René wasn't sure that she was ready for that, but she also knew that she didn't have a great deal of choice. If she was going to find out what was going on, she would have to return and start looking for a possible reason for all that had happened. Somewhere in Captain Del's papers, either in his bedroom or in his den, she might find something that would explain why someone was trying to run her off the estate. With some luck, she might even find a clue as to who it might be.

"You ready to go back?" Jeff asked disturbing her thoughts.

"Yes," she replied, somewhat reluctantly.

Jeff stood up and took her by the hand. They walked to the dock. As they stepped out on the dock, René hesitated at the sight of the boat.

Jeff looked at her, then at the boat. It didn't take but a second for him to realize why she hesitated.

"Wait here," he said as he let go of her hand and moved closer to the boat.

Jeff knelt down and looked into the boat. There didn't seem to be anything out of order. It appeared to be just as they had left it. But just to be on the safe side, he made a complete search of the boat and motor to make sure that it hadn't been tampered with and was safe. When he found nothing, he motioned for René to come and get in the boat.

As René sat down in the boat, she looked at Jeff. He didn't say anything. He simply started the motor.

"I suppose you think I'm afraid," she said.

"Yes, I think you are, but you have every reason to be. I'm just mad at myself for not thinking to check the boat myself."

* * * *

The ride across the lake was a quiet one. The only sound was that of the boat motor as it pushed the boat across the lake.

As they got closer to the dock and the burned out boathouse, René's heart began to beat faster. The sight of the remains of the boathouse and the burned and charred dock reminded her of what had happened there yesterday. It also reminded her that she could have been killed if she had started the boat or had been in the boathouse when it exploded, and that Sam was nearly killed when it did explode.

"Are you all right?" Jeff asked.

His question seemed a little out of place. Of course, she was not all right. She was scared to death, but then wouldn't anyone be scared whose life had been threatened?

She turned and looked at him. She could see by the look on his face that he was worried about her. She let out a soft sigh, then smiled at him.

"I'm all right," she said. "I'm glad you're here."

Jeff smiled at her, but he had a pretty good idea what was going on in her head. He could not blame her for being frightened. Anyone would be scared under the circumstances if he had been through what she had.

Jeff ran the boat up on the beach. He got out, then helped René out of the boat. As they walked up to the house, they saw Sam and Mildred come out onto the front porch.

"Everything okay?" Jeff asked as he stepped up on the porch.

"Yeah," Sam answered. "How about you?"

"We had company last night, but they didn't stick around long."

"Come in and tell us about it," Mildred suggested.

Jeff and René followed Sam and Mildred into the kitchen. They all sat down and talked while they drank coffee.

* * * *

When they were done, Jeff and René went to the den. René immediately sat down at the desk and began looking around the room while Jeff sat down on the sofa and watched her.

"What are you looking for?"

"I don't know for sure, but I'm looking for someplace where Captain Del might have hidden something that will tell us who might be trying to get hold of the estate," she replied as she looked at him.

"Like what? A letter or maybe some notes that Del might have made?"

"Maybe. I don't know what I'm looking for."

"What makes you think you'll find anything?"

"I don't know, but when Martin was here it seemed that he had a lot of interest in the fact that I had gotten the desk open. It was almost as if he knew there was something in the desk that he didn't want me to find, or something that he wanted. I've gone through the desk, every inch of it and found nothing."

"What about that cabinet?" Jeff asked.

René looked at the low built-in cabinet below some of the bookshelves. She really hadn't noticed the cabinet before as it was partly hidden by the sofa.

"I haven't looked there," she admitted.

"Would you like me to help?"

"Yes, I would like that," she said with a smile.

René was not sure if she was just glad that he was willing to help her, or if it was because he seemed to believe in her. Whatever the reason, she liked the fact that he was there and he was ready to help her.

Jeff stood up, moved the sofa out of the way and then pulled one of the drawers out of the cabinet. He set the drawer down on the floor in front of the cabinet, then sat down next to it. He began by taking out each piece of paper and skimming over it. When he finished with one, he put it in a neat stack and took out the next.

René watched him as he methodically examined each piece of paper and each letter in the drawer. René took her cue from him and did the same thing. She quickly realized that by doing it this way, they were not likely to miss anything that might prove important in their search.

It was almost noon before they had finished going through every piece of paper in the cabinet. When they were finished, René sat back in the chair and looked up at the painting of Captain Del. She wondered where he would hide something that he didn't want anyone to see. Something that might prove important in the future.

"You know that he was a sly old fox," Jeff said as he watched her look at the painting.

She turned and looked at Jeff.

"You probably knew him as well as anyone."

"I'm sure."

"Where would he keep important papers that he didn't want anyone to see?"

"I'm not sure, but the one room that I have never been in was his bedroom. Except for the time when Sam and Mildred moved him into the den, I doubt that they had been allowed in his room, either."

"You mean even when he was sick, you never visited him in his bedroom?"

"No. When he got so sick that he could not get up and down the stairs by himself and he needed almost continuous care, he had Sam and Mildred move him down here. They put a bed in here for him."

"Will you help me search his bedroom?"

"Certainly," he replied. "But I would like to get some lunch. We've been at this for several hours."

René and Jeff put everything back in the cabinet, then went to the kitchen for lunch.

CHAPTER THIRTEEN

After lunch, Jeff and René went to Captain Del's bedroom. When they arrived at the door, René reached out and turned the knob. To her surprise, the door was locked.

"The door's locked," she said as she looked at Jeff.

"Do you have the key?"

"No. It wasn't locked the last time I was up here."

"Maybe, Sam has a key. Let's check with him."

Jeff took René's hand and led her back down the hall and down the stairs. When they arrived at the bottom of the stairs, René glanced out the front door and stopped suddenly.

"What's he doing here?" the tone of her voice showing her disgust.

"Who? Who are you talking about?" Jeff asked as he turned and looked out the door.

"Hanover, Martin Hanover," she said, her voice showing her obvious dislike for him.

"So that's Hanover?"

"Yes, and he was told to stay off my property."

When Martin saw the front door open and René step out on the porch, a big smile instantly came over his face. But the smile quickly faded when he saw a man come out of the house behind René and move up beside her.

"What do you want?" René demanded, not waiting for him to show how charming he could be.

Martin seemed to be caught off guard. He had not expected to see a man there to support her, especially a man with a gun on his belt. He had to wonder if she had hired a bodyguard.

"I see you have a friend," Martin said as he looked at Jeff.

"This is Mr. Daily. He's the local Wildlife Officer. What do you want?" René asked, again ignoring the niceties of a proper introduction.

Martin breathed a sigh of relief. He was glad to know that Mr. Daily was not a hired bodyguard. He hesitated a moment before he spoke.

"I just came to see if you needed anything. I heard about the explosion."

"I'll just bet you did. No, I don't need anything, especially from you."

Martin turned and looked toward the remains of the burned out boathouse, then looked back at her.

"That was a terrible accident. It's a good thing no one was hurt," he said as a slight hint of a grin came over his face.

"Yes, it is. But it was no accident," René said as she glared at him.

"You don't say. I was told that your boat exploded."

"In case you have not received the message, you are not welcome here," René said flatly, not wanting their discussion going on any longer than necessary.

The slight grin disappeared from his face as he just stood there looking at René. It seemed to him that Jeff was watching him rather closely, but he had made no move to interfere. He looked from René to Jeff then back to René, trying to decide what he should say next.

Jeff got the impression that Martin wanted to say more, but did not want any witnesses to what he wanted to say. He was not about to leave René alone with Martin.

Jeff had taken an instant dislike to Martin. Since Martin gave no indication that he was going to leave as René had requested, Jeff decided it was time for him to step in.

"I think the lady just invited you to leave. I would strongly suggest that you accept the invitation and get off her land before she decides to press charges of trespassing," Jeff said as he took just one small step toward Martin.

Martin looked at Jeff as if to size him up while taking a step backwards. It was clear that Jeff was very well built and in good shape. And, of course, Martin had not missed the fact that Jeff carried a gun, although Jeff had given no indication that he might use it. Without a word, he glanced at René, then turned and walked around the house toward the back where he had left his car.

Jeff followed at a distance to make sure that he did leave. He stopped at the corner of the house and watched as Martin got into his car and headed down the driveway toward the road.

René joined Jeff at the corner of the house. She took hold of his arm and leaned against him as they watched Martin drive away disappearing in the trees that lined the road. All the time René was wondering what his motive for being there had been.

Martin had made it a point to direct her attention to the boathouse and the explosion that had destroyed it. Was his purpose to scare her? If that was his intent, he had succeeded. Just knowing that he was still in the area was unsettling enough for her.

René couldn't help but think that there was some other purpose for Martin being there. She remembered how interested he had been in Captain Del's rolltop desk. The search of the desk, as well as the cabinet, had proven fruitless so far. She had found nothing that could possibly be of interest to anyone other than Captain Del, but he must have thought that there was something there that was important to him.

"I don't like him," Jeff said interrupting her thoughts.

René looked up at him. She could not keep a grin from coming over her face. It was not what Jeff said that was so funny, but the way he expressed his feeling and the fact that she felt the same way.

"He's gone. Let's go back inside," René suggested.

Jeff simply nodded, then turned around. Together they walked back to the front of the house. Jeff glanced over his shoulder toward the road for one last look to make sure that Martin had really left before he followed René back into the house.

* * * *

It didn't take them long to find Sam and get him to unlock the door to Captain Del's bedroom. It turned out that Sam had locked the room. He had locked it just in case someone came into the house again without anyone knowing it.

Jeff and René searched the room from top to bottom and had found nothing that would help them discover who might be involved in the attempts on René's life. They were about to give up when Jeff accidentally bumped the shiny brass base of the ship's compass with his boot. To their surprise, a door to a hidden compartment in the base popped open. They looked at each other and smiled.

"I told you that old man was a sly old fox," Jeff said with a grin.

"He sure knew how to make it difficult to find things," René added.

Jeff and René knelt down beside the brass base of the compass. Inside the base they found several books. On closer examination they discovered that the books were really journals, or more accurately, ship's logs. The only difference was that the estate was Captain Del's ship. At least the logs made it appear that he ran it like a ship, which seemed to be logical as Captain Del had been a real ship's Captain.

René and Jeff sat down on the floor next to the base of the ship's compass and started looking through the logbooks. It seemed that the captain had kept a daily record that included everyone who had come to visit him, things that happened during the day, and records of important letters and phone calls. The logbooks contained dates, times and what took place. They even contained the number of fish the Captain caught on days that he went fishing. The logbooks were rather detailed, very much like a ship's log would be, and they were written in Captain Del's own hand.

After glancing over just a few pages, René began to realize that the information in these logbooks could prove to be important, not only to her, but to others as well. They might even lead them to who was behind all the things that had been happening.

René wondered if these logbooks were what Martin was looking for. She wondered if Martin knew that Captain Del kept such records.

She leaned back against the heavy brass base of the compass and began reading one of the logbooks. The logbook she had was dated about two years ago. The first entry in the book was July fourteenth. It contained a short entry that referred to a visitor. Although it mentioned a visitor, it didn't mention the person by name, or the reason that he had been there. René concluded that the visitor must not have been very important to the captain.

The next entry was dated the fifteenth. It told about the Captain going fishing and catching a couple of fish, which Mildred prepared for the Captain for his dinner.

René smiled at the thought of Captain Del eating what he had caught earlier that day. It brought back memories of when she was there as a child and caught a fish. Captain Del had the cook prepare her catch for her dinner that evening.

The next few entries were short and very detailed, but not very important to their search. They simply showed how simple a life the Captain led. It seemed that he spent a good deal of his time reading and fishing, two of the things he seemed to like to do the most and seemed to get the most pleasure out of.

René had gone through several days in the logbooks when one entry really caught René's attention. It told of a visitor who had been there earlier in the week. The big difference was that it put a name to the visitor, Randolph Smith. It also mentioned that Mr. Smith had asked Captain Del if he was interested in selling the estate.

"Jeff, do you know who Randolph Smith might be?"

"Sure. He's a big real estate developer from Albany. Why?"

"It seems he visited Captain Del and asked him if he wanted to sell this place."

Jeff looked at René. He remembered that Mr. Smith had asked him if he was interested in selling his place a couple of years ago. It caused Jeff to wonder if there was any kind of a connection.

"When was he here?" Jeff asked.

"About two years ago. Why?"

"About two years ago, Randolph Smith came to see me. He wanted to buy my property. I had inherited it from my grandmother and I wasn't about to let my property go, especially to a land developer. I told him that I was not interested in selling it. I didn't know that he had come over here and talked to Captain Del," Jeff said.

"Do you think there might be something to this?"

"That was two years ago. I haven't heard anything from Smith since, or from anyone else that wanted to buy my property for that matter. I doubt that Mr. Smith was the type of man that would wait that long to obtain a piece of land that he really wanted."

René had to think about that. Since Jeff and she owned all the land around the lake, and the lake was not very far from Albany or New York City, their properties could be worth a great deal of money. It would not be the first time that someone set in motion a plan to obtain something they wanted very badly from someone who did not want to let go of it.

Jeff was also thinking about it. He wondered if Smith was still interested in the property. If he was, why had he not contacted him again about it? Although he didn't know

Smith personally, he had heard that he was an honest person. He made his money the hard way. He earned it doing business fairly with people.

"I think it would be a good idea if we gave Mr. Smith a call," Jeff suggested.

"What would that prove?"

"I don't know, but we would be able to find out if he is still interested in our properties. If he's not, he might know who is."

"And if he is?" René asked.

"If he is, he might be involved in what has been happening around here. But then again, he might not be."

René quickly decided that there was nothing to lose from calling him. In fact, they may find out something important.

Jeff set the logbook he was reading on the floor next to the compass stand then stood up. He reached down for René. She took his hand and let him pull her to her feet.

"Do you think we should put the books away before we go downstairs?" René asked as she looked at Jeff for his thoughts.

"Probably a good idea, just in case we don't get back to them right away," Jeff agreed.

* * * *

After putting the books back in their hiding place, they went downstairs to the den. Jeff looked up the phone number for Mr. Smith's real estate office and began dialing the number.

René stood beside the desk and watched him as he dialed the number. An envelope lying on top of the desk caught her eye. It was from the law firm of Cosgrove, Wentworth and Smith. It was the very same law firm that had written to her to tell her of her inheritance. It was the name 'Smith' on the envelope that caught her attention. She had no way of knowing if it was the same Smith, but it could be.

She reached over and touched Jeff on the arm just as he finished dialing the number. He looked at her, then at the envelope. She pointed to the name of Smith on the envelope. He immediately hung up the phone before anyone had answered.

"You think it might be the same Smith?" Jeff asked.

"I don't know. There are a lot of Smiths in the world. If it is, it might explain how Martin got to know so much about this place," she suggested.

"Do you think he would have access to that information?"

"I don't know, but he works in the law office. I would think that he could gather a lot of information on almost anything going on there. I doubt that anyone would think twice about him going through files," René said.

Jeff had to give it some thought. He wondered if Martin was really smart enough to think this thing out for himself. There was something in the back of Jeff's mind that made him think that there might be someone else behind all this. Martin was too visible, almost too obvious in his approach. There had to be someone else behind it, someone with the brains and the capital to make it work. Someone who was willing to stop at nothing to get what they wanted.

"Do you know which lawyer Hanover works for?" Jeff asked.

"No. I think he just works for the firm. He sort of works for all of them, I think."

"I think I'll call the law firm and ask for Randolph Smith. If it is him, they will put me through. If not, they'll tell me."

Jeff picked up the phone and dialed the number of the law firm. He glanced over at René while he waited for it to be answered. He noticed that René seemed a little nervous.

"Hello. I would like to speak to Randolph Smith, please," Jeff said into the receiver, then waited.

René noticed a surprised look come over Jeff's face. She wondered what he had been told, but waited impatiently for him to tell her.

"I see. Can you tell me who has taken over his cases?"

Again René had to wait to find out what was happening.

"Oh. Thank you. By the way, did Mr. Smith have a realty business?" Jeff asked, then listened for a reply.

"He was a real estate developer? Interesting."

After listening for a short time, Jeff replied. "No. I'll have to think about it and call you back. Thank you for your help."

Jeff slowly hung up the phone as he looked over at René. He was trying to put what he had been told into perspective as well as to organize his thoughts.

"Well?" René asked impatiently.

"Randolph Smith was the third attorney in the name of the firm. He also had a real estate development business. It seems that he died suddenly during an attempted robbery of his home in Albany about six months ago. The robbers have not been caught."

"I don't remember hearing anything about that."

"I don't either, but that is what I was told. It seems that his cases, at least the clients that have stayed with the law firm, have been divided up between Wentworth and Cosgrove."

"What about the real estate part?" René asked.

"She couldn't tell me anything about that. Apparently, all the records went to a silent partner, but she couldn't tell me who it was."

René thought for a moment before commenting.

"That would mean that Martin is probably working for Wentworth," René said thoughtfully.

"What makes you say that?"

"I found a letter that indicated that Cosgrove didn't trust Martin. It may not have said that in so many words, but the implication was there. Mr. Cosgrove warned Captain Del to be careful about what he said to anyone about his personal affairs, and especially those involving the estate," René explained.

"That could mean just about anyone."

"I guess you're right," René conceded.

"I think we'd better go back and finish going through the logbooks. We might find something in them that will put us closer to finding out who is responsible for what has been happening here," Jeff suggested.

"That's a good idea, but I would like a cup of coffee."

"That does sound good," Jeff agreed.

Jeff took her hand, and together they went to the kitchen. They found the kitchen empty. Jeff looked at his watch and figured that Mildred should have been fixing dinner.

"I wonder where Mildred is," Jeff said.

"I don't know."

Just then the back door opened and Mildred came into the kitchen. In her hand she had a small bucket of freshly picked strawberries.

"I wondered if you were ever going to come down. I picked some strawberries for desert."

"That sounds great."

"What time would you like to have dinner, Ma'am?"

René looked at Jeff, but he gave no indication what time would be good. He simply shrugged his shoulders to indicate that any time was fine with him.

"About six?" René asked.

"That would be fine. Should I call you when it's ready?"

"Yes, please," René replied.

"We just came in for some coffee," Jeff said as he stepped forward and picked up a cup.

He poured a cup for René, then a cup for himself. After handing a cup to René, they left the kitchen and returned to Captain Del's bedroom.

* * * *

Once inside the room, they retrieved the logbooks from the brass stand and sat down to read them. Neither of them knew what they were looking for other than for some clue as to who might want the estate and why.

Time slipped by as René sat on the floor going over each entry in the logbook. Most of the entries showed nothing other than the fact that Captain Del loved his estate, and that he rarely left it except for an occasional visit to his friend, Franklin, in Albany.

Suddenly, René came across an entry that surprised her. It gave her the impression that Captain Del had been rather upset when he wrote it. She read it a second and a third time before looking at Jeff.

"Jeff?"

"Yeah. Did you find something?"

"I'm not sure. Read this and tell me what you think."

Jeff took the logbook and read the entry that René pointed out to him. He read it a second and a third time, too.

I had a visit from some SOB from Albany. He told me that I should be selling this place because I was getting too old to take care of it. He strongly suggested that I sell it to Randolph Smith.

I told him that I was not about to sell it. I told him that if I were going to sell it, that Smith would be the last person in the world I would sell it to. No one is going to turn this lake into a resort or sell it to some money grabbing developer that will ruin the lake and the woods surrounding it.

I told him to get off my property and to never come back. He left without having to call the Sheriff.

"It looks like Smith had someone come out here and try to strong arm Del. It doesn't sound like he took kindly to it," Jeff said.

"I know he didn't. I just wish that he had written down the guy's name."

Without further comment, they settled back into reading the logbooks. It wasn't long before Jeff stumbled onto something that didn't seem to make sense to him. It was an entry that made reference to Kathleen Cosgrove.

Kathleen came out to the estate without Franklin today. She had never done that before. She said that she had heard that I wanted to sell the estate and that she would like to buy it, if I was going to sell it

She seemed upset when I told her that her information was wrong and that I had no intentions of selling this place to anyone. I don't understand what difference it would make to her. When I asked her where she had heard that I was going to sell, she told me that she overheard it in Franklin's office.

Kathleen asked me not to tell Franklin that she had asked me if I wanted to sell. She didn't want to upset him. I told her that I wouldn't say anything to him. I almost wished that I had not promised her that, but I will keep my promise.

"You got any idea what this is all about?" Jeff asked as he showed the entry to René.

René read the entry, then looked over at Jeff. She had a puzzled look on her face.

"What's wrong," Jeff asked.

"I've got a funny feeling that Kathleen is mixed up in this."

"What makes you say that? Just because she asked Del if he would sell his estate to her doesn't prove anything."

"No, it doesn't. But I saw Kathleen come out of the studio house behind the Cosgrove home in Albany just seconds after I saw a car that looked like Martin's leave from behind the studio. I thought that maybe she was having an affair with Martin, but this makes it look like there might be more to it than just an affair," René explained.

"Are you sure it was Martin's car that you saw?"

"That's just it. I'm not one hundred percent sure. It could have been any one with a black BMW, but it did have mud on the back of it like was on Martin's car just the day before."

"Did you notice that she didn't want Del to tell Franklin that she had asked him to sell his place to her?" Jeff asked.

"Yes. That might explain why Franklin never mentioned it in any of his letters. He didn't know that she had tried to get Captain Del to sell it to her."

"I'm beginning to agree with you. I'm thinking that Kathleen just might have something to do with this," Jeff said thoughtfully.

"I know why I feel that way, but what makes you think she's involved?" René asked.

"I'm not really sure. Maybe it's because I don't care for her that much. She strikes me as a woman who would stop at nothing to get what she wants."

"I take it that you have met her?" René asked.

"Yes, twice. The first time was one afternoon while they were visiting here. I found Kathleen looking over the property while Del and Franklin were playing chess on the front porch. I can't put my finger on it, but it seemed to me that she was looking at the place as if she were appraising it rather than just enjoying it.

"The second time was when Del was sick. It was after he had been moved to the den. I came in to visit Del. She was here with Franklin. Franklin was sitting with Del, but Kathleen was sitting at Del's desk. She looked like she was looking for something in the desk. When I came in, she had the look of a kid that just got caught with her hand in the cookie jar."

"Didn't Del see what she was doing?"

"I don't think so. He was not well. It probably looked like she was just sitting at his desk. I don't even think Del realized that the desk was open."

Just then, they heard a call from downstairs. It was Mildred calling them for dinner. Jeff stood up and helped René to her feet.

After securing the logbooks back in the compass stand, they left the room. René locked the bedroom door, and then they went downstairs to dinner.

CHAPTER FOURTEEN

After dinner, Jeff and René went outside. They sat down on the porch swing at the end of the porch and looked out over the lake. The slowly setting sun left sparkles of bright lights dancing on the rippling water of the lake. A duck flew in and landed gracefully on the water near the tall cattails at one end of the small beach.

Jeff put his arm around behind René and gently pulled her close to him. He gently pushed the swing so that it would rock slowly back and fourth. He liked having her near him. He liked the light fragrance of her soft hair and sparkle of her eyes. In fact, there was nothing about her that he didn't like.

René leaned against him. She felt safe and secure with his strong arm around her shoulders. This quiet and relaxed time with him seemed so peaceful that it almost made her forget about her troubles. She didn't want to drag him into her problems. Yet, she was glad that he was there for her.

"It'll be dark soon," Jeff said as he watched another duck float down from the darkening evening sky and land on the lake.

"I know," René replied as she snuggled closer to him.

"I don't think this is over," Jeff said as he turned and looked at her sitting next to him.

Jeff didn't want to disturb those few moments of peace and quiet, but he didn't want her to get too relaxed, either. She needed to stay alert, just as he did.

"I'm sure it's not," she replied letting out a long sigh.

Jeff looked out over the lake again. He had been thinking a lot about last night and the visitors that had come to his cabin. He also thought about how easily someone had gotten into the house and left the dead rabbit in her room. Neither place seemed like a safe place where he could protect René. He needed a place where they could not be found.

"Are we going back to your cabin tonight?" René asked, disturbing his thoughts.

"I was wondering. How are you at camping?"

"Camping?" she replied with a surprised look on her face.

"Yeah. Camping."

"I've done a little. Why?"

"I don't think my cabin is any safer than it is here right now. And I think you will agree that it's not very safe for you here."

"Yes," she replied, wondering what he was getting at.

"But I think if we go across the lake and into the woods, they won't be able to find us. Even if they do, we'll be able to know they're coming long before they find us. Plus, we won't be trapped in my cabin. What do you think?"

"It sounds romantic," she said with a smile in an effort to make it seem less dangerous.

"Actually, it is romantic," he replied with a grin.

"I think all this is an elaborate scheme to get me alone in the woods where you can ravish my body," she said as she reached up and put her hand on the side of his face.

"Sounds good to me. Is it working?"

"Yes, but you could have just asked me," she said as she looked up into his eyes. "I would gladly go anywhere with you."

"Seriously, I don't think that either place is safe for you right now."

Jeff's last comment seemed to bring René back to reality. It had been a pleasant relief to forget about everything that had happened and to have at least a moment of playfulness, but that was not how it was. No matter how hard she tried to escape the seriousness of the situation, it was not going away.

"You're right," she replied thoughtfully. "What do we do? We can't just walk off into the woods."

"That is just what we are going to do," Jeff replied.

René looked at him with surprise. She couldn't believe that he would suggest such a thing.

"I have a hut in the woods where I go sometimes when I want to be alone to think. No one knows about it and there's no phone. I have some emergency supplies there if I need them. It's really very comfortable."

"Now that really sounds romantic," she said softly.

"There's only one problem. If we get caught away from the cabin, we don't have communications with anyone."

"I see. We would be on our own?"

"Yes. Do you have a problem with that?"

"No. Not as long as I'm with you."

"Do you know how to use a gun?"

"Yes. I have one in the desk."

"I think you should get it."

"Okay. When do we leave?"

"Now," Jeff replied, then stood up.

He took René by the hand and led her back into the house. He waited while she retrieved the small gun that she had found in the desk. Just touching the gun reminded her of how serious all this had become. Up until now, it had all seemed like some sort of bad dream. Now the dream was over and it was real.

René slipped the gun in her belt under her blouse so that it could not be seen. She looked up at Jeff as he watched her. She could see the worried look on his face.

She stepped up in front of Jeff, reached up and put her hands on his shoulders. Looking into his eyes, she smiled up at him.

"Everything will work out," she whispered as she slid her hands around behind his head and pulled his face down to her.

She felt the warmth of his lips as she kissed him, and the feel of his hands as he slipped them around her narrow waist. She let herself lean against him. The feel of his strong body pressing against her as they kissed reassured her that he would do everything he could to protect her. The one thing she had discovered was that she had fallen in love with him.

But if the truth were known, René was not sure if everything would work out or not. She had to believe that it would. She had to believe that once it was over there would be a future for them. To think otherwise was to give up hope. To give up hope was to give up.

After a couple of minutes, René leaned back and looked up at him. She was sure that she could see from the look in his eyes that he loved her, but she could also see that he was worried about her, too.

"We'd better go," he said softly, reluctant to let go of her.

"Shouldn't we tell Sam and Mildred what we are doing?

"Yes. We don't want them to worry."

René was not in any hurry to let go of Jeff, but she knew that he was right. She slipped her hands off his shoulders and took hold of his hand. Together, they walked to the kitchen.

René and Jeff found Mildred and Sam setting at the kitchen table. They took a few minutes to tell Sam and Mildred what they were going to do.

Sam thought it was a good idea. He told René that he would make sure the house was closed up tight before they retired for the evening. Once everything was arranged, Jeff took René's hand and led her toward the front door.

The sun was setting and long shadows lay across the lawn as they walked hand in hand toward Jeff's boat. They made no effort to hide their movements this time. It made no difference if they were seen. If they were seen, whoever was watching them would think that they were going to his cabin. By the time they traveled around the lake to get to the cabin, Jeff and René would have disappeared into the woods.

Before René got into the boat, Jeff checked it over to make sure that it had not been tampered with while they were in the house. Once he was sure that it was safe, he held out his hand to help René get into the boat.

* * * *

As they went across the lake, René looked back at the house. She wondered if she would ever be able to enjoy her new home as much as Captain Del had. So far, it didn't look like it.

The thought crossed her mind that she might never see the house again. That thought caused her to turn around and look at Jeff. She noticed that he had been watching her. He had a serious look on his face.

Jeff could see the sadness on her face. He had a pretty good idea what she was thinking about. If it were up to him, she would have many wonderful years in that old house, but he knew that there were no guarantees in life.

It wasn't long before Jeff moved the boat up along side the dock in front of his cabin. Jeff didn't have time to get out of the boat before Jake showed up on the dock, his tail wagging with excitement. After tying the boat to the dock, he got out and looked around. He reached down and patted the dog on his head.

"Good boy."

René looked up at Jeff as he again looked around. He seemed so serious, but he had every right to be. He was looking out for her safety. He also seemed a little relieved by the presence of his dog.

"See anything?" she asked.

"No," he replied as he turned his attention to her. "Jake would not be so excited to see us if anyone was around. He's kind of protective."

Jeff reached down and took her hand to help her out of the boat. He then hurried her off the dock and into the trees. It was clear to him that she was vulnerable any time that she was out in the open. Without delay, Jeff led her to his cabin. He made sure that the dog had food and water, then patted him on the head before he went inside, leaving the dog outside to keep watch.

Once inside, Jeff shut the door and went straight into the bedroom. When he came out he was carrying two dark brown blankets. He laid them on the table along with the rifle he had removed from the gun rack above the fireplace. He removed his pistol from the holster on his belt and checked it to make sure that it was loaded and ready for use. He also loaded and checked the rifle. When he was done, he picked up one of the blankets and handed it to René.

"Wrap it around you. Make sure you cover your head," he instructed.

René watched him as he wrapped one of the blankets around himself. She took her cue from him. It didn't take a genius to figure out what he was doing. The blanket would serve as camouflage in the growing darkness. It would not only blend in with their surroundings, but would distort their shapes as they moved through the woods. As soon as they were both ready, he picked the rifle up and led her to the back door of the cabin. It was almost dark outside by then.

"Keep the blanket over you, and keep quiet," he whispered.

René nodded that she understood. She watched him as he slowly opened the back door of the cabin.

Jeff took several minutes to carefully look around to see if anyone was out there. When he had convinced himself that it was clear, he motioned for René to come out of the cabin. He pointed toward a clump of trees and motioned for her to go there.

René ran over behind the clump of trees as he had instructed. Once she was behind the trees, she knelt down and waited for Jeff to join her.

"Follow me, keep as quiet as you can and stay close," Jeff whispered.

"What about Jake?"

"He'll be fine. He'll watch the cabin and let us know if anyone comes around."

René again nodded that she understood. When Jeff began moving away from the cabin, René followed closely behind him.

It was getting so dark that it was hard for them to see where they were going. René stayed as close to Jeff as she could. She didn't know how far they had gone when Jeff stopped and took the blanket off his head.

"I think it's safe now."

René took the blanket off her head, but she kept it wrapped around her shoulders. The night air was starting to get cool and damp. If it continued, it could get pretty chilly by morning.

"You all right?" Jeff asked in a whisper.

"Yes. How much further to your hut?"

"Not much further. You getting tired?"

"No."

Jeff smiled at her and took hold of her hand. He then turned around and started off again with René at his side. The last thing he wanted to do was to lose her in the darkness. He moved slowly through the woods being very careful not to trip over any stumps, rocks, or anything else that might be on the ground. The last thing he needed was to make noise.

He helped René find her way. It took them almost an hour of slow moving to get to a small clearing deep inside the forest.

"Here it is," Jeff whispered.

René looked around. The moon had come up, but she could not see anything that looked like a hut. It just looked like a clearing to her.

"Where is it?"

"Right there," Jeff replied as he pointed into the darkness.

René still didn't see anything. Jeff took her by the hand and led her across the clearing. He pulled a bush back out of the way to reveal an opening. René looked at it. The opening was small and would require her to duck down to get through it.

"What is this?" she asked in a whisper.

"This is my hut. I built it when I was a kid and would come out here to spend the summer with my Grandmother."

"It doesn't hardly look big enough for us."

"It is. It goes way back in there. The vines and bushes form a cover over a room that is about ten by ten. It also has a door in the back if we need to sneak out."

"Is it full of bugs and spiders and things?"

"No. In fact, I used it just a few weeks ago. I sometimes come out here to hunt turkeys. I've been keeping it cleaned up for just that purpose. Come on. Let's go in."

René shrugged her shoulders and followed him in. The room was completely dark when Jeff shut the door. He struck a match to light a small lantern that filled the room with light. He set the lantern on a table. The lantern gave out a pleasant glow over the small room.

René moved to the center of the room and looked around. The room had a cot for a bed, several small cupboards and a small gas stove. There was a small wooden table and a couple of wooden chairs. It wasn't much, but it had the things that they would need for at least a short stay.

"This is kind of nice," she said a little surprised at how nice it was for a room that had been carved out of the woods.

"Thank you. I sometimes use it to warm up when I'm out hunting in the winter. I've even come out and spent the night here when I want to get away and be alone."

"What do you have to get away from? You already live alone."

"I don't have a phone here. I often get calls from people to check out some stray animal at all hours of the day and night. I find that it is nice to come out here and listen to the quiet, or at least the sounds of the forest. You're the only one that knows this place is here, except for Jake."

"I promise not to tell anyone. I'm sure that Jake won't tell anyone, either," she said with a grin.

"Funny. How about a cup of coffee?"

"Yes, thank you."

René watched as Jeff put some water in a pot and put it on the stove. She thought he looked right at home in his hut.

"I hope you like instant, it's all I have here."

"That'll be fine."

"Are you going to sit down?"

René smiled. She looked around the room. The only place to sit down was on one of the two wooden chairs next to the table, or on the edge of the cot. She felt a little nervous, but she couldn't understand why. After all, she had spent the night in his bed just last night. She had even kissed him and let him hold her while she was wearing nothing but one of his shirts. There was certainly no reason to be nervous now.

René chose to sit down at the table. While sitting there, she took in the hut. She thought passed through her mind that it must have been very much like the homes of some of the first settlers. It had just the very basics, yet it was warm and comfortable.

"What are you thinking about?" Jeff asked as he walked up to her and set a cup of coffee on the table in front of her.

"I was just thinking about your hut."

"It is kind of small," he replied as he looked around it.

"No. Well, it is, but, you don't understand. I was thinking about how warm and cozy it seems."

"I guess it does, but I wouldn't think you would see it that way."

"Why not? Because I have a big house on the other side of the lake?"

"I didn't really mean it like that. It's just that I, well, I would think you would like the finer things in life."

"I didn't always have the finer things in life. I may have been raised on Long Island, New York, but I learned to appreciate what I had. After my grandparents passed away in a boating accident, I was on my own. I worked my way through college. Don't get me wrong, I do like the finer things of life, but I also can enjoy the simple things as well."

"I'm glad," Jeff said with a smile as he sat down across the table from her.

Jeff and René sat at the table and talked quietly about their past. Jeff told her what it was like growing up in a small town in upstate New York. How he went to college and became a Wild Life Manager for the state of New York.

René told him about her life growing up with her grandparents after the death of her parents. She told him about her college days and about the job she had just before she inherited Captain Del's estate.

Time passed quickly as they shared their lives with each other. They had not realized how late it had gotten until René yawned.

"Getting tired?"

"Yes, I guess I am."

"You can have the cot, if you like."

"Where are you going to sleep?" she asked.

"I'll sleep here in the chair."

"You won't get much sleep in a chair. I'd be more than happy to let you share the cot with me."

Jeff looked at her. René smiled.

"I meant you could lay down with me and sleep. I emphasize the word 'sleep'," she said with a chuckle.

"Oh," he replied with a grin. "I don't get to ravish your body as you so delicately put it?"

"No," she replied. "Besides, there isn't enough room on the cot for that."

"Then there's still hope?"

"Maybe," she replied with a grin.

Jeff stood up, took the empty cups to the counter. When he turned around, he saw René folding the covers back. He watched her as she sat down on the edge of the cot and took off her shoes.

She smiled up at him as she lay down on the narrow cot and scooted over next to the wall to make room for him. She held the blanket up while he sat down on the edge of the cot, then laid down beside her.

With the cot so narrow, they had to sleep on their sides. As Jeff laid with his back to her, René pulled the covers over him. She then laid down and snuggled up against his back, laying her arm over him.

Jeff laid still as he thought about the beautiful woman lying on the cot with him. He would like to roll over and take her in his arms, but even with all the kidding they had been doing he was not sure that she was ready for that. She had been pleasant, but she was still vulnerable. He didn't think it would be good for their relationship to take advantage of her.

René laid as still as she could. She didn't want to disturb him. She could not tell if he had fallen asleep or if he was just lying quietly.

She had difficulty falling asleep. Her mind was filled with thoughts of the man beside her. She could remember how it felt the night before when he took her in his arms and kissed her. And she could remember the feel of his strong arms around her as well as the feel of his hands on her body. She almost wished he would turn over and kiss her right then. After what seemed like an eternity, she finally fell asleep.

Jeff was having his own problems falling asleep. He could feel her arm wrapped around him. He wanted to gently rub it to let her know that he cared, but he knew that she needed her rest.

As he closed his eyes, he could also remember holding her in his arms in his bedroom the night before. The feel of her warm body pressing against him did little to help him sleep, but sleep finally came.

CHAPTER FIFTEEN

Jeff was a fairly light sleeper. A faint noise off in the distance woke him. He lifted his head from the pillow in the hope of hearing the sound again and understanding what it was that he was hearing. When he moved, he woke René.

"What is it?" she asked in a whisper.

"Sssssssh."

René laid quietly next to him, watching him and listening for any sound that might be heard. It was dead quiet for several minutes before the sound was heard again. It was a dog barking, but it was some distance away from the hut.

"It's Jake," Jeff said in a whisper. "There must be someone snooping around the cabin."

"What do we do?"

"You don't do anything. You stay here."

"Where are you going?"

"I'm going to check it out. Maybe I can find out who it is."

René didn't want him to leave her alone. She wanted him to stay with her and protect her, but she couldn't bring herself to tell him. She didn't want him to think of her as a frightened little child.

"I'll be back in a few minutes. If something happens out there and I don't come back, you stay here until daylight. Then go out the back and follow the narrow trail to the lake. Follow the edge of the lake around to your house and call the police as soon as you get there. Don't try to follow me, it could be dangerous."

"Are you sure it's a good idea for you to go out there?"

"No, but it's better to know where they are, than to have them so close that we can't escape."

René just looked at him. Her eyes pleading for him not to go and leave her there alone.

"Do you understand?"

"Yes," she replied reluctantly.

She understood, but that didn't make it any easier for her to let him go. She knew that it could be dangerous, and that Jeff could get hurt. But she also knew he was doing it for her, to keep her safe from harm.

Jeff swung his legs off the side of the cot and stood up. He looked down at René as she sat up on the edge of the cot. He smiled in an effort to reassure her that everything was going to be okay, but he knew deep down in his heart that it wouldn't help much.

"I'll be back soon. I have to find out what's going on," he said, then bent down and kissed her lightly on the forehead.

She watched him as he turned around and picked up his rifle. He glanced back at her and gave her a wink before he ducked down and disappeared into the darkness, closing the door as he left the hut. René sat there staring at the door for several minutes after he was gone, wishing that she had insisted that he either take her with him, or that he stay here with her.

As she thought of Jeff and what he was doing, it came to her that she needed to be ready to leave the hut at any moment. Just in case Jeff came back and they had to leave in a hurry, she would be ready. When she bent down to retrieve her shoes, she felt something cold and hard under her blouse. She touched her side and remembered that she still had the small handgun tucked in the waistband of her slacks. She reached in and took it out. She held it in her hand and wondered if she would have to use it, if she would be able to use it.

René tried to mentally prepare herself for whatever might happen. Time passed slowly as she listened for any kind of sound that might tell her what was happening out there, but she heard nothing. There were no owls making hooting sounds in the night like there had been earlier. There was no breeze to rustle the leaves of the trees.

The lack of sounds, any sounds, heightened René's senses. Every nerve in her body was tense, and her heart pounded so loudly that she could almost hear it.

In her nervous state, she kept turning the small handgun over and over in her hands. She kept feeling it and hoping that she would not need it. Yet, wondering if she would be able to use it if the time came when she did need it. The tension in her body continued to build, as did her nervousness.

The sudden sound of gunshots caused René to jump to her feet and turn toward the door. Before she even realized what she was doing, she found herself standing in the middle of the room with the gun held tightly in her hands. She was pointing it at the door as if she expected someone to come charging through the door at any minute to attack her.

Her heart beat rapidly and she held her breath, not sure what to expect. She waited breathlessly, staring at the door, but nothing happened. She listened, but she didn't hear anything. Slowly her mind started to come up with all sorts of things that might have gone wrong. The first thing to run through her mind was that Jeff had been shot. That he was lying out there somewhere hurt, maybe dying. That he needed her and she was not there for him as he had been for her.

As her mind played with that thought, she began to realize that she could not let her imagination run wild. She would have to think positively and clearly. Jeff was used to using a gun. He knew his way around the woods. He was not likely to walk into a trap.

As René began to gather her senses, she began to think about what she had heard. She tried to remember how many shots she had heard. She could not remember how many shots were fired, but at least two of them sounded like they may have come from a rifle. The rest of them sounded like pistol shots. She knew that Jeff had a rifle and a pistol. She also remembered that the rifle shots were not the first or the last shots fired.

René wanted to leave and go looking for Jeff, but that was not what Jeff told her to do. He wanted her to wait until morning. If that was what he wanted her to do, that was what she would do.

René, still gripping the small gun in her hands, sat back down on the edge of the cot. She listened and waited nervously as she stared at the door. She continued to worry about Jeff, but she managed to keep her emotions under tight control.

* * * *

It seemed like it was taking forever for Jeff to return. The hands on the clock next to the cot moved at a snail's pace. It clicked off the minutes so slowly that René was beginning to think that the clock didn't work. With each minute, she worried more and more about Jeff's safety and what might have happened to him. She had heard nothing since that one burst of gunfire.

The tension built inside her until she couldn't stand it any longer. She had to do something and do it now before it was too late.

Just as she was about to get up off the edge of the cot, she heard a strange noise at the door. The noise startled her causing her to jump to her feet and face the door. She again pointed the gun toward the door and listened. It sounded like someone or something was scratching at the bottom of the door.

René gripped the gun tightly in her hands as she slowly started to move closer to the door, her gun at the ready. As she got closer, she thought that she could hear the sound of a dog whining along with the sounds of the scratching on the door.

"Jake?" she called out softly.

The next sound she heard was that of Jake. He barked just once to let her know that he was there.

René quickly opened the door and looked out. Jake was almost frantic. He jumped up and down, ran toward her, then he would run a little ways away, then turn around and look back at her as if he expected her to follow him. When she didn't come right away, he ran back to her and did it again.

René was sure that he wanted her to follow him, but Jeff had told her to stay in the hut until morning. She wasn't sure what she should do. After looking around and not seeing Jeff, she decided that she couldn't leave him out there if he was hurt. If Jake was that excited, there must be something very wrong.

She took a deep breath as she looked out into the darkness. This was no time to hesitate. If Jake wanted her to come with him, she would go.

"Come on, Jake. Take me to Jeff," she said, determined to find him.

As soon as she started out the door, Jake took off down the trail quickly disappearing into the darkness. She wanted to call out to him, but thought better of it. Calling out might let someone in the forest know where she was. As soon as Jake was out of sight, she stopped and stood still. In a matter of seconds, Jake would show up to show her the way again. In order to save time, René took hold of Jake's collar. Now he could not run on ahead and disappear in the darkness, but he could lead her to Jeff.

She had not counted on Jake being so strong. The big dog practically dragged her along the narrow trail. Just before they got to the cabin, Jake broke free from her grip and darted off the trail into the trees. René turned and followed him, but then she had no choice. Within minutes, Jake had taken her to Jeff.

René suddenly came upon Jeff lying face down on the ground, his rifle off to one side half hidden under the brush. At first, she thought that he might be dead. She tucked her gun in her belt, knelt down beside him, then reached out to touch him. He moved ever so slightly. It was enough to assure her that he was alive, but not enough to assure her that he would come around. In the moonlight, she could not see how badly he was hurt. She needed to get him somewhere where she could tend to him. The closest place was his cabin.

Still kneeling down beside him, she looked around and listened for any sound that would warn her of danger. She could not see anything, nor could she hear anything. She wondered if it would be safe to take him back to his cabin. She looked at Jake. He was sitting close to Jeff and looking at her as if he expected her to do something to help his master.

"You're going to have to help me," she whispered to Jake as if she expected him to understand her.

She carefully turned Jeff over on his back, then moved to above his head and sat him up. She wrapped her arms under his arms and around his chest from behind him. Interlocking her fingers, she lifted him up and began dragging him toward the cabin.

As she dragged him along the narrow trail, Jake ran on ahead. She was sure that Jake would let her know if anyone was around.

Jeff was not light, and it took all the strength that René could muster to get him back to the cabin. She had to stop a time or two just to catch her breath and to get a better hold on him.

When she got close to the cabin, she laid him down on the ground behind some bushes off to the side of the trail. She was tired, but she couldn't stop now. She was the only hope that Jeff had. She had to get him to the cabin if she was going to help him, but she had to make sure that there was no one there.

"Jake, stay," she whispered.

Jake sat down beside his master and looked up at René.

She then turned and started toward the cabin, keeping low in among the bushes. She glanced back to see if Jake was minding her. She could see his outline in the soft moonlight. He was still sitting next to his master.

As René approached the cabin, she could not see any light coming from inside the cabin. If someone was inside, they either had the windows covered or they had the lights off. She hoped that whoever had been there was now gone.

René reached in under her blouse and gripped the small gun in her hand. She took a deep breath, then slipped around to the back door. As she approached the door, she leaned up against the cabin and listened. She could not hear anything. Her hands were sweating as she tried to get control of her frayed nerves. She wanted to return to Jeff and wait for morning light so that she could go get help, but the fear that Jeff might not last that long gave her the strength to reach out and put her hand on the doorknob.

After taking a deep breath, she slowly began to turn the knob. When the door latch came loose, she slowly pushed the door open. With her gun gripped firmly in her hand, she peeked inside. In the darkness, she could not see anything inside. The curtains were closed keeping out even the moonlight. Her heart was pounding in her chest, and she could hardly breathe as she stepped inside the cabin.

Moving carefully and slowly into the cabin, she worked her way over to the fireplace. There was a very soft glow coming from the coals. She found the lantern and the box of matches on the fireplace mantel. She struck a match on the stone front of the fireplace filling the room with a soft yellow light. Seeing no one, she lit the lantern.

As the glow of the lantern filled the room, she saw that the cabin was empty. Setting the lantern down on the table, she rushed out the back door and ran to Jeff. Jake was still sitting beside his master, waiting and watching.

"Come on, Jake," she said as she tucked her gun back in the waistband of her slacks.

Again, she bent down, sat Jeff up and got a good hold on him. She pulled him to the cabin. Once inside, she laid him down in front of the fireplace.

After making sure that both the front and backdoor were closed, she got a comforter from the bedroom and spread it out on the floor. She put Jeff on the comforter and covered him up. She then built up the fire and moved the lantern from the table to the floor near Jeff's side. She quickly checked him in an effort to find the extent of his injuries.

There was a nasty cut on the side of his head where a bullet had grazed his scalp, and there was blood running down the side of his face. She was unable to find any other injuries.

René got a cloth and some water, then began to clean up the wound on Jeff's head. While she was taking care of Jeff, Jake lay down next to his master and watched her every move. When she was finished, she sat down on the floor next to Jeff. She took his hand in hers and held onto it. René looked at Jake and could see the sad look in his eyes as he looked up at her.

"He'll be fine," she said softly.

She wasn't sure that she believed what she had said, but it seemed to be the only thing to say. Jake laid his head down next to his master's shoulder. He seemed to be waiting for Jeff to wake up. René was sure that he would stay at his master's side until he did wake up, no matter how long it took.

René gently rubbed Jeff's hand, and sat beside him for a long time. As the adrenaline wore off, she got very sleepy. Not wanting to leave Jeff's side, she laid down on the floor beside him. She never let go of his hand. She did not really sleep, either. It was more like dozing off and on the rest of the night. It was not the kind of sleep that produces any real rest.

* * * *

The time passed slowly. There was a slight glow of morning light seeping in around the edge of the curtains when a strange sound woke René. At first she didn't know what to think, but soon realized that the strange noise was that of Jake.

She glanced over at him. He was standing up with his head down and the hackles on the back of neck standing straight up as he looked toward the front door. He looked like he was ready to take on whatever or whoever tried to come through the door. He was alert to something outside.

She could hear rumbling coming from the dog's broad chest. She quickly realized that there must be something outside that disturbed him. She looked around until she found her gun lying on the floor next to her. She picked it up and ran to the door. She quickly and quietly slid the bolt closed, locking the door. She then readied herself for whatever might be out there.

"Easy," she whispered to Jake as she stepped back away from the door and knelt down next to Jeff.

Jake glanced over at her, but immediately looked back toward the door. He was quiet now, but still ready for whatever might try to harm his master.

Suddenly, the doorknob moved very slowly, then rattled as if someone was trying to get the door to open. René quickly stood up, still pointing the gun at the front door.

"I have a gun. Identify yourself or I will shoot," she cried out nervously.

René thought she heard someone move outside the door, then there was silence. The wait was hard on her nerves. In the silence, she thought that she could hear voices outside the door, more like two people whispering to each other. She could not tell what was being said, but she knew that they were very close to the door. The one sounded like it might be a woman, but she couldn't be positive.

The waiting was more than René could stand. She was sure that they were trying to decide if she really had a gun, and if she did, did she know how to use it. To René's way of thinking, it was time to let them know that she would defend her man. It was time to let them know that she was ready for them, and to remove all doubt that she did indeed have a gun and knew how to use it.

Slowly, René squeezed the trigger of the small gun as she pointed it at the door. The cabin filled with the sharp sound of a gunshot and the smell of burnt gunpowder as the gun jumped in her hands. There was a cracking sound as the bullet slammed through the front door of the cabin. In all the confusion and noise, René thought she heard what sounded like a scream but could not be sure.

René thought she heard the voice of a man say, "Let's get the hell out of here," and then there was the sound of running that quickly faded away.

René let out a sigh of relief. Whoever had been out there was now gone. She looked over at Jake and saw him looking at her. She smiled at the dog, then turned her attention to Jeff.

Jeff was still lying on the floor, but his eyes were now open. He was looking up at René.

René could not help herself. She quickly dropped to the floor and leaned down over him. She started kissing his face. Even Jake got in on it by licking his master's face.

"Careful," Jeff said, a hint of pain in his voice.

"Oh, I'm sorry," René said as she sat back on her heels and looked down at him.

"How did I get here?" Jeff asked as he looked around.

"Jake and I found you and brought you here. How are you feeling?"

"I have a splitting headache. Shooting that gun off in here didn't help much."

"I'm sorry about that."

"It's all right. You made them leave. It sounded like you might have hit one of them. I better get up," Jeff said as he started to sit up.

"No, you better rest a little more," René said when she saw the strained look on his face. "I don't think you're ready to get up. I'll fix you something to drink."

"Okay," Jeff replied, more than willing to lie back down.

René got up and went into the kitchen. She put a pot of water on the stove for coffee. When she looked back to check on Jeff, he was lying on the floor with his dog curled up beside him. Jeff had his eyes closed, but she could see by the rising and falling of his chest that he was just resting.

As soon as the water was hot, René made coffee. When she returned to the living room, she saw that Jeff and Jake appeared to be sleeping. She smiled to herself, then turned to set the coffee on the table.

"Would you care to join us," Jeff said, opening his eyes and looking up at her.

She turned around and saw Jeff lying there with his arm reaching out to her, inviting her to lie down on the floor next to him. René smiled down, then knelt down beside him.

"Will you get any rest if I lay down with you?" she asked teasing him a little.

"Probably not," he replied with a grin. "But I would like you beside me just the same."

René looked into his eyes. She was just so happy that he was alive that nothing else seemed to matter. She laid down and curled up against him.

Jeff wrapped his arm around her and held her to his side. He had his faithful dog on one side, and the woman he loved on the other. What more could life offer a man, he thought.

René laid against his side with her head on his shoulder. She closed her eyes, but she didn't sleep. All she could think about was Jeff. He had been shot, but luckily he was not seriously hurt.

Her thoughts turned to her house across the lake. She wondered if it was worth it to fight to keep it. If she kept the house but lost Jeff, what would she have? Her answer was clear - nothing.

She wanted to tell Jeff that she would put the place on the market this afternoon if it would stop all this. But when she looked over at him, she noticed that he was sleeping soundly. She didn't want to disturb his rest, as she was sure that he needed it.

She let out a sigh, then relaxed. It was only a matter of minutes before she was asleep, wrapped in the warmth of Jeff's arm.

CHAPTER SIXTEEN

René woke when she felt something move beside her. As the cloud of sleep cleared from her head, she remembered where she was and what she was doing. She realized that it was Jeff that had moved. She quickly raised her head up and looked up at him.

"Hi," he said with a smile.

"Hi," she replied, relieved that he seemed to be better. "How are you feeling?"

"A little better, I think. What time is it?"

René looked at her watch. It was getting on toward mid morning. After telling Jeff the time, she laid back down and put her head back on his shoulder. The fact that he was feeling better relieved her mind of at least one thing.

René was not ready to leave his side just yet. She didn't want to get up, but she realized that it was getting late. If they didn't get back to her house pretty soon, she was sure that Mildred and Sam would begin to worry about them.

Reluctantly, René sat up again and looked back over her shoulder at Jeff. He looked much better now that he had gotten a little rest. His color had returned as well as the sparkle in his eyes.

"Are you ready to get up and go back?" she asked.

"Not really," he said as he reached out and took hold of her arm.

Gently, but firmly, he pulled her down to him. René turned toward him and went willingly. She let him pull her down over him. The smile on her face faded away as she was drawn closer to him.

As soon as their lips met, she melted into his arms. The feel of his arms wrapped around her made her feel warm and wanted. It also made her feel safe again. She could not remember a time when she had felt so completely in love as she felt right now.

Their moment of passion was suddenly interrupted by Jake. He was growling again. They looked over and saw him standing with his head down, the hackles on the back of his neck were up and his nose pointed toward the door. He was once again ready to attack anyone who tried to come through the door.

"We've got company," Jeff whispered as René rolled off him.

Jeff quickly got to his feet, but he suddenly felt a little woozy and unstable. He grabbed the table for support then turned and quickly sat down in a chair.

René saw what was happening to him and scrambled to her feet. She went to his side and grabbed hold of him to give him support as he sat down.

"You all right?" she asked, her voice showing how worried she was.

"Get the gun," he said.

René hesitated only a second before she let go of him and bent down to pick up her gun from the floor. She quickly returned to Jeff's side, only this time she stood beside him with her gun pointed at the door. It was her chance to protect him from any further harm, and she was ready to do just that.

"Anyone here?"

Jake stopped growling and stood up straight, his head came up and his tail began to wag. Jeff looked at René. A smile slowly came over his face as René let out a sigh of relief.

"Just a minute, Sam," Jeff called out.

René set the gun down on the table and walked over to the door. She unlocked the door and opened it. She saw Sam standing outside. He had a worried look on his face.

"You all right?" Sam asked, the look on his face showing his concern.

"Yes. Come in," René said as she stepped back.

"What are you doing here?" Jeff asked as Sam came into the room.

"The two of you didn't show up this morning for breakfast, so I decided that I'd better come over and see if you were all right."

"We're fine," Jeff said.

"You don't look so fine. You look a little pale and that knot on the side of your head looks pretty nasty," Sam replied.

Jeff reached up and touched his injury. He flinched, as it was very tender to the touch.

"Looks to me like you had a little run-in over here. You have a knot on your head, and there's a bullet hole in the door that didn't used to be there."

"Yeah. We had company last night and they weren't very friendly," Jeff said.

"Do you know who it was?"

"No, but René shot one of them."

Sam turned and looked at René. His look of surprise quickly changed to a smile of approval. "Good for you, Missy."

"I didn't mean to hit anyone. I was only trying to scare them off," she said apologetically.

"It worked," Jeff said with a grin. "They left in one hell of a hurry."

"Good. Maybe they will think twice before they come back again," Sam said.

"Don't count on it. They'll probably just come back better prepared next time," Jeff countered.

"I think we should get Jeff back to my place where he can rest," René suggested.

"That sounds like a good idea," Sam agreed.

With René on one side and Sam on the other, they helped Jeff to his feet. He was a little unstable at first, but the dizziness soon went away. They walked him down to the dock. René held Jeff as Sam looked over the boat. As soon as Sam was sure that the boat was safe, they helped Jeff in. René sat down beside him and wrapped her arm around him while Sam tied his little fishing boat behind Jeff's larger boat. Just as they were about to leave, René noticed that Jake was standing on the dock. He seemed nervous and looked as if he wanted to go with them.

"Come on, Jake," she called to him.

Jake didn't hesitate. He immediately jumped into the boat. It took René a moment or two to get him to settle down. He was rather excited.

Once they were all in the boat, Sam started up the motor and pulled away from the dock, towing his little boat behind. He then turned toward the estate.

* * * *

It didn't take long before they reached the narrow beach in front of the estate. Sam and René helped Jeff up to the house, taking him into the den where he laid down on the sofa. His head was hurting, sort of throbbing. His injury had taken a lot out of him and he was tired.

"I'll get an afghan for you," René said as Sam turned and left them alone.

Jeff watched René as she left the room. When she returned, she had a large colorful afghan. She laid it over him and tucked him in.

"You get some rest. I'll be back in a minute."

"Where are you going?" Jeff asked as he reached out and took hold of her arm.

"I want to talk to Sam about last night. I'd also like some coffee. Would you like anything?"

"No, I guess not. I think I will just rest for a little while," he said letting go of her arm.

"Good. I'll see to it that you are not disturbed."

"Thanks. There is one thing I would like."

"What's that?"

"A kiss before you leave," he asked as he looked up at her.

René smiled down at him, then knelt down beside the sofa. She leaned over him and gave him a warm gentle kiss.

"I'll see you later," she said as she stood up.

As she left the room, she closed to door. She hoped that he would get the rest he needed.

René went out to the kitchen. Mildred and Sam were sitting at the table. They looked as if they were waiting for her.

"How is Jeff?" Mildred asked, her concern clearly apparent in the sound of her voice.

"I think he will be fine. He just needs to rest."

Mildred poured a cup of coffee as René sat down at the table. After setting the cup in front of René, she sat down to listen to what had happened last night on the other side of the lake.

Mildred was worried about René and Jeff. It had been a close call. She stood up and poured René another cup of coffee.

"I don't think you should go back over there tonight. I think it would be better if you stayed here. At least there would be four of us here," Mildred suggested.

René thought that she had a good point. She would talk to Jeff as soon as he was awake, but for now she wanted him to be left alone. She stood up. Taking her coffee with her, she returned to the den. She entered the den as quietly as possible.

Jeff was sleeping, his dog lying next to the sofa. She walked across the room and sat down at the desk. She swung the chair around so that she could look out the window. The remains of the boathouse and dock were all that scarred the view. If it had not been for that, it would have been a beautiful view of the lake and the surrounding woods.

René's thoughts turned to the things that had happened over the past few days. She had almost been killed, Sam was almost blown up, and just last night and this morning Jeff had almost been killed, and she had shot someone. She had to wonder if it was all worth it. There had to be a way to put a stop to all this.

The more she thought about it, the more she realized that it had already gone too far. Whoever it was that wanted all the property around the lake was committed to getting it. At this point, it was too late for them to turn back.

* * * *

Time passed as René sat there waiting for Jeff to wake up. There were a dozen things running through her mind all at once. But there was one thing that seemed to remain at the top. It was Jeff. No matter what happened to the estate, Jeff was the most important thing in her life. She knew that she would gladly give up everything for him.

Suddenly, her thoughts were disturbed by the sound of a car coming down the long drive. René stood up and walked over to the window. There was a big white Lincoln Town Car coming down the drive. She had seen the car before. In fact, she had ridden in it. It was Franklin Cosgrove's car. She wondered what he was doing here.

René quickly went over to the sofa and leaned down over Jeff. She reached out and touched him lightly on the arm.

"Jeff?" she said softly, hoping to wake him, but not startle him.

"Yes," he said as he looked up at her. "What is it?"

"We have guests."

"Who?" Jeff asked as he tried to shake the sleep from his mind.

"I think it is Franklin Cosgrove."

"What's he doing way out here?" Jeff asked as he sat up.

"I don't know."

"Maybe we should find out."

René smiled then stepped back. Jeff stood up and took hold of her hand. He leaned close to her and kissed her lightly on the cheek, then they walked to the front door together.

Just as they stepped out on the porch, Franklin and Kathleen came around the corner of the house. They noticed that Franklin looked out at the remains of the boathouse.

"What happened?" he said as he turned and looked up at René and Jeff.

Jeff and René could see the surprised look on his face. René glanced at Kathleen. It seemed to René that the loss of the boathouse had not come as a surprise to Kathleen. The look on Kathleen's face was more like that of someone who already knew about the explosion and fire that had destroyed it.

"The boathouse burned down the day before yesterday," Jeff replied.

"Do you know what caused it?" Franklin asked.

"Leaking fuel line in the old boat, we think," Jeff replied not sure that he should disclose the real cause of the fire.

"I hope no one was hurt," Franklin said as he turned and looked back at the remains of the boathouse.

"No. No one was hurt," Jeff said, intentionally leaving out the fact that Sam had come very close to being in the boathouse when it exploded.

It quickly became clear to René that Jeff had no intentions of telling Franklin about what had been going on here. She wondered if it was because he didn't trust Franklin, or because he didn't trust Kathleen.

"What happened to your head?" Franklin asked as he looked at the knot on Jeff head.

"I ran into a tree branch last night," Jeff replied.

"It looks nasty. Have you seen a doctor?"

"No. It looks worse than it is. Why don't we go inside?"

Franklin seemed to accept Jeff's explanation of what had happened. He reached out and took Kathleen's arm, then they started up the steps to the porch.

Just as Jeff and René turned to follow Franklin and Kathleen up the steps of the porch, they heard a second car coming down the driveway. René noticed right away that it was a black BMW, just like the one that Martin drove.

"What's he doing here?" René said to Jeff.

"Pardon me?" Franklin said as he turned back and looked at René.

"Nothing," she replied, but she noticed the look on Kathleen's face.

René wasn't sure if Kathleen had heard her, but she thought she could see that Kathleen was pleased that he had come to the estate. Kathleen also seemed pleased that René was not happy to see Martin on her property. René wondered what his arrival could possibly mean to Kathleen, unless she had been expecting him to show up.

"What's he doing here?" Jeff said loud enough for Franklin to hear.

"Oh, I'm sorry. I asked him to bring me some papers from the office. I hope you don't mind."

"No, of course not. What sort of papers?" René asked, she had thought that everything had been settled.

"From what I am told, it seems that Del had made some kind of an arrangement with a real estate developer to sell a large part of his estate. Since you are now the owner, it will be your responsibility to sign over the land."

"I'm not signing over anything that breaks up the land. You told me that no one else had any claim to this land," René said angrily.

"I didn't know about this until it was brought to my attention by Martin Hanover. It seems that he found the papers while he was doing some research for one of the other attorneys. They had been filed in the wrong file, by mistake, I'm sure."

"I'm sure it was 'by mistake'," René said sarcastically. "Doesn't it seem a little strange to you that Captain Del would agree to sell part of his estate without telling you about it?"

René could see that her statement caused Franklin to stop and think. But a glance at Kathleen gave René the feeling that Kathleen knew about the so-called agreement, and she was hoping that Franklin would not listen to René.

"It does seem a little strange, now that I think about it. Del seemed so set on keeping this place intact for you."

"Have you actually seen the agreement?" Jeff asked.

"No, that's why I had Martin bring it out."

"Don't you think it would be a good idea if you at least looked at it before you decide if it's any good?" Jeff suggested.

"Yes. Yes, of course. That is why I asked Martin to bring the agreement out here. I will want to look it over before any decision is made."

"Well, here are the papers," René said as Martin came around the corner.

Jeff stood at René's side while Martin gave the papers to Franklin. It was easy for Jeff to see that René was worried, but then she had a right to be after all that had happened up to that point.

"Let's go inside," Jeff suggested.

Jeff turned and opened the door. He then stood next to the door as Franklin and Kathleen passed by him. As René started to go by, he took her by the arm. As she looked up at him, he looked at her as if he wanted to say something to her that he didn't want anyone else to hear.

René took the hint. "Franklin, why don't you go into the den and take a good look at those papers. Jeff and I will get some coffee."

"That's a good idea. I'll need a little time to study these papers very carefully."

"You can wait out here," René said, as she turned and looked Martin in the eyes.

"Mr. Cosgrove might need my advice," Martin said in protest.

"I doubt that very much. You either wait out here, or I will call the police and have you removed," René said as she looked at him.

Martin was obviously upset at being excluded, but he had learned very quickly that René would indeed call the police and have him removed.

"He might be right. Mr. Cosgrove might need him," Jeff said, gently squeezing René's arm.

René looked up at Jeff wondering what he was thinking, but she trusted him. Jeff had to have a reason for wanting Martin inside with the rest. She would trust his judgment.

"Okay," she relented.

Martin grinned slightly, then walked past René. She wasn't sure it was a good idea, but she knew that Jeff must have had a good reason for wanting him in the den with the others.

Jeff and René went into the house and shut the door behind them. Jeff took René off to one side, then looked around to make sure that there was no one within earshot of them.

"Did you notice Kathleen?" Jeff asked in a whisper.

"Sure. What about her?"

"Did you notice the way she was holding her arm?"

René thought for a moment, but couldn't remember seeing anything out of the ordinary.

"No, not really," she replied, curious as to what Jeff was getting at.

"She seems to be favoring her left arm. It's like she might have injured her arm."

"What are you saying?"

"What I'm saying is, I think she was the one outside the door when you fired a shot through it. She probably got hit by either the bullet or a piece of flying wood from the door."

"I can't see her as one that would get that close to this. She's more the type to have someone else do her dirty work."

"Not if she doesn't trust her partner. If that's the case, I think she would be right in the middle of it, running the show. I think her partner is Hanover, and up to now he hasn't been getting the job done."

René thought for a moment. She had seen her come out of the studio behind the main house in Albany, and she had seen what looked like Martin's car leave there. René tried to picture Kathleen as a woman that wanted something she could not get easily. She saw her as a woman that would do whatever it took to get what she wanted, if she wanted it bad enough. She also saw her as a woman who could get someone like Martin to do what she wanted for her. They both struck her as greedy.

"You might be right, but how do we prove it?"

"I don't know, but one thing I do know is that we should get a call to the Sheriff and get him out here."

"I can arrange that. I'll have Mildred call from her apartment above the garage."

"Good idea. Now we best get some coffee and get back in the den before anyone gets suspicious."

Mildred was setting a pot of coffee on a tray that had several cups, a cream pitcher and a bowl of sugar on it. She was just picking it up to take it into the den when René stopped her.

"I'll take that. I have something I need you to do."

"Yes, Ma'am," Mildred replied as she set the tray back on the table.

René explained that she wanted Mildred to find Sam, then go to their apartment above the garage and call the Sheriff. They were to explain what happened at Jeff's cabin last night and early this morning. When the Sheriff arrived, they were to direct him into the den.

Mildred didn't understand what was going on, but she nodded that she understood the instructions and would do what René requested. As soon as Mildred was out of the kitchen, René picked up the tray. She looked at Jeff, let out a sigh, then nodded to him that she was ready.

Jeff held the door, then followed René to the den. As they entered the den, Jeff immediately noticed that Franklin was sitting at the rolltop desk carefully reading the agreement that Martin had brought out for him. Kathleen was sitting on a chair across from the chair that Martin was sitting on.

Kathleen was watching Franklin for some indication of what he was thinking as he read the document. It seemed to Jeff that Kathleen had a worried look on her face, and he wondered why.

René set the tray on the coffee table, then sat down on the sofa next to Jeff. Jeff nudged her. She looked at him, then at Kathleen. She got the impression that Kathleen seemed just a little too interested in what Franklin was reading.

René found it difficult to keep her eyes off Kathleen. She found herself glancing from time to time at Kathleen's left arm in an effort to see if she favored it.

René also found herself glancing over at Martin from time to time to see what he was doing. It seemed to René that he was also very interested in what Franklin was reading. It was almost as if he didn't know what it said, but something about the way he looked convinced her that he had read the document long before he got here. If that was the case, why was he so interested in it? He should know what it said. Then it hit her. It wasn't that he didn't know what was in the document that made him so nervous, it was whether or not Franklin would believe that it was a true and accurate document, one that would stand up in a court of law.

Franklin seemed very engrossed in reading the document. The look on his face caused René to wonder what was wrong. If the document was valid, then she stood to lose a large part of her estate. The one thing she knew for sure was that she would not break up the estate without a fight. She also knew that with a good lawyer, she could tie the whole matter up in court for a very long time, several years in fact. She didn't think those who were interested in her property would like that very much.

CHAPTER SEVENTEEN

Everyone was sitting in the den watching Franklin as he carefully studied the document. It seemed to take him forever, although it was really just a little over thirty minutes. René thought that he might have read it over twice and some parts of it more often than that. She got the impression that Franklin either didn't believe what he was reading, or he wasn't sure if the document would stand up in court. Whatever the reason for his reading it so carefully, she was sure that he was studying it to make sure that above all it was legal.

Kathleen and Martin would glance at each other from time to time, then turn back to look at Franklin. They were obviously impatient to hear what Franklin had to say about the document.

Occasionally they would look around to see if anyone had seen them looking at each other. It was apparent that they were trying not to be obvious about it, but they were not succeeding very well.

René certainly had not missed the glances that Kathleen and Martin had shared with each other. All it did was reinforce her belief that they were up to something. The only question in René's mind was what were they up to? The fact that this document suddenly showed up with no mention of it in Captain Del's logbooks or anywhere else was a good clue as to what the two of them really wanted.

The fact that Kathleen and Martin were showing some interest in each other proved nothing, even though René was convinced that they had been having an affair. René even noticed that Jeff had caught glimpses of them looking at each other.

René was as impatient to hear what Franklin had to say about the document as the others. After all, it was her estate that was in jeopardy. She was more than a little nervous. She could not tell from the look on Franklin's face what he was thinking or what was going through his mind.

Finally, Franklin looked up and scanned the room. He looked at each of those sitting around waiting for him to decide if the document was authentic or a fake. If it was authentic, was it enforceable?

"Well, it looks on the surface to be a legal document," he said breaking the silence.

That was disappointing news to René. Her shoulders sagged as she turned and looked at Jeff. She could see that he shared her feeling of disappointment. But a quick look at Kathleen and a quick glance at Martin indicated that they seemed to be very pleased with what Franklin had to say.

"However, I don't think it will stand up in court," Franklin added.

René happened to be looking at Kathleen when Franklin made his comment. Kathleen's jaw dropped at the news. It was clear that his statement came as a total shock to her, as well as a disappointment.

"Why is that?" Kathleen snapped sharply, her voice showing just a little too much interest.

She must have realized that she had spoken out of turn and with a little too much enthusiasm. As she looked around the room, she found everyone looking at her.

"A..am..I'm sure that René would be interested in knowing why it won't hold up in court," she stammered, looking a little confused as well as foolish.

It was clear by the look on Franklin's face that he didn't know what to think. He was obviously astonished by Kathleen's comment. He couldn't understand her outburst. What possible interest any of this could be to her was beyond him.

"Yes. I am interested in this document, but for different reasons, I'm sure," René replied.

"And just what do you mean by that?" Kathleen snapped back, again her voice was sharp and direct as she glared at René.

"I have no desire to break up this land," René said as she looked at Kathleen.

"Well, you might not have a choice in the matter," Martin said seeming just a little too self-confident and a little too smug to suit René.

"You are a guest in this house and I would suggest that you keep that in mind. You have nothing to say in this matter. If you don't keep quiet I will have you tossed out," René said flatly, her dislike for Martin was clearly evident in the tone of her voice.

The smug grin on Martin's face quickly turned to a sharp glare. It was clear that he didn't like René any more than she liked him. He wanted to tell René that her time there was limited, but he was sure that she would have him removed if he said anything more. The last thing he wanted was to be "tossed out" just when things might be going his way.

"Just a minute," Jeff said firmly, grabbing everyone's attention. "I probably knew Del better than anyone here, especially during his last few days. I got to know his mindset during those days when he was in pain and uncomfortable and needed someone with him. I spent most of my free time at his side."

"So? What difference does that make?" Kathleen asked with a tone of disgust in her voice.

"I believe it makes all the difference in the world," Jeff answered. "The only thing that Del talked about, at least when he was coherent enough to talk, was leaving his estate intact for René."

"You would say that. After all, you have been trying to get close to René and her property since the day Del died. I wonder why that is?" Kathleen asked rather smugly.

René looked from Kathleen to Jeff. One look at Jeff and she was sure that Jeff's interest in her was the same as her interest in him. He loved her and she loved him. The property was just something that existed.

"I resent that," Jeff said with a sharp tone in his voice.

"I'm sure you do, but maybe Del changed his mind," Martin said, his voice showing a hint of arrogance.

"I certainly doubt that," Jeff said. "What I think is that this document is a fake. And I think it was thought up after it was found out that René doesn't scare off as easily as someone thought she would."

"Are you accusing me?" Martin said with a sharp tone in his voice.

"I don't know who has been trying to scare her into selling the estate. But I do know that one of those who have been trying to get their hands on this property got hurt early this morning at my cabin," Jeff said as he turned and looked directly at Kathleen.

René quickly looked at Kathleen and watched for a reaction from her. Jeff's words had caused Kathleen to look at Martin and unconsciously touch her left arm at the same time.

René was now sure that she knew who was to blame for all that had happened. The problem was proving it.

Just as René was about to say something about Kathleen's arm, Mildred entered the room. René turned to face her.

"What is it, Mildred?"

"Sheriff Stone is here to see you."

"Please, show him in," René said.

As she turned around and looked over those sitting in the den, she noticed that Kathleen was glaring at her. She also noticed that Martin suddenly looked a little nervous. He apparently had not expected to see an officer of the law there.

René turned back around and stood up just as Sheriff Stone stepped into the den.

"Nice to see you again, Sheriff," René said as she stuck out her hand.

"Nice to see you again, Ma'am. I'm sorry if I'm breaking in on some kind of a meeting," he said as he looked around to see who was there.

"Can I get you anything?" René asked.

"No, thank you. I was wondering who owns that black BMW?"

"I do," Martin said sharply. "Why?"

"I have one of my deputies taking a look at it. It looks like one that we have been looking for these past few days."

"You can't do that without my permission. You can't search my car without a warrant," Martin said angrily as he stood up.

"No one said anything about searching it. I just said that he was looking at it. Do you have a problem with that?"

Martin suddenly realized that he might have over-reacted just a little. He stood in front of the chair and looked around the room. His outburst had caused all those in the room to stare at him. He found that everyone was looking at him as if they expected some sort of explanation or an answer to the Sheriff's question.

"Ah . . no. I have no problem with that," he said calmly as he stepped back and sat down on the chair.

"I really need to talk to Jeff, if you don't mind?" Sheriff Stone said.

"What can I do for you?" Jeff said as he stood up.

"I would like to speak to you and Miss Richardson in private, if you don't mind?"

"Sure."

"Excuse us, please," René said as Jeff took her by the arm and led her out of the den into the hallway.

"Thanks for coming so quickly," Jeff said.

"What's going on here? Sam said you wanted me to come here as soon as possible. He told me some story about the two of you being shot at and you shooting someone at your cabin," Sheriff Stone said looking over at Jeff and seeing the scratch and bump on his head.

"Well, that's partly true. René did the shooting," Jeff replied.

"You want to tell me about it?"

Jeff gave Sheriff Stone a brief rundown on what had happened last night on the other side of the lake. Sheriff Stone listened with a great deal of interest.

"That's pretty much the way Sam and Mildred told it. I called Trooper Busack. He wasn't far from your cabin. I asked him to go over to your cabin and look around. He just called me back. He said that he found some tire tracks on the road to your cabin that he was sure didn't belong to your truck. He said that they stopped short of the cabin. He also found footprints in the soft ground near the front door," Sheriff Stone explained.

"That's good. You should be able to find out if Hanover's car was near my place," Jeff said.

"Yeah, but we might have a problem."

"What kind of a problem?" René asked.

"We won't be able to take prints of Hanover's tires unless we have something solid to go on."

"I don't understand."

"We have to have more than tire prints to get a judge to issue a search warrant so that we can search his car. The tire tracks alone might not do it."

"What about the tracks his tires made on my drive?" René asked. "They lead right to his car and it's parked in my driveway right now. If the tracks here match the tracks at Jeff's cabin, and the car that made the tracks is parked right there, wouldn't that be grounds for a search warrant?"

Sheriff Stone looked at Jeff and smiled. He had the tracks for comparison and the car that made them. What more could he ask for?

"Jeff, you've got yourself one very smart young woman here," he said.

"Yeah, I know," he replied as he reached out and put his arm around her waist.

"What do we do now?" René asked.

"I want the two of you to go back inside and keep the rest of them busy for awhile. I don't want anyone to leave. I'll call Busack and see how he's doing."

Jeff nodded that he understood. Jeff turned René around and they went back inside the den while Sheriff Stone went out to his car.

Sheriff Stone called Trooper Busack on his radio. They discussed what they had found and if there was anything that they could use to determine if Martin's BMW was at the cabin.

* * * *

Meanwhile, when Jeff and René entered the den, they found Martin talking to Franklin. It sounded as if he was trying to convince Franklin that the document was not only legal, but that it would stand up in court. Jeff and René listened for a moment or two.

"Miss Richardson has no choice in the matter. This paper makes it clear that William Delcambra had agreed to sell the majority of his property to the R.D. Smith Development Company," Martin was saying.

"First of all, I am not William Delcambra so I don't know what he agreed to. So as far as I'm concerned, that piece of paper is just that, a piece of paper. Secondly, Mr. Smith is dead. In fact, both parties to this so called agreement are dead," Franklin reminded Martin.

"Mr. Smith may be dead, but his company is not. He was not the only owner of the development company," Martin said with an air of confidence.

"Who owns the company now?" Jeff asked, looking directly at Martin.

"Well, several people do."

"My guess would be that one of them is you. Am I correct?" René asked staring at Martin.

When Martin didn't answer, René was convinced that he was the one behind all the problems that she was having since she first found out that she was to inherit the estate.

"Your silence tells me all that I need to know," René said.

"What if I am? You can't prove that I had anything to do with any of the things you claim have happened to you."

"I'm sure you have covered your tracks very well except for one thing," Jeff said.

"And what was that?" Martin asked, still sure that every thing was going well for him.

"Your partner," René blurted out.

"My partner?" he asked wondering what it was she thought she knew. "I don't have a partner."

"We know better. Kathleen is your partner," René said as she turned and looked at Kathleen.

"What? How dare you," Kathleen said angrily.

"Oh, I think she dares because you were at my cabin last night," Jeff said as he stood up.

"I beg your pardon. She was not at your cabin," Franklin said, obviously upset by Jeff's accusation.

"But she was, Franklin," Jeff said. "She was there with Martin."

"You can't prove that," Martin said as he stood up.

"Sit down," Jeff ordered.

"You have no authority to tell me to do anything. You're just a game warden," Martin said as he started across the room toward the door.

"He might not have the authority, but I do," Sheriff Stone said as he stepped into the doorway.

No one had noticed that Sheriff Stone was standing just outside the open door to the den. He had been listening to what had been going on for several minutes.

"Sit down, Mr. Hanover," Sheriff Stone ordered.

Martin reluctantly returned to his chair and sat down. Franklin was staring at his wife. He couldn't believe that she had been with Martin.

"Go ahead, Jeff," Sheriff Stone said as he leaned up against the doorframe.

"Kathleen and Martin were at my cabin last night with at least one other person. Before the shooting started and before I got shot in the head, I saw them waiting in the brush while the other man was checking out my cabin. I heard them talking. I was some distance away, but it was Kathleen's voice that I recognized. I didn't really recognize it until just now. That accent of yours gives you away."

"I was not in the woods around your cabin last night. I was in Albany," Martin insisted.

"Not so. You were at my cabin."

"You'll never be able to prove that," Martin insisted.

"I will. Yesterday was Thursday."

"So what?" Martin said sharply."

"Thursday afternoon the county road workers drag the road to my house for me. They've been doing it for the past three years. Last night you drove part way down the road to my cabin and left tire tracks in the freshly graded road. The only tire tracks, I might add, since I had not used my truck for the past couple of days."

Suddenly, Martin looked a little sick to his stomach. It was clear to Jeff that he was searching his mind for some kind of an explanation that would explain how his tracks got there. He stared at Jeff for a moment or two before he decided that Jeff was bluffing. That thought gave him a renewed sense of confidence.

"You're bluffing," Martin said. "You can't prove the tracks are from my car even if you did find any tracks, which

I sincerely doubt. Besides, the tires on my car are just like thousands of tires."

"He's not bluffing. Trooper Busack is checking out the tracks right now. By the way, he's an expert on such things," Sheriff Stone said with a slight grin.

"You can't do that, not without a search warrant," Martin insisted.

"But we can. You see Mr. Hanover, your car is parked outside. We are going to compare the tracks that you left on Miss Richardson's driveway to the tracks we found on the road to Jeff's cabin. If they match, we are going to charge you with assault with a deadly weapon, attempted murder, along with conspiracy and possibly arson. There may be other charges later."

René thought the look on Martin's face was priceless. The confidence that usually showed in his face was gone. He looked more like a scared little boy, she thought.

"You can't do that. You can't do that," Martin yelled.

"Yes, we can. You see, the tire tracks are not on your property. They are on Miss Richardson's property and she has given us permission to use them. And I'm sure that I can get a search warrant for your car and most likely for your home if they match," Sheriff Stone said with a tone of confidence in his voice.

Martin sat back in his chair. He looked from Sheriff Stone to Kathleen, then back to Sheriff Stone. His mind was going a mile a minute as he tried to think of an alibi, something that would get him out of the situation.

"You'll never be able to make your charges stick," he said as he tried to formulate what he was going to say next.

"I wouldn't count on it. Once we compare the tire tracks we will have all we need."

"First of all, I was nowhere near this place when the boathouse exploded. I was in my home in Albany."

"How did you know it exploded?" Jeff asked.

"You said it exploded," Martin said confidently.

"No. I said it burned down. I didn't say anything about an explosion."

Martin looked around the room. Everyone was staring at him, even Kathleen. He was beginning to feel trapped. All he could think about was how to get out of there. He needed to get away, and fast.

He suddenly realized that nothing had been said about him being under arrest. He had not been read his rights, that much he knew. It occurred to him that if they had any evidence that they could prove, they would have arrested him by now. He felt that he had nothing to lose by getting up and leaving. He stood up and started across the room.

"Where do you think you are going, Mr. Hanover?" Sheriff Stone asked.

"Am I under arrest?" Martin asked with a renewed sense of determination and confidence.

"Not at the moment," Sheriff Stone replied.

"Then I'm leaving."

"No, you're not," Sheriff Stone said as he stepped in front of the door.

"You either arrest me, or let me go. And I can assure you, that if you arrest me, you better be able to prove your charges. Otherwise, I will sue you and the county for false arrest."

Jeff and René clearly heard the threat in his voice. They also realized that Sheriff Stone didn't have very much to go on at the moment. Without something to tie Martin to the scene, there was little that he could do but let him go.

"Let me put it this way, Mr. Hanover. If you try to leave, you will be arrested. I might suggest that you spend the next few minutes calling one of your high priced attorneys from Albany. I've got a very strong suspicion that you're going to need one real soon."

Martin took another quick look around the room. Everyone was watching him to see what he was going to do now that his threat of a lawsuit had been challenged. As his eyes returned to look at Sheriff Stone, he could see that the Sheriff had no intention of backing down. He quickly realized that this was not an idle threat on the sheriff's part. He meant it and would make it stick. Martin quietly returned to his chair and sat down.

* * * *

During the exchange between Martin and Sheriff Stone, René had been more interested in what was going through Franklin's mind. She noticed that he had been watching Kathleen, observing her as she watched Martin. Franklin was looking at Kathleen with a bewildered look on his face, one of total disbelief. It was almost as if he was seeing his wife for the very first time, and he looked as if he didn't like what he saw.

"Kathleen, what do you have to do with all this?" Franklin asked softly, almost as if he wished to have no one else hear him.

"What?" she retorted much louder than she had intended.

"I want to know what you have to do with this?" he repeated, the tone of his voice showing that he demanded an answer.

"I don't know what you're talking about, you old fool," she snapped angrily.

Franklin just looked at her as he slowly leaned back in the chair. He had come to realize that his suspicions about Kathleen and Martin might very well be true. He was convinced that they were partners in something, but he just didn't know what until now. The way she looked at Martin was a dead give away. It was clear to him that she was afraid that Martin would say something that he shouldn't, and end up implicating her.

* * * *

Just then Trooper Busack came into the room. He stepped up next to Sheriff Stone. He leaned close to Sheriff Stone and whispered something in his ear.

Jeff and René watched as Trooper Busack and Sheriff Stone talked quietly to each other. There was no change of expression on either of their faces so there was no way of knowing what they were talking about. After several minutes, Sheriff Stone nodded his head, then looked toward Martin.

"Mr. Hanover, would you stand up, please?"

Martin looked around the room as if he was wondering what was going on, then slowly stood up. The expression on his face seemed to indicate that he knew what was about to happen, but was having difficulty believing that it was actually happening to him.

Sheriff Stone moved across the room toward him. When the Sheriff got close to Martin, he reached behind his back and pulled out his handcuffs.

"Mr. Hanover, you are under arrest for the attempted murder of Jeff Daily and René Richardson, assault with a deadly weapon, and trespassing. There may be other charges added later," Sheriff Stone said as he turned Martin around and cuffed his hands behind his back. As Sheriff Stone cuffed Martin, he read him his rights.

"Do you understand your rights, Mr. Hanover?"

"Yes, but you can't prove any of this," Martin insisted.

"I think we can. The tire tracks in Miss Richardson's drive that were made by your car match the tire tracks across the lake on the road to Jeff Daily's cabin. And I think a search of your car will provide the rest of the proof we need."

"You can't search my car without a warrant."

"You're right, Mr. Hanover, but Trooper Busack has called into town and a warrant is being issued as we speak. Do you have anything you want to say?"

Martin looked over at Kathleen as if he expected her to come to his rescue, but she said nothing. He looked down at the floor for a minute. He could sense that she was not going to help him. He was on his own.

"Yeah. I want a lawyer," he said as he looked back at Kathleen with hate in his eyes.

"Okay. Do you want to call one now?"

"That won't be necessary. I would like Franklin to be my lawyer."

"Me?" Franklin said with surprise.

"Yes. You're the only one that I can trust," he replied as he glanced over at Kathleen.

Franklin looked at Martin, then at his wife. He could see the fire in her eyes. There was something going on between Martin and his wife, but Franklin couldn't seem to figure it out.

"I don't think that I should be defending you," Franklin said.

"You are the best one around. Oh, don't worry, I can pay you," Martin said as he looked at him, then turned and glanced at Kathleen.

Franklin seemed confused, but he had to know what was going on between Kathleen and Martin. If he was going to find out everything, he needed to speak with Martin alone. He also had to find out what Martin had in mind. He was sure that Martin had a very good reason for picking him to defend him, but he didn't have any idea what it could be.

"Would you mind taking the cuffs off Mr. Hanover?" Franklin asked the Sheriff. "And do you have some place where I could converse with my client in private?"

"You can use the room at the top of the stairs," René suggested.

"If he runs, I'll hold you personally responsible," Sheriff Stone said as he turned Martin around and unlocked the handcuffs.

"I understand," Franklin replied.

Sheriff Stone stepped aside and watched as Martin and Franklin walked out of the den and started up the stairs to the second floor. Sheriff Stone motioned for Trooper Busack to go outside and keep a watch to make sure that Martin didn't try to escape out a window. Sheriff Stone stood at the bottom of the stairs and waited for Martin and Franklin to return.

CHAPTER EIGHTEEN

Jeff sat next to René on the sofa, but his mind was not on the woman sitting beside him. He was wondering just what Martin had in mind. There had to be a reason for Martin to pick Franklin to defend him. After all, it was clear that Franklin didn't like Martin, and that Martin thought Franklin was just a used up old man. There had to be something that he knew that no one else seemed to know or had thought of. Martin was no dummy, and Jeff was sure he had something up his sleeve. Just what it was, was not clear at the moment.

René was also curious as to why Martin would ask Franklin to defend him. She was trying to figure out just what Martin was up to. As she thought about it, she looked across the room at Kathleen. Kathleen had gotten up and was pacing back and forth in front of the French doors that led out onto the porch. It was almost as if she was trying to decide if she should make a break for it and try to run.

It was obvious to René that Kathleen was very worried about something. There were two possibilities that came to mind at the moment. The first was that Franklin would find out that Kathleen's affair with Martin was true. Martin was sure to tell him about it.

The second was that Franklin would find out that she was involved with Martin in their effort to take the estate away from René. That would surely alienate Franklin from her.

In either case, it was more than likely that Kathleen would lose Franklin. More importantly, she would lose his money and her position in the community. There was no doubt in René's mind that money and position were the motives for everything that Kathleen did.

* * * *

Franklin and Martin went into the bedrooms at the top of the stairs on the second floor. Martin sat down on the edge of the bed, while Franklin stood just inside the room looking at him.

"Okay, Martin. You say I'm the only one you can trust. What makes you think you can trust me? I'm sure you don't like me, and I certainly don't like you."

"I don't care if you like me or not. The reason I trust you is because you cannot tell anyone what I tell you now. You are my lawyer. Secondly, if you don't get me off, I'll claim that you threw the case because of your wife and I'll get a new trial. And third, in this state you cannot testify against your wife," Martin said with a grin.

"And what do you mean by that?" Franklin demanded.

"Get with it, Franklin. Your wife is into all of this clear up to her pretty little neck."

"Into what? You better make yourself clear or I'll terminate this right now and tell the Sheriff."

"Tell them what? Don't get on your high horse with me. Anything I tell you here cannot be used against me in a court of law. The minute you said that you wanted to speak to your client alone, you became my attorney, like it or not. That's why I picked you as my attorney."

Franklin just looked at him for several seconds. As he walked across the room and sat down on a chair, he realized that Martin was right. He had walked right into Martin's trap with his eyes wide open. Franklin knew that if he talked about what was said between his client and himself, it would be thrown out of court. He also knew that he could lose his license to practice law for violating client/lawyer privilege. What he didn't know was to what extent Kathleen was involved in all of this, and just how many of the charges that the Sheriff had mentioned could Kathleen be charged with?

He took a moment to think about Kathleen. She was much younger than he was. He had often wondered if he could give her everything that she needed. It was slowly becoming clear to him that he apparently could not, although he had tried.

Franklin's future was looking a little dim. He had loved Kathleen from the very first time that he met her at a friend's home in New York City. He knew that she was much younger than he was, but that didn't matter to him. He hadn't thought that it mattered to her, but apparently it did.

"We don't have all day," Martin said in an effort to get Franklin to pull himself together.

Franklin looked up at Martin. His first thought was to kill Martin with his bare hands, but he knew that Martin was much younger and stronger than he was. And what would it solve? Nothing.

"How deeply involved is Kathleen?" Franklin asked as he stared at Martin.

"Like I said, 'up to her pretty little neck'. This whole idea was hers in the first place. She has wanted this property for years. Ever since the first time you brought her out here to meet your friend, William Delcambra."

"She never mentioned it to me. We had no secrets," Franklin said in disbelief.

"You had secrets, you just didn't know about them. That's why they're called secrets," Martin said sarcastically.

"I don't believe you."

"Did you notice that Kathleen was favoring her arm?"

Franklin thought for a moment before he remembered that Kathleen had complained that her arm was bothering her. She had said that it was from doing too much work in her garden.

"She strained a muscle while working in her garden," Franklin retorted.

"I'm sure you believed her. The truth is that René Richardson shot her when she fired that wild shot through the door of the cabin."

"You lie," he said, but he knew that Martin was probably telling the truth.

"Why don't you ask her?"

"I will."

Franklin remembered the look in Kathleen's eyes when she had lost her cool in the den. He could also remember the look on her face when Sheriff Stone put handcuffs on Martin and placed him under arrest. No matter how much he tried to deny it, Martin was probably telling the truth for once in his miserable life.

"How do you figure that I can help you?" Franklin asked as he looked up at Martin.

"First of all, you will get me out of this little jam I'm in. Secondly, you will make sure that the courts uphold that document that William Delcambra signed agreeing to sell a large part of his estate to R.D. Smith Development Company."

"I can't tell the courts what to do," Franklin said in protest.

"You have friends on the bench. You can get them to agree to anything you ask of them," Martin said angrily.

"I might be able to do that, but I won't."

"You don't get it, do you? If you don't do what I tell you, you will never practice law again, and I'll see to it that Kathleen grows old in the state prison for women," Martin threatened angrily.

Franklin again looked down at the floor as he thought about Martin's threat. It became clear that he had a choice to make. After all these years, he began to understand that Kathleen really didn't love him. It had become clear that she "loved" him only for what he could give her.

Franklin recalled that Kathleen had called him "an old fool". That one statement had done more to open his eyes to the real Kathleen than anything else. He had given her a nice big house in a very affluent part of Albany. He had given her money, prestige, and position, but that was apparently not enough for her. She wanted more.

Franklin had been a lawyer for a very long time and he was well past the age that most people retire. He wouldn't want to practice law with the embarrassment of having his wife accused of trying to kill someone. Even if he could get them off, he would not want Martin and her to get away with it. And he certainly would not want René to lose her land, land that was rightfully hers.

Franklin slowly looked up at Martin and asked, "Did you burn down the boathouse?"

"Since you can't tell anyone what I say here, I see no reason not to tell you. No, I didn't. I had someone else do it for me, but I won't tell you who. Too bad it didn't work."

"What do you mean?" Franklin asked.

"If it had killed René like it was supposed to, Kathleen could have easily convinced you to buy this place for her from the estate. Then all this would not have had to happen. All our problems would have been solved," Martin said with a slight chuckle of disappointment in his voice.

"Did you try to kill Jeff, too?"

"Yes, I did try to do that. Too bad it wasn't a little lighter out by his cabin. If I could have seen him better, he would have died of a hunting accident," Martin said with a grin.

Franklin looked into Martin's eyes. It was clear to him that Martin would have done anything to get hold of the estate, even kill for it. Franklin realized that no matter how it all turned out, he had lost Kathleen and everything else he had thought was important to him. He could not let Martin and Kathleen get hold of what rightfully belonged to René.

"Well, I have some news for you," Franklin said as a slight grin came over his face. "You're going to jail."

It pleased Franklin to see the smug look on Martin's face disappear. It was replaced by one of anger with a hint of fear mixed in it. For the first time it occurred to Martin that Franklin might not knuckle under to his demands.

"You're making a big mistake," Martin said angrily.

"Maybe, but I will not let you get away with this."

"I'll see to it you lose your license to practice law."

"I don't care. I've been thinking of retiring, anyway. After you and Kathleen are put in jail, I think I'll take a trip overseas to some place nice and quiet while the two of you rot in hell."

"You're bluffing."

"Try me," Franklin said as he stood up and started toward the door. "You're going to jail."

"I'll see you in hell," Martin blurted out.

"Probably," Franklin replied as he walked out the door and into the hall.

Fear quickly replaced the self-assurance that had been a part of Martin for so many years. He began to realize all that he would lose if he were sent to jail. His mind was working hard in an effort to figure out what to do next. He had never felt fear like he was feeling it now, especially when he heard the sound of Franklin's voice drift back up the stairs.

"He's all yours, Sheriff. I won't represent him."

The next sounds Martin heard were those of Sheriff Stone's boots as he was coming up the steps. Martin could feel the panic build up inside him. All he could think about was getting away, but there was no place to go.

Finally, panic overtook him. He grabbed the chair that Franklin had been sitting on and tossed it at the window. The chair went crashing through the window, falling to the ground below.

* * * *

The sounds of breaking glass alerted Sheriff Stone. He took the last few steps two at a time, then rushed down the hall to the bedroom. As he turned into the bedroom, he saw Martin trying to climb out the window.

"Halt," Sheriff Stone yelled as he drew his gun.

Martin was over halfway out when he stopped and looked back. Sheriff Stone had his gun in his hand and had it pointed directly at him. Martin turned and looked down. He could see Trooper Busack waiting below. He decided that there was no place to go and nothing else he could do but give up. He shifted his weight to get a better grip on the edge of the window. He started to pull himself back inside the room when a piece of loose molding around the edge of the window gave way from his weight.

As his hand pulled the molding off the window frame, Martin lost his balance and fell back out the window. He screamed as he fell to the ground some fifteen feet below.

Sheriff Stone got to the window just as Trooper Busack got to Martin. Busack reached down and checked for a pulse on Martin's neck. He looked up at Sheriff Stone in the window and shook his head. Martin was dead. He had broken his neck when he hit the ground, and one of the legs of the chair he had tossed through the window had pierced Martin's heart killing him instantly.

Sheriff Stone let out a sigh of disappointment. Without Martin, he had nothing. He was sure that Martin had not acted alone. There were others involved, but without Martin to point them out, it was not likely that anyone would be prosecuted for anything. Plus there was the possibility that it was not over for Miss Richardson.

* * * *

When Sheriff Stone returned to the den, he found Jeff was holding onto René. She had her head buried in his shoulder. Franklin was standing by the door looking out over the lake. Kathleen was sitting in a chair. She was the only one that didn't seem to be affected by hearing Martin fall from the second story.

"I'm sorry to report that Mr. Hanover fell from the window and died as a result of the fall," Sheriff Stone said.

Sheriff Stone watched Kathleen for some kind of reaction, but he saw none. He walked across the room and picked up the phone and called for an ambulance to come to pick up the body.

"Is there anything you can tell us about what you and Martin talked about?" Sheriff Stone asked of Franklin.

"You can't say anything about what Martin told you," Kathleen insisted abruptly.

"He's dead. Anything I say now will not matter to him."

"But, Franklin," she replied, the look in her eyes pleading with him not to say anything.

Franklin turned and looked at the Sheriff.

"My wife and Martin were trying to get this estate away from Miss Richardson. There was at least one other person involved, but I don't know who he is. Maybe Kathleen will tell you."

"Franklin!" she said knowing that he was not going to protect her.

"I'm sorry, René," he said as he looked at her.

"René was right," he said turning back toward Sheriff Stone. "Check her arm and you will find an injury caused by a bullet."

"Do you want to show me your arm?" Sheriff Stone asked as he stepped in front of Kathleen.

Kathleen looked at the Sheriff, then looked at Franklin. It was over and she knew it.

"Captain Del was your friend," she said angrily. "He would have signed this place over to you if you had just asked him. Instead, you insisted that he give the whole place to this wimp of a girl."

"I think she has proven that she is no wimp. She is entitled to it. She was his only living relative."

"What about you? You looked after him for almost a year while he tried to get over the death of his wife, and what did you get for it? Nothing," she screamed at him.

"I would have never asked him for anything. He was my friend, and he would have done the same for me."

"You're just a damned old fool. You could have had everything and you let it go. Now you have nothing."

"I think you better come with me," Sheriff Stone said to Kathleen.

Kathleen looked up at the Sheriff, then stood up. He gently turned her around. As he did, he pulled her arms behind her back and put handcuffs on her as he read her her rights.

Jeff and René sat on the sofa watching as the Sheriff led her out of the house. They didn't know what to say.

René looked over at Franklin. He was just standing there watching his wife being led away. There was no sign of anything on his face. It was as if the Sheriff was leading away a complete stranger.

René stood up and walked over to Franklin. She reached out and touched his shoulder. Franklin turned and looked at her.

"I'm sorry," René whispered.

Franklin tried to smile at her, but it was not much of a smile. There was no doubt that Franklin was feeling the weight of the world on his shoulders at that moment.

"I thought I knew her," he said with a sigh. "I think I knew all along that she only loved me for what I could give her. She never did really love me just for me."

"What are you going to do now?"

"I'm going to get her a good lawyer. I might be able to get her to tell us who her other accomplice was for a lighter sentence. Then after her trial, I'll divorce her, retire from law, and take a trip overseas to see some of the things I've put off seeing for so many years."

"You know you will always be welcome to come here and stay as long as you want," René said softly.

"Thank you. I might take you up on that some day, but I think I had better go now."

René stood at the door to the den and watched as Franklin walked out of the house. Jeff soon joined her and together they walked out onto the porch.

"Franklin's really hurting," René said.

"I'm sure he is, but he is also relieved. He knows where he stands with Kathleen, and that's important to a man."

"It's important to a woman, too," René said as she turned and looked up at him.

"I'm sure it is," he replied as he looked down at her standing by his side.

Jeff looked into her eyes, then slowly leaned down and kissed her. Their lips met in a gentle loving kiss. When it was over, he smiled down at her.

"You are beautiful, and I love you" he whispered.

"Will you stay with me tonight?" she asked in a soft sigh.

"Will you wear my shirt?" he asked with a grin.

"If you like," she replied as she squeezed him.

"Then I'll stay, but it will be forever," he replied.

René and Jeff turned and went back into the house. Everyone was gone and they had the place to themselves. Jeff slipped his arm around behind her and guided her up the stairs to the bedroom.

Once inside the bedroom, he turned her around and pulled her gently to him. She went willingly, wanting him to be with her forever.

www.ingramcontent.com/pod-product-compliance
Lightning Source LLC
Chambersburg PA
CBHW071141170626
46809CB00002B/716